Boy meets girl. Boy meets girl. Boy
meets girl. Boy meets girl. Boy meets
girl. Boy meets girl. Boy meets girl.
Boy meets girl. Boy meets girl. Boy
meets girl. Boy meets girl. Boy meets
girl. Boy meets girl. Boy meets girl.
Boy meets girl. Boy meets girl. Boy
meets girl. Boy meets girl. Boy meets
girl. Boy meets girl. Boy meets girl.
Boy meets girl. Boy meets girl. Boy
meets girl. Boy meets girl. Boy meets
girl. Boy meets girl. Boy meets girl. Boy
meets girl. Boy meets girl. Boy
meets girl. Boy meets girl. Boy meets
girl. Boy meets girl. Boy meets girl.
Boy meets girl. Boy meets girl. Boy
meets girl. Boy meets girl. Boy meets
girl. Boy meets girl. Boy meets girl.
Boy meets girl. Boy meets girl. Boy
meets girl. Boy meets girl. Boy meets
girl. Boy meets girl. Boy meets girl.
Boy meets girl. Boy meets girl. Boy
meets girl. Boy meets girl. Boy meets
girl. Boy meets girl. Boy meets girl.
Boy meets girl. Boy meets girl. Boy
meets girl. Boy meets girl. Boy meets
girl. Boy meets girl. Boy meets girl.
Boy meets girl. Boy meets girl. Boy
meets girl. Boy meets girl. Boy meets
girl. Boy meets girl. Boy meets girl.
Boy meets girl. Boy meets girl. Boy
meets girl. Boy meets girl. Boy meets
girl. Boy meets girl. Boy meets girl.
Boy meets girl. Boy meets girl. Boy

MEETS

GIRL

MEETS GIRL

a novel

WILL ENTREKIN

*O*nce upon a time I fell in love with a girl who didn't love me in return.

And while that may not be, as openings go, altogether novel (for who among us hasn't felt the sharp-barbed long-constant prick-pull of unrequited love?), still I've always known it's how I need to begin this story. I've always known I'm going to eventually need the big guns if I intend to make my way through, and I've known that since before I even started, back when I was sitting next to Veronica—the girl with whom I fell in love but who did not love me in return—and across from Angus Silver, about whom I will tell you more as we go along, because Angus Silver is an idea you need to be eased into.

Back then, when I understood, finally, how to tell this story and thus redeem myself, I also realized it wasn't going to be an easy story to tell, and even that I might not actually have the talent to pull it off.

Still, I understood, as well, I had to try.

And so I shall. So I begin to recall and to recount even if not for the first time; I have test-written and re-written this opening so many times I've lost count, but not a single one has yet worked. This is, in fact, the only opening so far that has carried me beyond false starts and falser endings, which I can tell you because, in the spirit of honesty, I have already finished this story, and am now swinging back around to revise it, to polish it and to make it gleam.

Then again, in the spirit of honesty, I must also admit that, though I finished it, I did not do so successfully. Much of the revision before me may be making the words gleam, but I am already aware I need to scrap the ending. The ending is the messy part, of course, and while I think I may be close, the conclusion has not yet felt as right as this opening. There are certainly other ways to begin—

It was the best of times, it was the worst of times.—

or perhaps—

Call me Ishmael.—

but those beginnings have only ever made me wonder why Dickens could never make up his mind, not to mention why parents might name their child Ishmael and whether that was only the beginning of the abuses the poor boy suffered.

But 'once upon a time?' This is how stories are supposed to begin if only because it seems like how they have always begun back since before there were any previous times to pin a 'once' upon. Even the phrase itself has a singular power you can feel in your gut, a primal quality that opens us as easily as a key a lock. Simply hearing it makes me believe my father is the smartest person in the world, my mother the most beautiful. Suddenly I feel like I am wearing my old powder-blue Dr. Dentons with the crinkly foot-pouches to protect me from whatever under the bed was drooling.

It runs silent and deep to find, within me, the memories of my mother reading me *Little Bear* and "The Leap-frog"—

A Flea, a Grasshopper, and a Leap-frog once wanted to see which could jump highest; and they invited the whole world, and everybody else besides who chose to come to see the festival.—

and *Alice's Adventures in Wonderland*—

Alice was beginning to get very tired of sitting by her sister on the bank and of having nothing to do: once or twice she had peeped into the book her sister was reading, but it had no pictures or conversations in it, "and what is the use of a book," thought Alice, "without pictures or conversations?"—

and stories about mist-shrouded castles overlooking emerald green realms. Wolves with big teeth, and evil stepsisters. Bears and chairs and porridge-eating intruders, evil witches and alchemical hobgoblins, grandmother's house and gingerbread cottages. It calls to my mind Disney princes with thick, black hair and big, blue eyes, who gallop trusty steeds through sun-dappled forests in enchanted lands to save from untold danger the women they love, because the one thing all princes charming have in common is the girls in whose names they pursue their noble quests.

Princes charming are silly like that.

But then, all boys are. I once heard a story about William Faulkner known to many as a Nobel laureate—

It is the writer's privilege to help man endure by lifting his heart, by reminding him of the courage and honor and hope and pride and compassion and pity and sacrifice which have been the glory of his past.—

but known to probably more as an Oprah pick, and known to some few besides as a Hollywood writer. My own favorite work ever by William Faulkner is his adaptation of Raymond Chandler's *The Big Sleep*, one of Hollywood's first, not to mention smartest, action movies, much of which one can attribute to Chandler himself—

When in doubt, have a man come through the door with a gun in his hand.—

and the thing about *The Big Sleep*, the reason it's among Faulkner's finest work, is simple: Faulkner knew what the story was about. It's ostensibly a crime-noir, with stolen pictures and missing persons and triple crosses, and it's easy to get lost in the complicated plot, but Faulkner understood the story was simple and reminded himself of it in a very simple way. His supervisors and managers did not know of his reminder until after he had left Hollywood and they cleaned out his desk to find two items.

The first was a bottle of Jack Daniels. Which I would say makes sense because Faulkner was a writer, but that would only propagate the myth of writers as drunks and bypass the truth: Faulkner was an alcoholic, who sometimes thought he wrote best when he was intoxicated but, given the state of his novels, perhaps should have waited till he had sobered up to revise them.

The second is more important: a single sheet of paper on which was typed, over and over and over again, in classic 12-point Courier font, a single phrase:

`Boy meets girl.`

Because that is what so many stories hinge upon. Not all of them, I know: some are about whales or a young girl's adventures in a strange world or even—

well, I'm not entirely certain what *A Tale of Two Cities* was about, but then, who is?—but many of the real ones, the true ones, begin with a boy meeting a girl.

Because that's what we do. We meet girls, and we fall in love with them, and then the real silliness begins. In ode to their beauty we compose poetry—

Who will believe my verse in time to come?—

and in honor of their faces we launch a thousand ships. In pursuits of their oft-capricious affections, we undertake quests of monumental foolishness. We tilt at windmills. We storm castles using only a wheelbarrow and holocaust cloak despite that we were mostly dead mere moments before and have been revived solely via ingestion of miraculous chocolate dispensed by Billy Crystal in bad prosthetics. Hell, I'm not sure what sort of motivation Melville said Ahab had, but he gave his character a peg-leg and an obsessive quest for a marine creature whose most distinguishing feature, besides a 'hump like a snow-hill,' was a blowhole, both of which sound more than a little Freudian to me.

Being a boy myself, I am no different, which is why I need to tell this story hoping for redemption, and that girl with whom I fell in love—who did not love me in return—was Veronica Sawyer. Veronica Sawyer has wavy, black hair highlit blonde and eyes the color of natural emeralds in mahogany. Veronica has a quick laugh and an easy smile and dresses like she belongs in a Banana Republic catalogue. Veronica speaks no fewer than three languages and knows how to request wine in several others besides. Veronica believes there is some point to graduate study in philosophy, and if you think, now, that I have somehow idealized Veronica Sawyer, I will say, simply, well, yes, that's very much the point, isn't it?

Because it truly was that sort of Love. Veronica is that sort of girl whom boys meet and fall in love with and do spectacularly blunderous things for. Veronica Sawyer is the sort of girl who makes writers capitalize words, who in times of yore would have inspired gallant knights to find dragons solely that they might fight and slay them. Veronica is the sort of girl the memory of whom could have inspired Cervantes, in his squalid prison cell, to write of Quixote's Dulcinea, to dream the impossible dream, to fight the unbeatable foe. All of which, of course, is why I felt I needed to begin with those four famous words.

Because, you see, once upon a time, a man who told me to call him Angus offered me what should have been a very simple choice between someone I thought I deeply loved and something I very deeply loved to do. I, being the sort of boy who would, if not storm a castle (for want of a cloud) nor launch a thousand ships (for want of an armada), certainly compose bad poetry to win the affections of a girl I loved who did not love me in return made a spectacularly bad decision.

When she discovered what I had done, Veronica became the kind of infuriated I would need phrases like 'hellfire and brimstone' and words like 'venomous' to adequately describe, and even then I'd be comically understating her degree of righteous indignation. Then again, she certainly had every reason to become so righteously indignant, because the choice I made had every bit as much to do with her and her future as it did with me and my own, even if I didn't quite realize that at the time.

I didn't realize a lot of things at the time. If I had, I might not have made such a spectacularly bad decision, a choice so bad, in fact, that the only way I can make it right, the only way I can redeem it, is to tell this story. I'm very much aware that much hinges upon my ability to tell it, which is in addition why I began with 'once upon a time'—not just because of old stories or big guns or fairy tales or romanticism, but because two futures depend on my ability to tell this story through to its rightful end, and beginning with those four words inspires some hope, however small and however distant, of three other small words.

I think I can reach them.

So help me, I'm going to try.

And so help me, I promise you one thing: I will pull out every damned trick I've got to do so. You can look up my sleeves and examine my hat to confirm that I have absolutely nothing in either, but in the end I promise you that I will either produce the flowers and the rabbit you so desire, or I will fail spectacularly and conclusively to do so, and really, isn't it worth reading even if only to find out which one occurs?

On my honor, I will do my best.

Words, don't fail me now.

Chapter Two (I didn't start with 'Chapter One' because I wanted to open with 'Once upon a time'), in which we encounter the reason this story has a conflict (because a boy meeting a girl is not one)

*W*hat should come next, according to conventions of both literature and drama, is my eloquent recounting of the moment I first glimpsed Veronica Sawyer. I'm supposed to tell you that sunlight cast her in a halo that burned her very image onto my oh-so-sensitive soul; that the beautiful smile upon her perfect lips made mine quiver with want of her; that she stirred within me the calls of both wild and poet alike; that I, to put it simply and to paraphrase Eddie Izzard alluding to Albert Schweitzer, quite fancied her.

Unfortunately, I can't, mainly because I don't actually remember meeting her—

and yet her name was like a summons to all my foolish blood.—

which is, perhaps, not the most romantic way to continue this story, but then again might be the most realistic. I played in a tee-ball league with Veronica's brother, Tom, back when Tom and I were kids. The only things I remember about back then are the lopsided tees, the coach who would yell at me to ask what I was swinging at, and the Big League Chew. My teammates and I would stalk across the parking lot between innings to purchase from the snack-shack stale nachos smothered in half-melted Velveeta. My puking on second base became the highlight of an otherwise low season.

Quick and agile and preternaturally athletic, Tom was the shortstop for our team the Jacksonboro Bobcats, whereas I was small and uncoordinated and had instincts better suited to deep left. One day, Tom stopped Jacky Malone, the opposing team's big, slow catcher, from beating the shit out of me, and from that moment forward, Tom and I became fast, if unlikely, friends. We were probably ten years old, and we wore cotton tee shirts as uniforms and hats that cost a dollar. Our folks and siblings came to our games, all of which were held on the field behind the local grade school, and I met Veronica for the first time at some point during the three seasons that Tom and I played in the league.

Three seasons of shredded gum and adolescent chaos, and the sole reason I'd ever joined was that I wanted to knock the stitches off a slowball. I think I believed that if I could just hit a single homerun, I might wake up the following morning taller and faster and better.

I spent three seasons playing deep left, and no ball I ever hit made it past the pitcher's mound; hits fair and foul alike dribbled off the end of my bat.

Eventually I gave up the idea that I had any athletic potential and turned instead to school and grades. I sucked at math and hated recess, but then I discovered books. I fell in love with stories, and instead of returning to the league during sixth grade, I whipped through our town's small library, which included everything H.G. Wells—

The stranger came early in February, one wintry day, through a biting wind and a driving snow, the last snowfall of the year, over the down, walking as it seemed from Bramblehurst railway station, and carrying a little black portmanteau in his thickly gloved hand.—

and more Lewis Carroll—

'Twas brillig, and the slithy toves
Did gyre and gimble in the wade—

I mention all this because this story is not solely about how hard I fell for Veronica. Any real story must contain conflict, and falling in love with a girl who didn't love me in return isn't one. That's the way life so often happens. You fall for some girl or some guy who barely even notices you, and you can't understand why you fell so hard for them, because you know, rationally, logically, they're no great shakes, but you don't care and you do it anyway. It's a lopsided smile, a carefree smirk, a winking eye. Calloused fingertips with crescent moons of darkness under the nails or slender hands with elegant knuckles. It's never chests or asses or anything so common, though you don't look away from those, either.

No, the reason this story has conflict is simple; one day, the librarian at my grade school set aside for me a book she thought I would like, about an orphaned boy wizard who had a mop of unruly black hair over a zigzag scar. The big, bright cover seemed a little more colorful and a little more childish than I had begun to read by then (the Hardy Boys were always running from explosions), but I took the book home and began that evening to read, and by the following morning, I wanted nothing less in the world than to be . . .

Neville Longbottom.

You thought I was going to say Harry, didn't you? The Boy Who Lived, as he was always known in those books? But no, because, you see, though Harry was the titular hero who fought the bad guy, if you read that first book, the character who actually came through in the end, the character who saved the day for Gryffindor, was Neville. I remember laughing with glee when Dumbledore awarded those final points to Neville, and I also remember realizing right then, as I closed that book, precisely what I wanted to do: I wanted to tell stories. Exciting stories. Awesome stories. I wanted to make some reader, somewhere, somewhen, feel what I did during that moment: a sense of infinite possibility.

The following day, I found myself scribbling through class, missing most of the notes I was supposed to take in favor of a story about . . . well, you know, I want to say I don't recall that first, earliest story, but I do; two young boys very similar to Tom and me met space aliens who gave them special superpowers.

That story never made it past the acquisition of said powers, and neither, for years, did any story I ever started. What can I say? I only ever wanted to fly.

Progression finally began as I started to read more. After blazing through both the Hardy Boys and *A Wrinkle in Time*, I moved on to Poe—

Let me call myself, for the present, William Wilson. The fair page now lying before me need not be sullied with my real appellation.—

before I found Stephen King's *Needful Things* and *Eyes of the Dragon* and Dean Koontz's *Strangers* and *Watchers* and *Lightning*.

Is it too melodramatic to say those stories saved me? It's not as though there was ever anything particularly malevolent in my life, not like I sought in my library refuge from a drunken step-father. Still, in those stories, I found the potential for the possibility I so wanted, and I'm not sure what my life would have become without books. I grew up in that small town, where everyone knew the quarterback but nobody really cared about the valedictorian, nevermind whoever finished second (as I did), and most people just kind of stuck around. Most of the residents of my hometown had grown up there, often just as their parents had.

Those books and stories made me want more, and when I started writing myself, I began to seek new experiences. Writing, if it didn't make me cooler and better and more interesting, at least made me believe I could be if I stuck with it. Most of all, writing made me believe I could find something more interesting, and for a young kid in high school who can't quite find a place no matter how hard he looked, in that sort of possibility lies salvation.

I found mine through studying. I found mine in Jack London's adventure stories, which inspired me to join the Boy Scouts and earn Eagle. I found mine because I realized I would need a car to go anywhere worth visiting, which made me get a part-time job working at a local hardware store, where I learned how to solve the sorts of domestic problems to which one can apply a wrench. By the time graduation came around, my activities around the community earned me several scholarships that allowed me to go to college.

All through those years, I wrote. I graduated from pens and ruled notebooks, first to my family's computer until my parents surprised me with a desktop for my sixteenth birthday. My parents had never been particularly well off, which made the gift that much more significant, and I made sure, over the next few years, to earn their money's worth from it. I used it to write the application essay that earned me a full academic scholarship to college, all the English papers that helped boost my GPA, and, of course, the first stories that weren't just adolescent fantasies of super powers and space aliens.

No, they were bad Dean Koontz rip-offs.

But that was okay. By then I was reading Douglas Adams and Richard Cox and Neil Gaiman, through whom I eventually found Jonathan Carroll and Will Shetterly and then the Nielsen Haydens, Patrick and Teresa, two editors at TOR, a major science fiction publisher. By then, in other words, I had begun to read more books by better writers, and most of all, was seeking them on my own, beyond the confines of the classrooms where my teachers were still trying to convince me Shakespeare was a genius and *Pygmalion* was how every suitor in the world was supposed to feel—

Women upset everything. When you let them into your life, you find that the woman is driving at one thing and you're driving at another.—

And okay, so maybe it really was.

***

By then, I'd long outgrown little league, but Tom and I were in the same patrol in our local Boy Scout troop, and so I saw Veronica often over the years, at courts of honor and various scouting functions. She seemed to get prettier every year, bypassing awkward adolescence to blossom into the beauty of oncoming adulthood. You could tell just by looking at her she was going to break some hearts, while I, on the other hand, remained pretty much a set of thick glasses with a squeaky voice and parted hair. Plus, of course, my pen.

When Tom and I began to hang out more often, playing PlayStation tournaments of martial arts fighting games, I began to see Veronica more often, as well. Some people are lucky when the people they fancy never give them the time of day, or realize they exist, but with Veronica, I had the opposite problem: I became such good friends with Tom that I basically became a second, honorary, older brother, more a best friend than a crush.

Which was why I decided to write her poetry before I left for college upstate.

God, I was such a cliché, wasn't I? That's what I'm thinking as I recount those gawky, awkward years— part-time job at a hardware store, Boy Scout, track and swimming, second in my class. Christ, it's like I was the supporting character actor in my own damned life. Those poems, too, were wholly unremarkable; imagine every cliché every high school senior has ever come up with, every groan-inducing stanza and cringe-worthy metric foot. The details of those poems are hazy, now—
and just before dawn I burn with desire
while I attempt to extinguish this delirious fire
that burns at my core and all the while,
I think of you.
Just before dawn.—
but I know I wrote nine of them, each worse than the one previous. About the only original aspect of the endeavor was its title: "True Images of Beauty," as I'd read that 'Veronica' was Latin for "true image."

(I discovered later it's actually derived from the Greek *Berenice*, meaning "bringer of victory," which means that even when I was original I was wrong, which may become a running theme here.

I wanted to let her know how I felt. I had spent so many evenings with her in her family's kitchen, just chatting, often eschewing another round of UltimaFighter just to talk to her. I got butterflies watching her pour a glass of water. I'd never actually told her that, but my major mistake was believing she hadn't already known; I'm not sure it could have been more obvious had I skywritten it on her living-room ceiling.

I composed those poems and bound them and then left them, one evening, in her mailbox. Just an hour or so later, Mrs. Sawyer called my house; considering I left my feelings behind on paper so I didn't have to look Veronica in the eye when I told her I was so in love with her, is it appropriate Veronica confirmed her solely-platonic feelings for me through her mother? That's exactly what happened.

It's not like I hadn't known she loved me like an older brother, no more and no less, but the actual confirmation made the world seem smaller, and darker. I can't say I had hoped otherwise; one of the reasons I hadn't said anything before then was that I had convinced myself that, so long as I never said anything, so long as Veronica never had to tell me—either outright or through her mother—that she only loved me as a friend, there might still be hope for more.

Of course, there was not.

Not until I met Angus, anyway. But first, college and some years after.

Chapter Three (College and some years after)

I started college in August 2001, at Montclair State University, barely three weeks before those men flew those two planes into the World Trade Center. College, then, began in an initial, froshy blush of flusterment and excitement that turned too suddenly into something far too somber and solemn. When once we had been undecided, we declared majors in philosophy and theology and biology and physics, as if we believed we might study our stumbling ways to understanding. Montclair was close enough to Manhattan that, during the subsequent autumn, our campus smelled like a construction site when the wind blew just right, and we students made it a point to always be aware of the national threat level before we left for classes. I remember the Anthrax scares and the admonitions to stock up on duct tape and plastic covering.

I pitched myself into my studies like they could be my salvation, burying myself so deeply in extra credits that I had very little energy left over to devote to much else; one of the benefits of doing this was that I stopped pining after Veronica. I put my head down and got the grades and studied literature and science, and by the time I graduated, I was engaged to a girl I thought I loved, which prompted me to find a crummy little apartment in Hoboken. My fiancée was Polish and came from a very strict, very conservative, very traditional family, which strained our relationship until finally it cracked under her pressure. Just a few weeks after I had graduated, and not even a full week after I'd moved into an apartment I'd chosen mainly because it was within walking distance of her house, my fiancée told me our relationship wasn't fair to me.

It came at first as a shock until, a few dark, empty-feeling days later, I discovered a newfound sense of something I can't describe as anything besides immense possibility. I suddenly had no ties, no commitments, and I could do anything, go anywhere, be anyone.

I think I reacted like most people in any such situation might: by remaining resolutely me. Waking up in the same bed, studiously checking the same hairline, buttoning the same shirts and shaving the same cheeks, walking the same streets and entering the same building to climb the same stairs to sit in the same desk . . .

There is some degree of comfort in the familiar. It may not be much to subsist on, but for a while it can be enough. Just after I'd graduated, I'd applied at a temp agency that had placed me at the *New Yorker* as an assistant to the advertising sales director, and there I stayed, performing menial tasks like updating databases and collating business cards into a rolodex. I'd leave my desk in the afternoon, usually at 5:30 or so, just late enough to be noticed as I squeaked out an hour or so of overtime every week but never so much to actually accomplish anything. PATH train back to Hoboken, take-out, and then writing. I was working on my second novel by then, after having completed my first, the afore-mentioned Dean Koontz rip-off, while an undergrad. My second, back then, wasn't much better; I'd had the idea while still in high school, and its origins showed through in places.

By then, I'd also begun to split my weekends between home in Hoboken and home in southern New Jersey. Tom had formed a band called Foolish with some other guys from our hometown, and I started blowing off steam by attending their gigs all over South Jersey and Philadelphia. There are few things like a dance floor to get you feeling loose and young and without trouble, especially when the lights are dim and you have a few in you and you truly believe the night could last forever.

I saw Veronica a few times at those gigs. Each time I would buy her a drink, and each time we would talk in precisely the ways you're just not supposed to in that sort of situation. Those situations are built for drunken debauchery and gratuitous youth, one-night stands with girls whose numbers you don't try to forget solely because you never made the effort to remember their faces in the first place. Those nights are alcoholically and rhythmically engineered to exist in a nether-place between recklessness and responsibility, and though they might support crooked smiles and tipsy kisses, wondering if there is more to life and the world out there is the sort of tear-soaked question that usually signals the person asking it should be cut off.

But not Veronica and I; when we weren't dancing, we were talking about what we planned to do in the coming years, and where and how we planned to do it. I'd graduated the year before, but still I was unsure, and still I felt as though I were in some vague, quarter-aged purgatory with fluorescent lights and blink-lighted telephones on fiberboard desks. Still I only wanted to write, and Veronica—a philosophy major who'd taken up acting in school plays and written her thesis on Ionesco—and I most often found ourselves nursing lite beers while talking about drama and words and books and life. I remember those nights as dimly as those bars: blurs of golden and pink neon, Tom's loud music, the way Veronica moved when she danced.

If there is a better way to spend your mid-twenties, I'm not aware of it.

But like all such times of perfection in one's life, it could only last so long. No matter how idyllic life might seem at any moment, it's always in danger of tipping dramatically over; when it's as good as mine was then, it can only get worse, and when it does, it can only get worse hard:

***

Coming on autumn, 2006: I was still at the *New Yorker*, still in advertising sales, performing in addition any go-to work anyone needed completed, PowerPoint slides for the CFO, Excel spreadsheets for the VP of Marketing. Part of the reason I remained on was in the hope that it might provide me an in if I decided to write a short story; I'd met some of the people in editorial, and I figured that handing someone a manuscript at least skips over the slushpile.

I can't pretend that coordinating ads was the most fascinating job in the world, but I enjoyed it. I always was a people person and, as my ex had once told me, I gave good phone. Plus, I was popular in the office, which was gorgeous; the entrance to Condé Nast is just off Times Square and its building looms above it, a great gleaming skyscraper among thousands very much like it. Those walls house multiple magazines—*The New Yorker*, *Wired*, *Vogue* for both men and women, *Glamour* and *GQ*, *Details* and *Vanity Fair*, a handful of *Bride*s and a couple of *Golf*s—all with distinct floors and departments and teams of workers, and if you really want to know just how achingly metropolitan it really is, how hip and modern and urban, how it embodies everything about Manhattan without ever really trying, you need look no further than its cafeteria: designed by Frank Gehry and featuring great, waving walls and Spartan fixtures. There, in the cafeteria, no cash is tendered; all transactions use debit cards. There in the cafeteria, the floor seems off-white but is, in fact, ash, and the custom-designed booths sit a handful of people each, all of whom wear designer suits and designer shoes and designer watches, and the blue titanium walls undulate like City waves without ever actually moving at all.

I went on a few dates during that time, or at least I think I did. I might have. I'm pretty sure I did. I "did lunch" with pretty girls in midtown. Heirloom tomatoes as an appetizer at Grand Central Station and clam chowder at some famous soup place near the train platform. Drinks at happy hours after work, where all the gals sipped pink cosmopolitans and probably should have been smoking menthol cigarettes long and slender as their legs but couldn't because it was recently illegal. I went out with artists who daylit as administrative assistants, directors who spent their afternoons maintaining records for a dental office, and dancers of hip hop and ballet alike, but I still alternated weekends between Hoboken and home, and so very few of those oft-awkward first dates ever made it onto slightly less uncomfortable second dates.

I never minded much, as I'd continued to work on that second novel. After a while, I gave up on short stories, as I discovered that I was more interested in, long fiction, not to mention that I finally realized that the only people who really get published in the *New Yorker* have names like McEwan, Proulx, and Moody; basically, writers I'd never gotten into because I much preferred the action and fun to fancy writing. I'd begun to expand my reading, picking up Michael Chabon and then the Nicks, Hornby and Earls, trying Dickens—

Whether I shall turn out to be the hero of my own life, or whether that station will be held by anybody else, these pages must show.

and then Austen—

It is a truth universally acknowledged that a single man in possession of a good fortune must be in want of a wife.—

which at the time only made me relieved I wasn't yet in possession of a good fortune.

***

I thought I was doing fine until my dissatisfaction caught up with me. It began gradually; I started to wonder if I really wanted to stay on at the *New Yorker*, and why. I started to consider that I was nearly 24 and still working temp jobs; I didn't want to become an aspiring anything daylighting in an office.

Perhaps I put too much into the idea that all I wanted to do was write: I began to devote more time and energy to it, eventually to the point that I basically stopped dating altogether in favor of focusing on words and pages. I even started bringing a flash drive with my novel on it into work, keeping the document open while I laid out ads. If my bosses ever suspected, they never said, but then again I have a feeling they were all doing the same thing; the cliché is that everyone in Hollywood has a screenplay, and I think everyone else, everywhere else in the world, either thinks they can write a book or is already working on one. Most of the people I spoke to were at least somewhat interested in writing, and all universally believed that they could pen either the next bestselling memoir or the Great American Novel.

Me, I wasn't sure about the Great American Anything, though I'd already begun to realize that working in advertising at the *New Yorker* wasn't really going to get me anywhere besides that fiberboard desk.

And that was when I had one of those perfect moments the likes of which remain indelibly with you all your life.

***

Perfect moments—you know the ones I mean, tight little barbs of time that cling hard enough to your heart to draw tears—don't come often, but if you're lucky, you recognize them when they occur. Perfect moments: the first time you see a new woman nude; the first time you hold your child. Moments that, should you be so lucky, you recall when you're old and grey and ready to move on from this world to what happens next.

That night, I was sitting on my big ugly yellow chair I'd picked from a neighbor's curb, in front of the piano bench I used as my desk. I could feel the heat of the processor or harddrive or whatever else spins hot in a laptop even through the gym shorts I was wearing, and I remember the white screen with its blur of black text, though in my memory the words are neither legible nor intelligible. I remember I was on page 68, and I had begun to read what I'd written the day before when suddenly, instead of characters and images and plot, I realized I was just reading words—

words, words, words—

without any meaning. Words without any magic behind them. Words like lightning bugs in the middle of an August thunderstorm, words—

full of sound and fury, signifying nothing—

that were no more than the sum of the letters that made them up.

And what difference did they make?

Because isn't that the question? Hamlet might have mused otherwise—

to be or not to be—that is the question—

but really I think we all seek little more than a way to make a difference, and I realized, then, that I hoped to somehow change the world by writing about it.

But how might I do so if I was just sitting there with a laptop and a blinking cursor? How might I do so by putting one letter after another? Surely better men than I had done so many times upon a time, and where had that gotten the world? Sitting there in my ugly chair, staring at those thin words on that glowing white screen, I realized I didn't know—

When a man is in doubt about this or that in his writing, it will often guide him if he asks himself how it will tell a hundred years hence.—

and I don't know that I've ever been more scared than that moment I doubted something I had always been so certain of. Prior to that moment in that chair in front of that screen, I'd never once considered that I might not become a successful author. Not that I thought it was anything so overstated as my destiny, but I had never for a moment doubted that if I just worked hard enough and put in the proper amount of time to tell the stories I wanted to tell, I would be successful.

And not just successful in the sense of publishing a handful of novels, either—perhaps it was because Jo Rowling and her bespectacled hero had prompted my realization of my own vocation, but writing novels and becoming a mega-bestselling billionaire author had always, in my head, gone hand in hand. Even to the point that, as an undergraduate in college, my plan had been that I would sell my novel by the time I graduated and could, rather than enter the workforce, instead go out on a massive, multi-venue and international author tour in support of said novel.

Obviously, we see how that worked out for me.

Which may have been the prompt for that moment of sitting there, in front of that screen, and realizing, for the very first time since I had closed *Harry Potter and the Philosopher's Stone*, that there was no guarantee any story I wrote would go anywhere. I could write all my life, I realized, and never sell a book. Never find a reader.

This is, I think, where I'm supposed to tell you that I closed my eyes and took a deep breath and allowed that next word to come. That I typed it, and then I typed the next one, too, and the next one again, because that's what I was supposed to do, right? That's what separates the novelists from the hobbyists; no matter what, no matter when, no matter how, when the going gets tough, the tough write it down, and I'm supposed to tell you that when it came right down to it, when I faced that moment, I stared it down and said—

yes yes I said yes I will yes—

and I kept writing.

But I didn't.

I'm not proud of that. In fact, if I'm to be honest, I am embarrassed to say that instead, I closed my laptop, set it back on my piano-bench desk, and walked away. I am ashamed to admit that, when the going got tough, I walked away.

I left my bedroom and crossed the hallway of my crummy little apartment, where floorboards I could see between groaned beneath my feet, into my kitchen. I figured I would grab something to eat, read a magazine or watch some television, get my mind off writing, off my job at the *New Yorker*, off being in the City, off living for an hour or so, but I opened the fridge to discover pretty much nothing in it: a six-pack of Corona, half a lime, and a packet of chocolate-frosted donuts. I decided to order some Thai instead, and I speed-dialed the local place as I popped a Corona. I finished that six-pack alone that night while I ate my chicken panang, watched bad network reality television, and surfed Internet porn.

***

The following morning, I woke up with a tongue so alien I had difficulty enunciating to my supervisor that I would be unable to report to work (now, years later, is the first moment I've ever wondered if they called in a temp to replace me for the day). In fact, I ended up calling out the following morning, as well. I remember those being a dark couple of days, though not in the sense of daylight and brightness; outside, November glittered even if it didn't do so warmly. Rather, I spent those couple of days venturing into Midtown to skim the bargain CD racks while I considered what I wanted to do from there, and all the while I did so I tried to determine whether writing truly was a part of it.

I had always thought it was, but where, I thought, had it gotten me? I was far enough beyond college I should have begun to think about an actual career, and I was realizing there was no guarantee writing would be part of it, which made me wonder if I really cared to devote so much time and energy to it. I could see doing so for something that would offer some reward, but I realized I no longer knew, and hadn't ever, that writing would.

I returned to work on a Thursday, and I asked my supervisor, who had a perfect head of salt-and-pepper hair and called me 'sport,' if I might have a moment of his time. He agreed to fit me in during his lunch, and so, while he chowed down on a chicken teriyaki salad from the lunch place around the corner, I asked him if he thought there might be a place for me on staff. I told him I had thoroughly enjoyed my time there, and really, I wasn't asking for a position I hadn't already fulfilled for nearly a year by then.

He listened carefully while I made my case, then told me that it might be a problem if only because of the budget. My position, apparently, took funds from a budget for freelancers and temporary workers; that money was separate from human resources and payroll. "Which means that it would have to go to board approval to allocate the necessary resources. I won't say it's unlikely, sport, only that it would require some budgetary juggling the board might be reluctant to attempt. You know how the board is," he told me.

I'm sure I probably nodded even though I actually hadn't a clue how the board was.

As it turned out, the board was composed of a group of individuals who were good at having meetings but somewhat worse at keeping track of their finances.

When my supervisor brought it up to them, rather than realizing they had a dedicated worker already on their staff, they realized instead they had a freelance contract employee whose paycheck pulled from a fund they had forgotten existed. The sudden discovery of my presence caused a minor kerfuffle among the board and its members, and a week before Thanksgiving, the not-so-delicate task of revealing that our company was freezing the fund they used to pay my salary fell to my supervisor. He told me the board regretted the decision, but it could no longer keep me on, and then he handed me the bottle of Scotch he'd already bought me for Christmas.

As severance packages go, it's more than some contract employees get.

***

So there I was, out of work and uncertain about both what to do and how. Luckily, knowing that the holidays were coming up (which meant both travel and presents), I'd saved enough to pay my rent through the upcoming January. Unluckily, that meant I had pretty much cleaned out my savings, so I called my temp agency to find out if I couldn't pick up a few short-term assignments. Being that it was the middle of November, though, the job pickings were slim and far between while most companies slowed for the holidays. My contact at the agency assured me that there should be more openings come January, and in the meantime, why not take a couple of weeks off? Hadn't I mentioned I was working on a novel? Why not finish it?

Not something I particularly cared to be reminded of. Why not indeed. Mainly because I hadn't actually written anything since the moment I'd seen all that work as nothing more than words; I had signed up for direct deposit when I started temping, so I hadn't even had to endorse a check. I won't say the well was dry, because after all I still had ideas, for the novel I was then working on and for several others besides, but rather I was wondering if the water was still any good, and that wasn't conducive to getting anyfuckingthing done whatsoever. I've always been the sort who refrains from doing anything until I just can't hold back anymore, and I didn't have that feeling with writing right then, that feeling that I wanted to, that I had to. I had always thought there was something perfectly Zen about a blank page, all that white, all that possibility, but I had also always believed that the intention to disturb such perfection came with responsibility. When it came down to it, I thought those pages were better off blank than with my random words spewed onto them.

So I did what any self-respecting creator of something should do at precisely such a moment: I high-tailed it out of Dodge. One can only make so many pointless treks into midtown, shopping for used CDs you can't actually afford anyway, and it was already too chilly to relax in Central Park. So I told my agency I'd be unavailable for a couple of weeks, and I hopped on a Greyhound home the week before Thanksgiving.

That was when the trouble really started.

Chapter Four, in which the trouble really starts, and which introduces a gun above a mantle, figuratively if not literally

*T*hanksgiving Eve, I saw Veronica at a Foolish gig, and we made plans to get coffee that Saturday at the local Barnes & Noble in the only strip-mall complex for miles, a classic-casual outing that on occasion flirts with being more than it is, date-wise, but never actually manages it. I don't know what you'd call the fringe collar of the black suede coat she wore when she showed up, but it looked like short strands of fine, grey yarn all around her neck, which only brought out her green-blue eyes, lending to them the gravity of an imminent thunderstorm and all the ferocity of lightning. But still she smiled, and it made her float.

I don't remember much about that conversation, but I'm sure it was like any conversation Veronica and I have ever had—long, digressing discussions of classes and life and movies and music, lyrics and dialogue. I'm sure it wasn't long before conversation came back around to me and what I was doing, and when it did . . . well, it all just came out in one long, stream-of-consciousness soliloquy Kerouac would have needed Benzedrine and toilet-roll typing paper to keep speed with. I told her about how writing had ground down, how I just didn't know if I had the juice left to say much of anything worthwhile, and that, at the worst possible time, when I thought about devoting my energy to something else, that was when there didn't seem anything else to devote that energy to.

"So what're you doing?" she asked.

I told her I'd paid rent through January. I told her I'd tried to find other ways to occupy my time, but Manhattan was expensive, and without a regular gig my financial resources were limited at best and running on fumes at worst.

"So what're you going to do, then?"

And I stopped, because I had to admit, I didn't have a damned clue. A few months, hell, a few weeks before, I would have had an answer ready even if that answer probably would have lacked any real specificity: "What am I going to do? Ah, I dunno. I'll figure something out. Always do, right?"

Right then, though, I discovered I couldn't find the confidence for words like that. I shrugged. "I don't— you know, I don't actually know. I'm trying to pretend I can make the best of it, really, but I don't have a clue what the best of it is," I told her as I pushed my waxed-plastic cup away. Talking about everything had made me restless.

"You want to get out of here?"

I tried to chuckle. "I'm probably not the best company at the moment, am I?"

"No, it's not that," she reached forward, squeezing my forearm. "It's just—you seem anxious, and I figured sitting here, in the middle of a bookstore, glugging down caffeine while the loudspeakers play Christmas carols . . . makes you want to jump out of your own skin, doesn't it?"

"That obvious, huh?"

"So I was just thinking, we've been sitting here, and we drank our coffee and all, so why not take a walk? Get out of the mall, away from crazy shoppers and discount crap?"

Never hesitated: Veronica was right that I damned near wanted to jump out of my own skin, and probably the only reason I didn't was I knew that I would only become a very confused skeleton still completely uncertain about what to do next. So we left the bookstore, into bracing cold and the kind of near-on winter world you feel like a brick to the nose. The mall itself was big enough, but just like everywhere else, various retail stores and chain eateries had sprung up all around it: Target and BestBuy, Outback and Red Lobster. Nothing ever actually closed, just changed: the Ground Round gave way to some generic Western-BBQ themed family joint, and the Olive Garden had once been a TGI Fridays. Veronica and I headed away from there, and just around the corner, the blatant store-lights gave way to a mom-and-pop diner and a few plazas we both knew well because we'd grown up only a few towns over.

We didn't talk much as we walked. By then, I was used to walking in Manhattan, block after block of tall buildings more spectacular than you ever imagined, life on not just the most enormous scale possible but also in time-lapse—a New York minute passes like a by-rushing subway train. I got preoccupied by how startlingly different it was where I'd grown up. I spent a lot of time shuttling—between Manhattan and home, between home and Foolish gigs—but so rarely did I venture much beyond the routine of certain pre-set routes that I realized, as I walked with Veronica, how much I had forgotten about where I grew up. When you live in Manhattan, you can forget the frustrated strip malls and desperate shopping plazas of suburbs. Manhattan is so fast and so . . . well, itself, really, that you can easily forget not only that the rest of the world has problems but even that it exists.

I realized, then, that Veronica had said something, but I'd been so preoccupied I hadn't caught it. "Huh?"

"I think I've got change coming."

"What?"

"I offered you a penny for your thoughts."

"Oh. Sorry. Just thinking about how different it is down here. Compared to Manhattan, I mean. As obvious thoughts go, way up there, so you probably actually deserve a refund."

"You like Manhattan?"

"It's—," I said, but I broke off. Because I realized, then, I didn't know how to finish that thought. Manhattan doesn't just transcend any adjective you can think of so much as it laughs them off with a self-awareness somehow divorced from either arrogance or hubris. Manhattan isn't proud if only because it's so busy doing other things it rarely stops to bask in how completely awesome it is. "It's New York," I finally settled on.

"Well, yes, that is true. But that's not what I asked."

"It's hard to say. It's like Manhattan exists beyond liking it or not liking it. Like Shakespeare."

"Well, except that one is a major metropolis and the other wrote plays—."

"No, I mean it's a bit beyond liking or not liking it. You can call a play like *Titus Andronicus* weak when you compare it with *Hamlet*, but it's still *Titus*, and it still has beheadings and action and all the brilliant stuff Shakespeare managed to pull off later. I remember I never actually used to get Shakespeare until I got to sophomore year and took one of those random lit survey courses, and we got to *King Lear*. My professor asked me to read one of the early speeches, either Edmund or Edward or Edgar, whatever, but I started to read it like I'd always read Shakespeare, and he stopped me to say I was hitting the linebreaks too hard, and then he suggested another way, and suddenly Shakespeare was an epiphany. Suddenly I got it. And I think that's what Manhattan's like. It's not good or bad or you like it or don't; it's something you either get or you don't. It's not like there's anything wrong with not getting it, but if you do, well, it's fucking Manhattan, isn't it?"

"And you get it?"

Leave it to Veronica to ask that sort of question. I could pontificate and bloviate all I wanted, but she'd nail it in a go, just like always. "Mostly, I think, yeah, I do. There are moments it's exhausting, but mostly it's Manhattan, and mostly it's the kind of awesome that's hard to cope with." We rounded the corner and found ourselves on a sidewalk, walking down the street with a row of houses on one side and a park opposite. Up ahead, we were coming up on a strip plaza with a Blockbuster and a Wawa convenience store. "I heard this story, once, about this town whose citizens had this brilliant idea to use lightning for power. So it did what any normal town wanting to use lightning would do—."

"Installed a lightning rod."

"No, this giant reactor. Kinda thing that could absorb, like, a go-jillion watts."

"I guess that's one way to go."

"This town sank millions into this absorption-reactor thing that could handle trillions of watts, like more energy than is generated by ten or twenty atomic bombs, and then it basically said, okay, now all we need is a good storm. And along comes a storm. And you know what happened?"

"Something suitably ironic, I hope. Otherwise it's not that interesting a story."

"The reactor blew. And not like it just shorted out, I mean, went off like the devil in a church in a crowded room. Just the one little strike of lightning, and the reactor just explodes. Like, they build it strong enough to withstand a nuclear damned blast, and a flash of lightning, and *puuf*," I waved my hand to emphasize the sound.

"So, what, Manhattan's so amazing it blows out your awesome receptors?"

I remember thinking, right then, that I wasn't surprised she had put it together like that. Sure, the story was only tangentially related (and arguably not very good at that), and even as I told it I planned to pull it all together in major revelation, but I distinctly remember thinking, "Of course she got it right away. She's Veronica."

I know that continues to paint her as some outlandish ideal, but what would be the point otherwise? Maybe she's not; maybe her eyes have a little more brown in them than green; maybe her smile is a little crooked; hell, maybe she twists at the mirror to eye with chagrin her hips, her waist, her thighs, lamenting genetics and that most recent beer she didn't need, but that's not the point, is it? When you meet someone like Veronica, all that gets cast straight out of your head. You don't mean it, and you don't realize it, certainly, but I know that if you don't know the feeling, you've probably never been in love, because in love does that to you. Being in love is like living in Manhattan; it blows the same awesome receptors, and like mason jars attempting to restrain lightning, reason and logic and rational thought do their best impersonations of fireworks, zing-pow into the night and the darkness, a calm but rushing whistle bursting into Roman candle brilliance and hyperkinetic light-crackles.

"Yeah," I told her. "Pretty much that exactly."

"So maybe you just need a bigger reactor."

"What?"

"You said it was exhausting. So maybe you need a bigger reactor to hold all that awesome."

"But it's not like I can just buy a reactor. Especially since we're speaking metaphorically. Metaphorical reactors are hard to come by."

"Maybe. But—last semester, I took a theology class. My professor was a trained Buddhist, and he once mentioned a belief Buddhists have about cups and faith. Like people say their cups runneth over? He said that one of the tenets of Buddhism is not just that we need more faith to fill our cups, but also that we spend our lives trying to grow our cups so that we can hold more faith. So maybe you're all full of awesome right now, and you need a bigger cup."

"I might be full of something, but I doubt it's awesome. But hey, at least metaphorical cups are easier to find than metaphorical reactors."

"You just need a challenge."

"I just lost my job."

"Since when was your job challenging?"

"It was a good job—."

"Maybe it's not about work. Maybe you need something more important, like writing."

"But I just told you—."

"Right. You told me you had some existential writing crisis, and maybe that's just it. Writing wouldn't be worth anything if it came easily, would it? Doesn't there have to be some challenge? Something you have to fight for, to finish it? Otherwise it's just too easy, and you end up with cookie-cutter books like Dean Koontz writes."

"Hey, dude makes some good coin. And I used to like his books."

"Key words being 'used to.'"

I conceded her point as we came to a stoplight and rounded its corner, and that's when we both simultaneously seemed to see up ahead the sign for a psychic reader: a great big eye in the center of a stylized hand on the palm of which were scribbled symbols that were as likely Arabic as Tibetan or Japanese or Pagan or somehow more esoteric. Squiggles and whorls, crinkled juts and zaggy lines, all of which made Veronica next to me squeal. I felt her hand on the inside of my elbow, an insistent squeeze. "Oh, we should totally stop in there."

"Since when are you into psychics?" As long as I'd known Veronica, her family had always been so Catholic she attended midnight masses on both Christmas and New Year's Eves with her parents and siblings, and I'd always thought Catholicism had dismissed as heretic any of the arts that hadn't to do with the Christ Jesus and his holy parents. This I mentioned.

"One of my roommates hired a fortune teller for a party we threw. She read my tarots earlier this semester. It's not like I'm sacrificing goats to the dark lord."

"Well, no, but aren't you divining the future by way of questionable means?"

"It's not about divining the future. It's about seeking guidance considering present circumstances, and honestly, given present circumstances, I think you could use all the guidance you can possibly get. So come on," she said. She grabbed my elbow to guide me down the gravel driveway of a non-descript house. Around the corner, up a concrete stoop to a screen door marked solely by an "open"-calligraphed sign. Through the screen wafted a sweet scent that stung my sinuses and made me want to blink.

"It'll be fun," Veronica said. A small, silver bell wrapped with a fresh shoot of some indiscriminate herb tinkled when she opened the door for me, then followed behind.

***

Inside, that scent was even stronger. The room beyond the door looked like a cross between someone's living room, someone else's curio closet, and a third person's sitting room, and none of them appeared to get along. Dark-patterned threadbare rug over a hardwood floor, two metal folding chairs next to a cabinet that looked like it should have been filled with fancy plates but instead contained makeshift, wooden figurines; a few crystal balls; and a few good-sized shards of quartz. A doorway, hungdown with wooden beads, close enough to obscure whatever was in the next room.

"Lovely," I whispered.

"Give it a chance," Veronica said.

"Yes, please do," came a voice as a woman parted the beaded curtain. It's silly to say, and it feels sillier to write, but something about that woman struck me hard enough in the gut I couldn't speak for a moment. It wasn't that she was beautiful, though yes, there was that: she was short and petite, slender with long limbs and the kind of body that moves like it would rather be dancing, and she wore her spectacular red hair down, layered in waves highlit by a streak of white like a jagged edge to a sunset. She wore her green, crushed velvet dress tight enough I could probably guess her measurements (34c, 23, 33), and it scooped down from her pale, slender neck above her ample cleavage. And her eyes: green like jungles and foliage, green like growing things.

But it was more than that. It was a sudden feeling of comfort, which inspired vulnerability; I think, in the weeks previous, I had worked hard on restraining my emotions, preventing them from showing, putting up a brave face and a convincing façade. I didn't realize it until that moment, when the appearance of that woman in that room, so close to me, caused it to slough off like so much dead skin. It was like she had a cool, clear aura, and the scent of her, like citrus and freesia, like a slight breeze across a lake on a warm summer day, cut through the smell of incense like, well, a breath of fresh air. I breathed it deep, and I couldn't help smiling.

"Come in, come in," she ushered us slightly forward and closed the door behind us. "You must be cold. Can I get you anything? Tea?" She asked as though we were guests in her house, and not prospective customers.

"We just saw your sign," Veronica told her. "And we thought—."

"You seek truth?" the woman said.

"Doesn't everyone?" I asked.

The woman chuckled, a bright smile with bells. "Not everyone, no. Many seek hope, or glamorous lies, or placation. Many still come to be told the future, and many more again desire guidance," she said, but she did so implying that she couldn't help those customers.

"So you turn them away?" Veronica asked.

"Heavens no! Hope and glamorous lies are among the many services I provide. I only ask that question up front to decide how best to serve you. So long as you seek the truth, we can do away with the window dressing."

"The window dressing?" I asked, surprised at her candor.

She nodded toward the curio cabinet I had noticed.

"They're fake," Veronica said.

"That's authentic quartz, and those figurines were carved by wise shaman of ancient tribes with greater knowledge than mine. But none are required for the truth."

"Only for the glamour," I said.

Her amused smile made her eyes sparkle, less like emeralds than like leaves after a recent storm. "Exactly that," she said, and she looked me up and down, as if in appraisal or curiosity. I wondered if she would say more, and then she did: "You're tired," but more as if to herself than to either me or Veronica.

I looked at Veronica. "We said we wanted the truth."

"So you did. And there are as many ways to tell the truth as truths to tell. I could read your palms or—."

"Do you do cards?" Veronica asked, a little eagerly.

"You ask as if you know them."

Veronica's cheeks colored just slightly. "I've been—I guess I've been practicing with them? At school—."

"They teach the tarot in colleges now? Whatever will they think of next?"

"No, no, just on my own. I bought a deck from a card reader we hired for a Halloween party—," she said, opening her purse and withdrawing from it a small, lavender velvet pouch, which she opened just a little before the woman stayed her hand.

"Oh, dear, someone who read your cards at a college party sold you a deck? And you've been using it to study yourself? You're a sweet girl, and so pure," the woman told her, and she said each as though she had commented on the color of Veronica's eyes or that she was wearing jeans.. "If you're going to study the tarot, you're going to bring something very special, and very beautiful about yourself, to it, and so you'll require better cards than these. Wait a moment, let me just see," she said, and she opened the curio cabinet to reveal beneath the visible glass sections a set of drawers. She opened the top one and pulled from it several small, velvet pouches, each much like the one Veronica had withdrawn from her bag but also somehow very different. I'm not sure how they could appear more dense, there in her hands, but somehow, they managed it; the only way I can describe it is that they looked more real or more intense, like a high-def television.

Across from the curio cabinet was a small display case with a glass top, beyond which was a chair and the sort of old cash register that popped numbers for sales, and the woman moved around the case. She set each bag, five in all, down on the glass, and from each she withdrew two cards, placing one face-up and the other face-down in front of each bag. A black pouch with pink backs like hot neon and art-deco faces; from a light blue pouch came backs like cresting waves and nautically themed fronts. The middle pouch: turquoise cardbacks and faces like open books. Besides those three, a leopard-print pouch with faces like animals, and finally a white pouch with grey backs and techno fronts.

"Choose," the woman said.

"Oh, I wasn't planning to buy a new—."

"I'm not asking you to buy them, dear. Simply to choose among."

Veronica hesitated, eyes glancing toward each card, each deck, in turn. "They're all so beautiful," she said.

"But each is also unique, and comes with its own qualities. And as you study and practice, you will imbue your deck with your own energy, which is why it's so imperative you have the right deck, the deck that's going to absorb and complement your energy, and why it's so imperative you choose carefully. So please . . ."

Veronica seemed to deliberate, then to decide. "I do like the black pouch."

The woman looked at the neon pink backs and smiled. "There's a lot of energy in that deck. Some people might argue there is too much, in fact, because it can be difficult to control it," the woman said as she picked up the two cards and returned them to her pouch, which she cinched tight and then offered Veronica.

"But I said, I wasn't—."

"You said you hadn't planned to purchase a deck, and I am not offering them to you for sale. I offer them to you with two conditions. The first is that you study the tarot well and you apply as much discipline to them as you would to school."

"Okay," Veronica said, but like she was a little unsure of doing so. Then: "And?"

"And that you chuck those other cards. There's a wastebasket right behind you."

Veronica turned, hesitated just a moment, then took the pouch again from her bag and let it fall into the trash. "Deal," she said as she took the pouch from the woman. "Thank you."

"It's my pleasure. Now, you said you were interested in having your fortunes read—."

"Actually, I was more interested in getting his fortune read," Veronica said.

"Mine?" I said. I hadn't realized it was a one-person pitstop.

"I can do my own, and you're the one with so much going on."

"Lots going on," the woman said as she came back around her counter. "I thought as much. You're at a crossroads."

"I am," I tried to ask, but it didn't quite come out with a question mark on the end of it. It wasn't exactly a statement, but neither was it something I didn't already know, merely something I hadn't realized until she pointed it out. "Yeah, I am," I said again. In a way, it felt good to say, as though I were asserting my own power in the universe by acknowledging that I no longer knew either my place or my direction within it. Letting go came with a certain amount of power, a certain sense of: "Bring it. Hit me as hard as you can with whatever you've got. Go on. I can take it."

Because I could. Or I thought I could, anyway.

"So you'd like your cards read," the woman said.

I shrugged. "I guess so, sure. Why not?"

"Oh, no, no, that simply will not do. You can approach the cards skeptically or dubiously, confidently and hopefully, for personal knowledge or personal gain, but the single way one must never approach the cards is ambivalently. You get from the cards what you bring to them, and if you bring nothing to them, they will offer you nothing in return. So I ask you again: would you like me to read your cards?"

"Yeah," I told her. "I would." And then I had a thought: "Only, could you use that deck? The one with the books on the fronts?"

The woman smiled. "The deck speaks to you."

"I guess so," I told her, then, quickly, "Which I don't mean as ambivalence. Just, I'm not quite sure what you mean, but yeah, I like the deck. It seems cool to me."

"It's probably the books," Veronica said.

I nodded. "Partly. I like the backs, too, though. It's such an interesting color," I said, even as the woman scooped up the two cards she'd put on the counter and slid them into the bag.

"You just wait here, and you use the time to familiarize yourself with your new cards, shuffle them to your heart's content, while I bring your friend into the next room to read his," the woman told Veronica, even as she took my hand in a gentle but forceful grasp and pulled me through the bead curtain.

Chapter Five, which may or may not reveal my fortune,
or my heart's content,
but certainly contains a first-act gun above a mantle

I t was like walking into an alternate dimension.
If you had asked me what I expected while I'd
stood in the curio-foyer with Veronica, I'm not
sure what I would have guessed. Nothing much after
having seen that other room; mismatched furniture, a
threadbare rug, an old coffee table. Something ordinary,
the kind of sitting room you grew up in, the kind of
living room your great-aunt had, perhaps with plastic
covers on the furniture.

Instead: a hall grander than I would have imagined
and larger than seemed possible, given the dimensions
of the house Veronica and I had entered. A marble floor
with a deep, dark rug that could only have come from
Persia, so intricate I would have believed it had taken
several generations to handweave. A large, rough-hewn
stone fireplace, in which crackled away bright orange
flame that smelled like autumn and above the mantle of
which rested a large, antique rifle—

If a gun is on a mantle in the first act, it must go off in the third.—

with a coal-black barrel and mahogany finish. Solid, dark wood rafters decorated the high ceiling in even intervals; I could have believed we'd just crossed the pond to end up in a castle in Scotland.

"Wow, it's—," I started to say, turning back toward the beads, but the woman pulled me farther in. Two burgundy leather chairs in front of the fireplace, between them a small table that looked as if it had been carved centuries before.

"It's home. Come, sit," she ushered me toward one of the armchairs as she sat opposite me. "Let's get to know each other," she said, as reflections of orange flame danced in her eyes, so lucid that I could have believed they weren't actually reflections at all.

"Um. Okay. Well, I'm—," I began, but stopped when she held up her hand.

"While there is much power in names, our little fireside chat will use other energy. You're a Taurus," she said.

It took me a little aback, but I smiled. "How could you tell?"

"You're very . . . intense," she said as if choosing wisely the word. "You have a lot of energy about you, and it's very dynamic. I'll bet you have a Taurus moon, as well."

"I didn't even know I had a moon."

She laughed. "It's just another aspect of your chart. We all have different signs in different houses, and we are all born under a certain sun and moon, with another sign rising."

"Oh, I've heard of that. I don't know what mine is, though."

She looked at me, her eyes a little narrowed. "I can't tell yours straight off. I'd have to do a chart. So instead, let's talk about what brought you here——."

"Veronica."

"You're very close to her."

"We grew up together."

"She's very special to you."

"She's a good friend."

"But there's no more to your relationship? I find that difficult to believe. Two such attractive young people as yourselves . . ."

"Well, there's—I mean," I said, and then I hesitated, took a breath. The woman looked at me expectantly, and so I let it out. "When I was younger, I fell for her. Pretty hard. We were always so close growing up, and I guess part of me just couldn't help it."

"And did you ever let her know that?"

"Once. I was a senior in high school. Just about to leave for college. And I thought it was a great idea to let her know how I felt. But it wasn't, and you know how that conversation went," I said, because how could the woman not? All those sorts of conversations tend to go the same way: I love you like a brother but no more, and our relationship is just too important for me—

"This was how long ago?"

"Before college, so must be going on, what's that, six, seven years ago? Something like that." Because, man, how time does get away from you.

"So what's made you so tired?"

I wondered how much to tell the flame-haired beauty sitting across from me, but her eyes seemed so sincere, so genuine, and before I knew it, I found myself unloading almost like I had unloaded to Veronica back at the Barnes & Noble coffeeshop. I told her just about everything.

"There are many possibilities all around you right now, and a lot of energies coalescing and dissipating almost simultaneously. Times like these can be very stressful."

"Tell me about it."

She set the pouch on the table before us. That green-brown color: there was something so old about it, almost medieval. "I didn't say it back in the other room, but did you realize, when you chose these cards, that their backs and the pouch from which they came arc precisely the color of Veronica's eyes?"

I looked at the pouch more closely. The dancing, flickering light of the fireside cast shadows and brightness like a picture show around the whole room, but I could see right away she was right. "I hadn't noticed."

"I thought not. Which is something I'm sensing about you. You're a very intense, very perceptive young man, but you've got some blind spots, one of which is the girl now shuffling cards in the next room. I don't tell you this to criticize you, mind you, only to make you aware of it," she said, then: "Now, are you ready to be read?"

I smiled. "I'm an open book."

The woman laughed. "Oh, my dear boy, of the myriad things you may in fact be, an open book is not one. You may be open to new things and accepting of dynamic energies, but you're also very guarded, and intensely private, am I right?"

The more she spoke, the less skeptical I became. Not that I believed there might be something more to the cards or the quartz or whatever else, but I was certain there was more to that woman and that she sensed there was more to me. Which I liked; I felt like she saw me sitting opposite her, but she also sensed my potential, whatever it may have been.

She had opened the pouch and removed the cards, which she slid across the table to me. "I'd like you to hold these for a moment. Don't shuffle them; just feel them. And I know that might feel like an affront to your oh-so-practical sensibilities, but humor me for a moment."

If she hadn't mentioned my hypothetical protestations, I might have made them, but her noting them engaged my defiant streak. Reverse psychology, perhaps, though I'm not sure psychology had anything to do with it; I think she had me pegged dead to rights.

I didn't mind. Letting go had never felt so easy or right, so I closed my eyes and did as she asked; the deck felt stiffer and sturdier than I had expected, as though the stock itself were not just heavy paper but also run through with cloth and perhaps even embossed with metal and gemstones and leaves. I felt life in those cards. I felt like they wanted me to shuffle them.

"Go ahead," came her voice, and I swear I could feel her voice in my ear, her hot breath against my neck, the proximity of her body to mine. I swear in the darkness of closed eyes I could feel the color of her hair and the sparkle in her eyes just as I could feel the textured features of those cards, and I did as she told. I could feel the power and energy of the cards as my fingers slipped each one past the next past the next past the next, over and over again. My fingertips became more nimble, my hands suddenly more dexterous, over and under each other like I had recently been practicing for a poker gig in Atlantic City, flippling and cuttling one past the other until I suddenly realized I should divide the deck in two. I cut it down the middle, then placed both halves on the table and flipped them one into the other like they were a blackjack rainbow, then started again to whip them over each other, whip whipwhip—

It is not in the stars to hold our destiny but in ourselves.—

until finally I clapped my hands together, as certain I must stop as I had been I should begin, and I slapped the cards face down onto the table with the decisive quickness of a killing blow. I realized, then, my breathing had become heavy, rushing in and out of my lungs, and it seemed as though I had broken a spell. Looking back, I realize it's more likely I fulfilled one.

The woman smiled as she pulled the cards toward her, and she started to flip the cards and set them onto the table, one by one. I craned my head slightly to get a better look, but she put her hand out and looked at me: "Don't bother. There's more to the cards than just what comes up on their faces, so let me finish, and then I'll explain them to you."

She laid down ten cards. Two formed a center cross with four cards surrounding it, and then another four along the right-hand side. Some came down reversed in relation to the other cards, and the last card she placed was face down.

She frowned at the cards a moment, then looked at me. "I sensed you were at a crossroads, but this spread—It's more serious than I had realized. I don't say that to scare you, only to make you aware that it's not happy. It says a lot for your character and your resilience that the stress you must feel is not as obvious as it certainly deserves every right to be. So that said, are you sure you want to hear this?"

"You're not going to tell me I'm going to die tomorrow or something, are you? Because Veronica said that's not the sort of thing——."

"The cards don't read the future. They read you and your situation. Which is not happy."

"Which only makes sense, though, no? I mean, I'm not altogether happy, am I?"

She exhaled, then pointed to the first card she'd put down, moving the sideways card on top so that I could see it better: a verdant field with three people, a man with a woman on either arm. One blonde woman dressed every inch in maiden white, the other a redhead in red and black the colors of seduction. Beneath them: "The Lovers."

"Well, that's not so bad, is it? Isn't a threesome every guy's fantasy?" I asked. I wasn't sure it was the fantasy of every guy, and I wouldn't even call it one of mine, but then again, had I a woman on each arm I wouldn't necessarily send either away. "Everyone needs a lover, right?"

The woman, however, shook her head. "This card can sometimes mean a new person is coming into your life, or that you're about to form a union, but it only means those things right-side up. Notice how so many of the cards are upside-down in relation to the others? That's called 'reversed,' and every card has a different interpretation when it's reversed. Like with this one, for instance, notice this man has a woman on either arm? That means he will need to make a choice: on one arm the virgin, and on the other, the seductress."

"Neither of which seems an altogether terrible option."

"Neither is. But each would have vastly different consequences."

"So, what, like a dilemma?"

"If it were in a different spread, it might be that simple. But in this one? With all these cards reversed? In this one, it means you don't even know what a dilemma is yet."

I considered that. Not so much on account of being scared, more just letting myself process what she was telling me. When she asked if I wanted her to go on, I nodded.

She indicated "The Lovers" again: "This card is the heart of the matter, but this second one, here, the Two of Swords, is your opposing factor. It relates to the heart of the matter but also encompasses another issue entirely, and see how she's blindfolded, and the two swords she's got crossed over her chest? She obviously can't see, but the two swords indicate it's willful: she's closed off to possibility, and she's closed her heart. She doesn't want to act. And now this one," she indicated a card just next to those first two: "This Four of Pentacles is your root cause. It's the unknown factor here, and upside down, or reversed, it indicates you're trying to assert control you can't. You're being stubborn, which doesn't surprise me. You're a Taurus, which means you're sometimes inflexible in your methods."

"I can be flexible," I said, but I said it a little too quickly—

the lad doth protest too much—

which made me counter: "But, it's true, when I see something I want—."

"Something you want is what's going to get you into this mess, and force this choice." She indicated the next card in the sequence of four: the Heirophant, a wizened scholar surrounded by books. "This is your past. It can mean education, but I've always thought that's the superficial aspect of this card. When you consider it more deeply, though, I think it's more about one's analytical nature than one's education."

She wasn't wrong about my analytical nature.

"These other two feed off each other. This one is what's most immediately on your mind, and the Nine of Cups is the sort of card that indicates a multitude of options but a lack of direction. Given that it's reversed, it indicates that you probably sometimes make major decisions without thinking carefully enough about them. Given the Heirophant and the Two of Swords, it's probably less that you don't think about them and more that even though you do try to analyze everything, you keep yourself unintentionally closed or blind to real factors in the decision. Which might be what's going to get you into the most trouble considering this upside-down Page of Swords: you've got a major choice coming, and it's going to be a doozy. It might even be a choice that someone is going to offer you, but either way it's going to force you to decide something that's going to impact your whole life."

She had finished with the first six cards, and she moved on to the four along the side, starting with the one closest to me:

"This is the King of Wands, and it represents you. And it's the right-way up, which might be the most encouraging thing I see in this whole spread. This is you as you are and as you could be, and the King of Wands is very creative, very strong, and very charismatic. He has style and presence, charm and beauty, and he inspires others, and you're blushing, so I think you like that, but I wonder if you really know or believe it."

"What? That I'm awesome? I mean, it's okay to hope, but to really——."

"No," she said, reaching across the table to touch my arm, sliding her hand down to mine, which she grasped with a light squeeze: "Modesty is commendable, but one mustn't be so modest as to deny one's true nature. Especially considering a spread like this, denying your power could have dire consequences. I knew the moment you walked in that you were special, and I wasn't even in the room you walked into. If you don't cultivate what strengths you have, whatever dilemma is before you could seriously unhinge you. But you're right to be careful," she said, tapping the next card, an upside-down Knight of Wands: "This card is you as others can see you, because that is often something you will find you cannot control. Some will see your confidence as arrogance, and some will believe your charm superficial. This card indicates that you can let their opinions, and your own insecurities, undermine your real strength. You mustn't let that happen."

She moved on to the next card. I had, as she had spoken, become more acutely aware that the final card, the one she was building toward, was face-down. All I could see was that green-brown back, and I realized I wasn't sure I wanted to know what it actually was.

"This card, this upright Magician, is good. Notice how one of his hands is in the clouds while the other is grounded? The magician is a conduit for greater things, and this is what you need to remember when you face whatever is coming. I have to say, though, that coming as it does in the middle of a spread like this one, I wonder if your own power doesn't frighten you. You may be a conduit, but I sense you fear your own ability to fulfill your purpose. Maybe you're worried about those other people who would call you arrogant, or that you won't be able to do your magic justice."

I didn't say anything to that, partly because I knew she was right. I wanted more than anything, and always had, to be better than I was, perhaps because I believed I had talent I simply never did justice. Sometimes, I knew, when I hit a stride in writing, when I really got into the zone, I often felt like I'd tapped into something, that the story hadn't actually come from me, that I was just its teller, and being a storyteller comes with responsibility, both to the story and those who would hear it.

"You write a lot," she told me.

"I used to. There was—up until a month or so I'd written pretty much every day for as long as I can actually remember. But then—well, I don't know what it was. I had this weird moment of uncertainty, and I haven't really written much ever since."

"It's very important to you, but I know you're holding something back. Not least because this last card," she tapped the table, "Is face-down. This is the outcome card, the card of consequences. I told you this is a troubled spread, but this is one of the few times I've seen this card come up face-down. This card could be a lot of things: the outcomes, certainly, but also the way out. It's not about the future, though. It's about seeing the situation as it is and understanding what such a situation will bring. But the fact that it's face-down indicates you don't want to see it. Maybe you think you do, but subconsciously, it's similar to this Two of Swords in that it's about what you want to see and what you choose not to," she said, leaning back from the table, settling into her armchair, as she did so. "Which is why I leave the choice to turn it over to you."

I hesitated, and that moment took on the preternatural reality only a moment like that can possibly hold: colors seemed brighter, and the fire crackle constant as television static but lower and deeper. A wood knot popped, and reflections of flames and their shadows danced like smoke on the walls. I couldn't decide if the room felt warmer or I did.

I hesitated, but only because I needed a moment. I knew she was probably right, that somehow I might be holding myself back or blinding myself to something I wasn't sure I was ready for, so I took a deep breath, and then reached out and turned the card over. That long moment continued as we considered that card between us.

"It—."

"I know," I cut her off. I didn't need her to tell me what the card was or what it meant. Its image depicted a large heart as perfect as any one might find on a Valentine, full of red and love, but pierced through by three silver swords, each with a thick, crimson drop of immaculate blood at its point.

A guy doesn't need a psychic or a fortune teller or . . . well, whatever that red-haired woman would have called herself to know a broken heart when he sees one. I could feel mine beating in my chest, strong and confident, and it didn't feel in danger of breaking, but I had to wonder, in light of those cards and what that woman told me, if it was just putting up a brave front it thought I needed to see right then.

Chapter Six, in which I finish a novel, get drunk, fall in love with Veronica again, buy a tattoo, and finish up the first act, pretty much all at once (though perhaps not necessarily in that order)

*B*ecause that's just about what happened. That woman brushed aside the curtain to allow me entrance back into the foyer, where Veronica looked up and asked: "Already? I thought you'd take longer."

I didn't think much of her question then.

The woman chuckled and ushered us out of her home as she admonished me that my fortune and reading were mine and mine alone; I could share them if I so chose, but nothing required me to do so. She told me, too, that if I chose to tell anyone, I should choose those people carefully.

Veronica and I walked back toward the mall, where my car was still parked, and I attempted to tell her about the reading, but she stopped me. "You heard her. That was yours. Maybe you should keep it for yourself for a while. Besides, what's really important is what you're going to do."

I considered that, the woman's talk of choices and changes. I would've given anything for that threesome.

"I think you should finish your novel."

I didn't respond.

"What else are you going to do? You're just going to stick what you've written in some drawer and forget about it just because it's a little tougher than you thought it was going to be? I think we both know that's bullshit. You're all paid at your apartment, so I think you should take the next couple of weeks to finish it. And when I say finish it, I mean do it right. I'm not talking about just writing on and on until you hit a spot where you can type 'the end.' I mean finishing it like a sprinter just totally shattering the world record at the Olympics, the kind of finishing where people aren't like, 'Well, he won,' but where they're like, 'Sheeit, I didn't realize a dude could go that fast.' That's the kind of finished I think you need. And you know your novel deserves it."

She was right, of course.

Because there's no point if you can't finish like that, is there? I think of all my favorite stories—*Macbeth* and *Rift* and *Hamlet* and *Stardust* and *Harry Potter* and *King Lear* and *Needful Things* and *The Lovely Bones* and *The Time-Traveler's Wife*—and none of them end like Shakespeare or Cox or Gaiman or Rowling or King or Sebold or Niffenegger just kept writing until the first moment an opportunity to stop writing presented itself. Those are novels and stories and plays that make you believe their writers finished in a white heat that caused (to extend Veronica's metaphor) blisters on their feet. I don't know about you, but I want the kind of ending it feels like the author had to sweat and bleed for.

And so, at the end of that weekend, I took another Greyhound back to Manhattan, where I caught a connecting PATH train back to my crummy apartment, and I sat down, and I started sprinting.

***

One hundred thousand words and two weeks later, I set my laptop on my desk. I want to say that I was breathing heavily and sweating profusely—wouldn't that be cool?—because I want it to seem dramatically more difficult and strenuous than it actually was, but I wasn't, because no matter how much author-types might want you to believe otherwise, that's not what writing is about. It's not the sort of debauchery that earned Bret Easton Ellis and Morgan Entrekin the legacies and reputations they deserve, nor the sort of Benzedrine-fueled sprint for which Kerouac is canonized; it is, in fact, a solitary gig writers accomplish best on their own, alone in a room with nothing but a blank page as a challenge.

It's challenge enough.

But I kept going. I set them up and knocked them down. I turned my hat backward and I stared down every blank page I found and I put my story on them like it was my job. I put one word in front of the other, and about twenty thousand words in I started to realize that I wasn't going to stop anytime soon.

That was when I called Veronica to read her the most recent scene in the novel. Which earned me a "Wow, that was terrific," from her, and "Wow, that was terrific" is not praise to be lightly taken, especially coming from Veronica. Veronica had become precisely the person who could challenge me, and whom I trusted to call me out on things, the person who asked the right questions at the right times.

Based on that "Wow," I continued on through another eighty or so thousand words. I sat at the piano bench that doubled as my desk and I just kept going, word after word after word so long as they continued the story.

I'd say I fell in love with Veronica all over again at some point during those hundred thousand words, but if the aim here is truth, I can describe it to you more accurately that I suddenly realized, hearing her voice, writing those words, that I had never actually fallen out of love with her. The more I wrote, the more deeply I understood that I had attempted to bury those feelings, partly because I realized that writing is not a process of building so much as digging; I dug deep for those words, disregarded life and time and college and everything else and attempted truly to strip myself onto the page.

I realized as I stripped away the layers that my love for her had never gone away. It was like writing was a magnet and my feelings for her were iron ore, and page after page brought those feelings finally again to the surface after years during which I'd tried to push them aside or move past them. Part of it was also that I felt, as I wrote it, as though Veronica were my own personal Burgess Meredith; finishing a novel requires more effort than most people care to invest, at least if you want to do it well, and sometimes you need someone in your corner to get you through it. Sometimes you need someone to cut your swollen eyelids and squirt water into your mouth, someone to rub your aching shoulders and whisper into your ear, when that bell sounds, that you can go on, you can go another round, you got this, Rock, you got this. Sometimes the body blows become sounds long after they've actually stopped hurting, and that's when you need the coach to urge you on and the girl at the side of the ring to keep fighting for, and I know I'm now mixing characters, if not metaphors, but I think you get what I mean. Veronica had become my coach and my Adrienne combined, my reason for fighting and the training to get me through it, and it can't be unbelievable that I fell for her all over again.

I don't know if I would call Veronica my muse, if only because I find the idea uncomfortable; it seems to put the impetus and the origin of the creative process beyond us, and my argument there is that we can't, or at least shouldn't. I fear that, if we do, we end up with empty art that might superficially display excellence in craft and mechanics but, more deeply, lacks honesty and soul. A guy named Walter Smith, whom people called Red, is famous for commenting on how easy it is to write—

All you do is sit down at a typewriter and open a vein.—

and while I know most people read irony and sarcasm into the truth of that, I think there's more to it. I think that if you really want to create something worthwhile, instead of seeking the help of some mythological muse whom you hope might show you the truth, you've got to reach way down deep within yourself to find it.

What I'm getting at is that I think too many people regard writing and literature as spiritual and metaphysical, and my feeling is that for it to really work, you can't feel you need to look beyond yourself for inspiration. The real process is finding the inspiration inside you and hopefully using it to inspire others, whether by word or by deed.

Not to put too high a value on the whole thing, mind you. But then again, I'm not sure one can.

My point is, Veronica wasn't my muse because I don't believe in one, but I think I once read that D.H. Lawrence told someone that all novels are a perfect letter to a particular person. I don't argue with that sentiment as vociferously as I might with the idea of a muse, and though I'm not altogether certain I wholeheartedly agree, I can nod and say that, if it's true, that novel was my letter to Veronica.

***

While I can't say I finished in the sort of white heat that would require you to shield your eyes, I can say that I was elated to finish that story by closing that document, and I decided to celebrate. I considered ordering in before I remembered the bottle of Scotch my supervisor had given me, and I figured that if ever there is a time for one's first glass of Scotch, celebration of the completion of one's first real novel—bad Dean Koontz rip-offs don't count—is probably as fine an occasion as one might find. I poured a small glass and realized how strongly it was about to hit me even as I brought it to my lips, its scent so deep and visceral I could smell the stories of Macbeth and William Wallace, while in my gut I felt the same pull as on hearing the first few notes of "Ave Maria" blown through a bagpipe.

I nearly hacked up that first sip. Caught me like a dagger in the back of the throat, and I coughed like an adolescent trying to pretend it wasn't my first cigarette, trying to stifle great wheezing hacks, while I dumped what little I had poured from my glass and filled it again with water from the faucet, which I glumped down like a thirsty man straight out of the desert. I realize that might be a horrible cliché, but I had just finished my first novel and felt entitled to horrible clichés, thank you very much. I then refilled my glass with Scotch, because, I figured, surely the second sip would go down more easily.

It didn't, but the third did. The fourth finished my first glass, by which point I had decided Scotch wasn't half bad and warranted a second glass, after which I decided I actually enjoyed the glass and would prefer a third while I ate dinner. Of course, I didn't find much in the way of food when I opened the refrigerator, just a half-full 20-ounce bottle of Sprite, some old bread, and a doorful of condiments, all of which made me reconsider ordering in until I remembered the pizza joint just a couple of blocks away. I thought I might grab a couple of slices until I realized they would probably be cold by the time I got back to my pad to wash them down with the Scotch, and then I had what I then thought was a brilliant idea.

I poured the Scotch into the Sprite bottle until it was full, then stuck the Scotch on the inside of the refrigerator door because I wasn't sure if I should refrigerate it after opening it, like salsa, and I took my bottle of Scotch-Sprite and left my apartment aiming for the closest pizza joint. I believe its name was Three Guys from Italy, and it was a completely nondescript restaurant save one extremely (at the time) important feature; it was just fifteen or twenty feet away from the escalator that led down to the PATH trains and, by extension, New York City.

Could I have had a better idea than to grab a slice and bring it into Manhattan proper? Sure, the trains featured signs banning both food and beverages, but I'd seen people scarfing down Big Macs on their way from the 33rd Street to Hoboken, so I didn't figure there'd be much harm. The pizza counter guy shoved a couple of slices into a triangular box, and I descended that escalator with my pizza in one hand and my Scotch-Sprite in the other (which, incidentally, made it more difficult than expected to withdraw my PATH card from my pocket, but still I managed), with the City on my mind and stories pulling me forward. I considered calling my friends, invoking the ever-popular "Hey, I finished a novel, let's celebrate" clause (affirmative response is obligatory), but in the end I took my seat and rode the PATH into the tunnels. Not sure where to go, exactly, but I figured 9th Street seemed a pretty decent destination: the Village. Grungy and leather and studs around universities and brownstones.

I followed the stairs up and around the corner to the street, where the first thing I saw was a blackboard placard advertising health food specials and the second thing I saw was the Gray's Papaya sign. Hung a left down 8th, and there, among shops that sold leather jackets and pipes ostensibly crafted for fine tobacco but obviously meant for marijuana, saw a sign adorned with Cassiopeia neon-pinpricked against all black, in the window the sorts of tribal markings and glittering jewels that indicate a tattoo and piercing parlor—

What better way to commemorate the completion of a novel than the celebration of permanent ink upon my skin?—

it made sense at the time.

Here I would like to ascribe to the receptionist and tattoo artist the same quasi-mystical aspects as were possessed by that red-haired Tarot reader from just a chapter ago, but the truth is, nothing could have been more completely ordinary than the evening I got my first tattoo: the Japanese symbol for "dream" upon my chest, over my heart. After paying the brunette at the front counter, I ascended a narrow, spiral metal staircase up to a room that appeared to be a cross between a dentist's office and an extraordinarily clean residential bathroom, and in that room, a man named Paco, who spoke only enough English to indicate how little he knew, applied to the skin above my left pectoral muscle a handful of strokes that have since become a three-dimensional character. One of the few words he spoke sounded like "valor," and he told me, as he pressed that needle into my skin, that the particular area I had chosen for my tattoo counted among the most painful for men, as it was short on fat and close to the bone. At first, I felt each vibration shudder through my body, but eventually it got to a point where my brain decided the pain it was feeling wasn't actually a signal for anything dangerous, at which point the whole thing took on a more surreal feeling, as if I were feeling the tattoo pricked and pierced into someone else's chest, as if the pain I was feeling were more a result of sympathy than stimulation.

All of this, Paco told me, signified my bravery.

But I tell you now I am not a brave man. Looking back, it scares me to consider that I might never have finished that novel had it taken longer than two weeks, because I am, if nothing else, a man of short attention and brief tenacity. Part of me hoped that getting a tattoo of the Japanese symbol for "dream" on my chest would ensure that, no matter where I went or what I did, my heart would follow it; the rest of me hoped there would no longer be a choice in the matter, because sometimes, given a choice, I will choke. Sometimes, given a choice between what's easy and what's right, I choose to attempt to demonstrate that the former is, in fact, the latter, when even I know it's not the case . . .

Scotch-Sprite neon whirl cacophony of leather and gleaming silver and pounding asphalt, shouts and murmurs and the hot scent of . . . what the Hell is a hot dog, anyway? Fried pork? . . . ketchup and kraut, the sort of fragrance so thick you can crunch it between your molars, and I'm pretty sure I picked up a hot dog as I stumbled my way back to the PATH, bandage over my bleeding heart, giant pump-bottle of Jerkins Vitamin-E moisturizer tucked under my armpit, if only because I can't figure out how else I might have gotten a mustard stain on the knee of the jeans I found crumpled on my bedroom floor the following morning. Brushing my teeth the following morning, the previous evening remained little more than a fluorescent rush on tracks through tunnels but don't touch that third rail for fear of the jolt through your soul. I wasn't sure it needed to be anything else; my novel was done, my rent was paid, and even as I brushed, even then again as I showered, even as the water struck my neck and coursed down my body, still my heart beat behind my dream as if propelling it ever forward. Tender to the touch, raised beneath my exploring fingertips: this is what I want.

I would have thought, then, it would also be what I would have chosen, but I hadn't yet exchanged Christmas presents with Veronica, and I hadn't yet met Angus, either.

But all that's gotta start:

A New Act

I think I want some quotes here; writerly types call them 'epigraphs,' and I'll even tell you I briefly considered opening this whole thing by quoting the first stanza of Nickelback's "How You Remind Me," but ultimately I decided against it, for the same reason there is no 'Chapter One' head—that 'once upon a time' opening.

Which I got.

Which means it's okay to tell you that, as I begin this here brand new act, I'm thinking of lyrics of popular music. I would quote them, but doing so would require obtaining licenses from the artists' record companies, which costs quite a lot of money I would presume the artists themselves rarely see—Neil Gaiman tells a story that he'd wanted to quote a song by the Brit band Blur, but their company demanded ludicrous remuneration that worked out to something like a hundred bucks per "ooo-wwo!"

So: do you remember *City of Angels*? That depressing movie with Nicolas Cage as a melancholy angel and Meg Ryan as a doctor? Because the Goo Goo Dolls wrote a song called "Iris" for it, and I can't imagine it would be difficult for you to Google it to check out the lyrics, or even to bust up the iTunes store and download a copy. While you're at it, check out the last few lines of their song "Name," which was one of the earliest hits. Those are songs I'm listening to right now, plus one called "Driving With Your Brakes On," which is by an Irish band named Del Amitri I would know only for its single "Roll to Me" had I not heard "Brakes" on a Greatest Hits CD I borrowed from my local library.

I mention all those not only because I'm listening to them right now but also because all those feelings those songs convey help set the mood for all the events about to occur. I'll tell you now it's going to be another chapter before I end up in the bar where I met Angus, and another chapter again before his nature in the story, or at least his function in it, becomes completely apparent, but suffice to say for now that Angus perhaps knew that I thought about Veronica all the time but wasn't sure I needed to write. As for the offer he made . . . well, first Christmas at the Sawyers, and then Angus can enter stage right and you can see for yourself.

Chapter Seven: Christmas at the Sawyers

*C*omin' on Christmas, people decorating their trees. I printed out my newly finished manuscript I had dedicated to Veronica and jammed it into the backpack I wore across midtown Manhattan as I made my way to Port Authority to catch a Greyhound home. One of those slate-grey, nondescript buses down the Jersey Turnpike blur the spindly trees along the side of the highway, all the way back to my hometown by way of connections and cars, at which point I called Veronica to ask if we could meet up, because I had a serious surprise for her. I guess she could hear in my voice how eager I was to see her, and perhaps even that I had specific reasons for being so eager. She told me she didn't have much free time, but I could attend Christmas Eve mass with her family.

Perhaps that's the most you need to know about Veronica: not that she is beautiful, though she is; nor what she studied; nor what she's accomplished since college; nor any other thing, because perhaps nothing will tell you so much as that Veronica Sawyer is the kind of girl for whom you attend Christmas Eve Mass at midnight. It's the crowded mass, full of not just the fervent but also all the people who go to church solely on Christmas and Easter. I can't tell you I was among the faithful; by then, I'd swung closer to agnostic, which was a major step in my own spiritual evolution—finally accepting that I didn't know all the answers was slightly out of character for me. I had grown up attending Catholic schools but had transferred out on the first day of my junior year, after which I'd swung hard enough the other way that other people might call it over-compensating, filling my days and studies with classes about cold, hard, rational science and the kind of philosophical discussions that excluded God in favor of morals and "quality."

But Veronica told me I could meet her at the mass and then return, with her, to her family's house, where she and Tom would be up until the wee hours, wrapping presents over hot chocolate and Christmas tree cookies. I wrapped the manuscript folder I'd bought in my mother's leftover wrapping paper and set it on the front seat of my car as I drove to the church and then, afterward, her house.

"Is this the big surprise?" she asked when she saw it. We were sitting in her family's living room, her tree to one side, the cream-colored carpet littered with wrapping implements and the sorts of gifts you get from Marshall's and L.L. Bean.

I offered it to her. "Sure is."

When she took it, her hands moved like it was heavier than she had expected. She hefted it, considering it, then, "I think I might know what this is."

"Not for sure until you open it."

"Should I open it now?"

"I wish you would. I'm dying to find out."

She chuckled as she tore aside the badly taped paper, which fell away to the floor, leaving nothing but the folder in her hands. It was a clear, plastic, accordion-type number, full of nothing but a bunch of typing paper. If I could have gotten it bound for her, I might have, but technology had not then advanced so far as it has today.

She turned the folder in her hands and read the title, then, "A novel." When she smiled, there seemed to be at least a little excitement in it, the sort you feel when your favorite musician puts out a new CD or you finally get the ticket to a movie you've been looking forward to for months, and I'll tell you, as feelings go, there's nothing quite like that one. "Is this what I think it is?"

"That depends. If you think it's a copy of the next Harry Potter manuscript, unfortunately not. If, on the other hand, you suspect it's a manuscript of the novel I finished over the past few weeks, mainly because you told me to, well, then, yes, it is."

Her eyes lit up as she hugged me. "Oh, that's so awesome! See, I knew you could do it."

I couldn't respond, too distracted by the sudden tangibility of her body against mine, not in a sensual way—not in the feeling of her curves against me, though there was that—but rather her weight, her tactility, so close to me I could feel, as I returned her hug, first the soft give of her big, fuzzy sweater and then the warmth and solidity of her body. Fine strands of her hair against my cheek, and she smelled like Christmas cookies, all sugar and vanilla.

I clutched her as I regained my voice, then, "Well, that makes one of us."

"This is so great," she said as she pulled back—I gave up that moment in my life with reluctance, like a kitten claw-clinging to a cardigan. "When did you finish?"

I shrugged. "It's still pretty fresh."

"So this is a first draft?"

"Pretty much. Which means it's rough. There are probably spelling mistakes. But I'm still dying to know what you think."

"Coincidentally, I'm dying to read it."

"Unfortunately," I told her, "What with paying rent in advance and not having a job, I wasn't really able to get you, like, a real present—." Because really, the damned thing was most of a ream of copy paper jammed into a plastic folder, which is, as we used to say back in college, kind of ghetto fabulous.

"Are you serious? This is awesome—."

"But there is a surprise for you, on the first page."

She turned the folder over and nearly tore it open, pulled it close to her as she withdrew a page, turning it over. "Looks like a pretty plain first page to me."

"That's the title page. The next page is the first one."

She smiled. "Right. Title page. The one with the title. Which I like, by the way."

"Really? I'm not thrilled with it. I just stuck it on for the time being until something better comes along. I mean, 'All Our Yesterdays'? Sounds like a soap opera, doesn't it?"

"They've lighted fools the ways to dusty death—."

I laughed, surprised she'd picked up that it was a phrase from *The Tragedy of Macbeth*—

Tomorrow and tomorrow
creeps at its petty pace from day to day
until the last syllable of recorded time,
and all our yesterdays have lighted fools the way
to dusty death. Out, out brief candle!
Life is but a walking shadow, a poor player
who struts and frets his hour upon the stage
and then is heard no more. It is a tale, told by an idiot,
full of sound and fury, signifying nothing.—
and I told her so.

"Are you kidding? It's one of my favorite plays. I came this close to doing my thesis on Shakespeare, rather than Ionesco. Still, I can see what you mean about its sounding like a soap opera title, at least if you don't have the context for it."

"Exactly. I was just thinking about seeing it on the shelf, and 'All Our Yesterdays' just didn't have to it the ring that I'd want, you know? But regardless, next page."

She pulled that one out, too, eyes scanning down the page, until they squinted with the sort of familiarity that crosses with recognition of one's own name, and when she saw it, her finger traced along the page, in her gesture nearly a reverence.

Having been raised Catholic but then diverging from religion to favor science like a cane to support the favored leg of my faith, I've wondered, often, about the nature of Heaven. I learned for many years the world of saints and sinners and pearly gates, Saints Peter and Francis and Gabriel, even a Purgatory in which waited desperate souls who hoped for fervent prayers in their own names, the accumulation of enough of which would get them past those aforementioned Gates, where the aforementioned Peter was the bouncer. Over the years, however, that became less believable to me, especially when I read a theory that Heaven is merely an instant that comes at final moment of one's life, so close to the end that sense of time and space would have already been irrevocably lost, which makes that instant technically last forever. I don't know if I believe that one, either, but if it is the case, I would have given anything to have Veronica's slender finger tracing reverently along that white page I'd dedicated to her be my eternity.

She read and then looked at me, smiling, reflections of the fire and the tiny bulbs on the Christmas tree flickering in her deep green-brown eyes, and I took my last thought right back. Forget those fingers on that page; if my Heaven wasn't Veronica's eyes, I didn't want to go.

"To me?" she asked. "But I don't—."

"You helped me out more than I might ever really be able to tell you, Veronica. Between getting me to start writing again in the first place, and then supporting me when I did—I don't think I could have finished it without you. You didn't need to say or do anything for me to know you were there, and it made all the difference."

She looked at the page again, smiling still with recognition and (I like to think) some small degree of honor, and then she hugged me again. "It truly was my pleasure," and then she pulled back, turned and pulled a package from her sofa. "And now I've got one for you," she told me, handing it to me. "It's not much—."

But I was already tearing into it. I'm not good about presents; I want to know what they are yesterday, and the excitement always gets to me. I know some people who can open a gift so carefully they can reuse the paper, and I just don't get it. Tearing the paper away revealed a plain white box with a tape-secured lid, and I slid my fingernail along the lip to sever it, then opened it to reveal tissue paper, under which I found nestled a picture frame of plain wood. Within that frame: a black pictogram of the word "dream" in Japanese.

Dead in my tracks would be one thing, so how about this: consider again the night I got my tattoo in the Village—the neon subway blur of Scotch-Sprite and hot mustard grease, enough movement and verve to make your eyes feel as gritty as the City itself and your teeth feel like asphalt, the sort of night that spins you right round so hard you haven't any other choice besides holding on for dear life for as long as you can until finally you find your way to that glorious orange seat, where you sit in a daze as the night sprints sideways toward onrushing dawn—and now imagine mainlining all those hours in the span of a single breath. Imagine smoking that night like a cigarette, quick burn cut through clear air, or perhaps even better, imagine touching that night like a livewire, that sudden, nearly eviscerating shock through your whole system that you just know is going to leave you tingling for hours afterward.

"Do you like it?" she asked. "I know it's not much, but I saw it in the window of this shop in the mall, and it made me think of you, so I just had to get it. I hope you like it."

"It's—," I said, but I stopped, because I didn't know how to tell her what it was without relaying the whole Scotch-tinted story, beginning to end, and so I did, and then I opened two buttons on my shirt to show her my tattoo.

"No way," she said. "And when was this?"

"Like a week ago?"

"That's when I saw this in the mall. That's so funny!"

I nodded. Funny was certainly one word for it, I supposed. I couldn't think of any others, but I was reasonably certain they were there.

"Anyway, if you'll excuse me a minute," she hoisted that folder into the crook of her hip as she rose, "I'm going to put your book away before it gets crazy around here. Don't want anything happening to it. Be right back."

With that, she left me to sit dumbstruck in her living room, still staring down at the frame she had given me, at the Japanese character on that parchment paper the color of cigarette-stained teeth. I thought again of the character over my heart, and I thought of synchronicity. Many people believe in signs and ascribe higher meanings to events either largely coincidental or completely random, movements of stars and the positions of cards in decks, but standing there, in Veronica's living room, staring down at her gift to me, I understood that position if only because I wanted to give it more meaning than it probably held. I wanted it to mean that our destiny was shared, that we were meant for each other in the way of soul mates, and mostly that she had greater, deeper, and more romantic feelings for me than she ever really let on. So absorbed, in fact, was I in those couple of characters and my own thoughts, as if I might will them real, that I didn't look up until I heard Tom bumble into the room, arms laden with packages he could just barely see over, which is saying something considering that Tom is a tall guy with long arms.

"'Sup, bro," he asked as he brought his packages to the tree, where he set them down, pulling a medium-sized giftbag from the top as he stood. He offered it to me.

I blinked, clearing my head, and took the giftbag automatically. "What's this?"

"Funny thing. Apparently, a small but dedicated population of individuals has begun a tradition of exchanging with each other small tokens of material appreciation aroundabouts this time of year. They even have this weird name for said tokens, which they call 'gifts.'"

"You—you got me a Christmas present?"

"Christmas! That's the name those people gave their quirky tradition! So you've heard of it."

I wanted to laugh but: "I—I didn't have a chance to—."

Tom waved his hand in dismissal. "Ah, but it is in giving that we receive, so why don't you just shut your damned mouth and open the damned thing?"

I set Veronica's present on the couch and opened the bag, which was stuffed with enough black tissue paper to choke a Goth. I found a CD, its cover a child's crayon-scribble of a band on stage—with tiny notes dancing out of each instrument—on which was scrawled what I assumed was the title. "Music we done played?" I asked as I turned the case over, scanning the back, but there was only a crayon-scrawled track listing. "Never heard of them."

"It," Tom said.

"It?"

He nodded. "It's a CD."

"Yes, thank you, Captain Obvious. So that's the title? Or is that the band?"

"They didn't put their name on it?"

I turned the CD over again. "No, Tom, it doesn't appear that they did."

"Well, that seems rather foolish of them."

"Only if they want people to know who done played their music, but yeah, a bit foolish, I'd say."

"Only a bit foolish? I'd say a lot foolish."

"Okay, a lot foolish."

"Totally foolish, in fact."

"Okay, totally f—," I started to say, before finally I got his meaning. Which just goes to show: hey, me? Not the sharpest knife in the drawer sometimes, right? Because the CD? "Are you serious?" I asked, unable to keep the happy-for-him out of my voice.

"But also foolish," he said.

"That—that's awesome. When did—how did you—?"

"We just thought the gigs have been going well enough, and enough people have been showing up and actually dropping our name at the door, and Lord knows we had enough songs together already. So we all sat down, put our heads together, and Glen knows a guy who knows a guy whose sister cuts some other guy's hair, you know how these things work, and suddenly we're all sitting down in the studio, and in the general parlance of the classic rockstar vernacular, we start what they apparently call 'laying down some tracks,' and our schedules worked well enough around themselves that we had all the work done way more quickly than we really expected. We had a good time and made something we like, which is why that's more an invitation than a present."

"An invitation to some super-secret live show?"

"We've never done one before, but we heard bands like to call them 'launch parties,' so we thought we'd have one, too, and no, ain't nothin' super-secret about it. It's going to be a week from last night, coinciding New Year's Eve, because, we figure, what better way to celebrate a new CD and a new year than by getting a little foolish? Copyright and registered trademark Foolish the band, all rights reserved, et cetera but only ad nauseum if you drink too much at the gig."

"Dude," I said, because sometimes I'm so totally eloquent it's jaw-dropping. I hugged him congratulations.

"Thanks," he said. "So, you gonna crash here tonight, or—?"

"Oh, nah—is it—?" I hadn't realized it had gotten so late, but I looked at my watch to see it was getting on near three in the morning. "Wow. It is late, isn't it? Yeah, I should get going."

"Dude, it wasn't a hint. You can totally stay."

"Nah," I told him as I shrugged on my leather coat. "Big day tomorrow."

"Well. Today, technically."

"You know, one year I was in college, I had this roommate who always said it wasn't tomorrow until everyone had gone to sleep and woken up again, so it wasn't Christmas until you woke up to presents under the tree. Which I think is kind of true, in a way."

"Well, sure, if by true you mean factually inaccurate," Tom said. "Come on, I'll walk you out to your car."

Cold outside, deep and dark and quick like a thief. The Sawyers lived on a cul-de-sac, and all the other houses were dark and still as Tom and I crossed his lawn, bone-grey in the light of the moon, to my car.

Which was when I felt compelled to say: "I have to tell you, I think I might be falling in love with your sister." I don't know what compelled me to say it, to be honest: bro-code, perhaps, but either way I thought I should tell him before I pursued it any further—if, in fact, I intended to, and I wasn't yet sure I did.

"Yeah," Tom said. "I gathered. Congrats on the novel, by the way."

"I'm just realizing it myself, and you gathered?"

"Don't beat yourself up. You always were a bit slow on the uptake."

"You think she knows?"

"I wasn't sure you did."

"And now?"

Tom shrugged. "Ronnie's my sister, and you're my best friend, and you're both adults, so you'll both work whatever's going on between you out without my helping you along, and truth be told, given that she's my sister and you're my best friend, I'd rather it be that way. I really would rather have little to do with it."

We'd arrived at my father's car, which I was driving while in town as I no longer owned one, and I unlocked the door. "Fair enough," I admitted, my breath a steam-plume in the air in front of me. "So you're not going to say anything?"

"I'm fucking Switzerland here," Tom said.

"Except without the knives and cuckoo clocks," I said as I opened my car door.

"Don't make me cut you."

"I'll see you next week. Merry Christmas," I told him as I slunk down into my seat. I started the car, wincing at the squeal of a belt protesting so much effort demanded in such cold darkness.

"Awesome. See you then. Drive safe," he pushed my door closed, slapped the roof of the car as punctuation as he walked away, back to his house. I considered honking but then realized I shouldn't, given the late hour, and so I pulled away from the curb and started home.

Christmas morning 2006, a night long into sleep and still hours before dawn, dark so deep presents seemed a long way off. I turned on the radio to hear Robert Downey, Jr. gravel over Joni Mitchell's "The River," which is not really a song you expect to hear on Christmas, but it seemed to fit that car ride through a hometown that no longer seemed quite so familiar as it always had. I'd gotten used to the underground trains, rush hour like time-lapse in realtime, to a world that was always on, where the lights were always lit and the trains always ran and people always rode them; darkness that clear and deep can make you dwell on thoughts you otherwise might not even have. The street lights cast everything in paler shades of orange, and I didn't pass anyone as I drove; there, in the darkness, the world didn't seem to expect to wake up to presents and breakfasts and family. It seemed liked the world expected just another day to live and love and cry and die, just another day when life goes on like it always does, and the main reason that seemed so sad a thought was that it was so true.

Which I realize may sound melodramatic, but then again, I remember that car ride, wishing along with Robert for a river so long I would teach myself to fly. I remember thinking about Veronica, wondering if she might ever actually love me or if fraternal respect and admiration were the most I'd ever receive from her, and I also remember wondering if there was any way I could tip the scales in my favor. I wondered if there was anything I could do that would make her suddenly see me differently, if there were any way I could send her chocolates or save a cat or change the world that would make her stop and think that I was not only not the man she had thought but also a viable romantic prospect. I remember thinking of her hair and how I wanted to run my fingers through it, the thought of staring into her eyes while brushing my fingertips down her cheek or grazing them across the back of her neck just before I pulled her close to kiss her delirious lips. I remember thinking of the way she had smiled when she had opened my novel and wondering if there was any chance whatsoever I might one day kiss that smile.

I wondered what she would say if I told her. I remember thinking I had, once, but I also remember thinking that revelation had come what felt like ages before that Christmas morning, and there's always a chance for things to change, isn't there? I remember recalling that awkward conversation with her mother, the words of rejection and consolation, but I also remember wondering if those words might be different, those several years later.

I also remember knowing I wasn't going to tell her. Not right then. Not yet. Because so long as I didn't tell her, there was some hope. So long as I didn't tell her I had fallen in love with her all over again, our relationship could exist in a state of the sort of quantum and romantic uncertainty that would have made Schrodinger bury his safe simply so that no one could ever open it—

(Erwin Schrodinger was a quantum physicist best known for a thought experiment involving a cat in a safe, a vial of poison, and a single atom with a known but unpredictable rate of decay, which would, upon decay, release the poison that would kill the cat. So long, he argued, as the safe remained closed, so long as the outcome remained unobserved, the cat existed in a state of uncertainty, observedly neither alive nor dead. I remember thinking, that night, that so long as I didn't tell Veronica how I felt, our relationship could exist in that similar sort of uncertainty, neither actually romantic nor completely platonic, emotionally involved and intimately connected even if never physically consummated, and now I'm intruding on a parenthetical aside, so I'm going to take you back to that car ride)—

with Robert Downey, Jr., on the stereo and the world so dark and cold but yet so clear, knowing that I was falling in love and trying to enjoy the moment of it rather than worry about the consequences it might bring. I was trying to simultaneously avoid the thought that I should tell her how I felt and how much even just having that thought made me feel like a coward.

I didn't know how she would react if I told her. I was fairly certain she wouldn't tell me she never wanted to speak to me again for fear of the complications to our relationship my romantic feelings might have caused, but then again, I was also fairly certain she didn't reciprocate those feelings I had. Which may sound diffident, but then again that's just one of those things you just sort of know, isn't it? Romance and attraction may both be nebulous enough that science and psychology still bend over backwards in their efforts to explain them, but that's only because things like love and chemistry can't be confined to either the laboratory or the classroom; half the fun is in the chaos, in barroom Brownian motion and the particle-wave of lust. We dismiss reason and logic for those calloused fingertips, that brilliant smile in an otherwise dim dive, those sweet eyes that tug you like you just don't expect and can't ever really fight. You know that moment— you've felt it mid-slug of lite beer, bottle raised to your lips and bubbles halfway down your throat, when the whole world has stopped on account of her laugh or his voice (or, let's be honest, her butt or his chest, or vice-versa). You just sort of know those things, and I just sort of knew Veronica and I had the bright, clear warmth of sunshine on a beach, not the hot, slow burn of embers in the darkness.

So what was I to do?

Well, right then, I was to drive home. I was to park at my parents' house and carry inside Veronica's present tucked beneath my arm, if only because I have always felt that it's better to concentrate on what is concrete in front of you than to expend too much effort on speculation.

I'm no longer exactly certain of that, but it's what I told myself as I slipped my key in the door and let myself into the house in which I'd grown up. Comin' home Christmas, so very different from comin' home New York: the different scents, for one, mom's homemade cooking and sugar cookies as opposed to the oddly neutral, gritty fragrance of the subway, but also . . . the home where you grew up always feels different from the home you make, even if you sometimes only realize it on Christmas morning long after the rest of the world has gone to sleep. It's not just the scent, not just the different warmth, but trying to decide exactly why— is it the knowledge of your mother's soft snoring a few bedrooms over? That you fall asleep in the same bed you slept in when you were a sophomore in high school?—is difficult at best. Sometimes, in fact, all you can really do is pull the blanket up knowing that Christmas morning is only a few hours away, and thinking all the while that maybe it's not such a bad thing to be in love, even if you're not exactly sure how she would feel if she knew.

Laying there, in that same old bed, I thought again of D.H. Lawrence, he of perfect letters to particular someones, and something else he said: that desire is holy. Which it is, and which makes longing a state of grace.

And then I slept.

*Chapter Eight, in which I demonstrate some initiative,
not to mention: meet Angus (finally)*

*C*onventional wisdom dictates that, upon completion of any first draft, a writer should step back. I think Stephen King noted (in *On Writing?*) that the magic number is six weeks; finish your first draft and then stick it in a drawer, and for six weeks do anything at all that doesn't include reading that finished draft, after which time you may retrieve your manuscript from your drawer to mark it with your editor's pen, and you may moan and groan and lament your general lack of creativity when you're not admiring your own genius, though you may be in a spot if there don't exist more moments of the former than of the latter (which may sound backward but, when revising, better to groan than preen). After all that time, you may proceed onto work on another draft, which, mathematically (at least according to Stephen King) should equal approximately your first draft minus ten percent.

I note all that because it's so totally not what I did. After attending a brunch at my grandmother's house, I spent part of Christmas evening polishing the first chapter of my manuscript, then wrote a single query to my dream agent—Merrilee Heifetz, an agent with Writers House, who represented Neil Gaiman, my own personal writing hero/mentor. Gaiman's a guy who, since the events of this story took place, has topped nearly every bestseller's list the *New York Times* can offer him, who's not only had several novels and stories adapted into television series or movies but even written a few himself (including an adaptation of *Beowulf* directed by Robert Zemeckis). Neil maintains a blog in which he manages to refer to Zemeckis as "Bob" without its ever feeling like name-dropping, and of all the writers I can think of, I think I'd like a diverse, varied, and successful career most like his, which is why Heifetz was not just at the top of my list of agents to query but managed to be the list in its entirety, at least to start.

Because why not, right? What had I to lose?

(you'll find out)

So I wrote up my query and polished up my first chapter, then printed both out. I signed the query with my lucky fountain pen, folded query and sample and a self-addressed, stamped envelope into another envelope, and headed down to the post office to mail it out. I wasn't sure it was the best idea to send it out so fresh and new, but then again, I figured, most agents cite a response time of no fewer than two months, and many request two to three times that many before you even hear from then, and even then, that's usually only in the case of a rejection. So if a rejection can take six months to arrive . . .

***

I hadn't been sure when I planned to return to Manhattan, but Tom's gig on New Year's gave me a reason to stick around for another week during which I'd be lying if I told you I did anything productive. The agency through whom I was temping assured me they'd probably be able to find something for me, if not at my previous wage then close to. I poked around on other job sites to see if anyone was looking for literature-slash-science majors, but funny thing that combination, because not so much.

I didn't mind too much. I had a few weeks before February rent would become an issue, and my parents didn't seem to mind the idea of my staying with them for a little while as I figured things out. Besides, I thought, taking a week off to gather my thoughts might do me a world of good, though that makes it sounds like a more formal or official process than it actually was, makes it sound like I didn't spend most of that week reading and watching television and pretty much slacking off to such a degree that you might as well picture me on the sofa in my boxers, scratching my balls, and it wouldn't be far off from the truth.

Thing was, I didn't know what to do. I wasn't worried much about money if only because I trusted my temp agency at their word and didn't think it would take long to place me well; I'd basically fallen into the job at the *New Yorker* as it had been, and Lord knew those sorts of gigs were a dime a dozen in the Big Apple, or so I thought. What else are you supposed to do in Manhattan, besides things like investment banking and driving cabs? Or maybe retail . . .

I spent most of that week thinking (for various definitions of the word), and by the time Tom's gig rolled around I was ready for a break from my melodramatic self.

***

On New Year's Eve, 2006, Foolish launched *Music We Done Played* at the Grape Street Pub in Manayunk, Pennsylvania, a hip and swinging establishment that had once been host to a Tuesday music night when it had been located on the nominative Grape Street. It had since become popular enough to move to new digs on the cool Main stretch, just beyond the ice cream parlor and the sushi joint. Manayunk is ten or fifteen minutes from Philadelphia proper and is a sort-of post-collegiate town, the kind of place where twenty-somethings whom a decade before would have been called yuppies go to polish the teeth they've already cut. It's the sort of place where an Apple store would not only not seem out of place but would also be able to find every one of its employees within a ten-block radius.

The perfect place for Foolish, whose music I have only just now realized I haven't yet described to you. If you imagine a network dramedy in which Patrick Dempsey's dreamy-but-troubled lawyer courted Mariska Hargitay's harried-but-optimistic forensic psychologist, and then play through an entire season to that singular moment when, after months of extended courtship, the two characters finally kiss, Foolish is playing the song you hear when they finally lock lips. It's bombastic mid-tempo pop like Coldplay decided Justin Timberlake's "SexyBack" should be more than a danceable pop tune and had to be both sultry and emotional simultaneously; like Mutt Lange and Rick Rubin collaborated on producing an album for a band equal parts Def Leppard and matchbox twenty; straight-up rock and roll crossed with massive pop.

I've never seen Foolish not get the room dancing, no matter the venue, no matter the crowd. Which was why Grape Street hosted the launch party on New Year's Eve, and probably why the show sold out days before it was to occur. Grape Street is not a small place—besides a main room large enough to hold a few hundred people, it has a secondary bar, an outdoor bar, a sidebar that's almost a lounge (generally where the acoustic open-mike nights go down) and an upstairs room that's totally a lounge when it's not a dance floor—but the entire place was packed by eight in the evening, and most of them were there for Foolish, which had built a loyal following around the Philly/South Jersey area.

It was very much like a massive New Year's Eve Party among good friends and their families; the crowd wasn't just mutual friends and their husbands or wives but also moms and dads and aunts and uncles—I'm pretty sure there was a grandmother around somewhere. It was hard to keep track, crowded as it was. Foolish played for several hours, mixing what seemed like dozens of covers among the songs on their CD, as well as the songs I'm pretty sure are required for all New Year's Parties, "Auld Lang Syne" and what not, and I danced and drank and partied and mingled and basically had more fun that single evening than during the entire previous year. If the New Year is supposed to begin as it may continue, I should have by all accounts expected a year that would have made Gehrig relinquish his whole luckiest-man-on-the-planet title.

It was also the night I met Angus.

That was at the end of the night. Tom had invited me to the Foolish afterparty; the guys and their wives and girlfriends were headed to a local strip bar where one of them had worked as a bouncer years before. An afterhours type of joint, and I was happy to join them even though I'd never really been into strip clubs (I just don't understand them. Don't get me wrong, I like looking at women as much as the next guy but Chris Rock has taught us nothing if not that there is no sex in the champagne room. Ever. And while I enjoy a good tease, the one thing a good tease demands is satisfaction), so I was waiting around for the guys to break down their equipment. I'd maintained a pleasant buzz for a solid several hours, very proud I'd spent only the first hour fully sober but had never once tipped over into full-on drunk.

I was nursing a Yuengling at the bar, when Veronica approached. "Just wanted to say goodnight before I left."

"No afterparty?"

"The strip club? Nah. Not my thing."

"Yeah, I hear you. Not really mine either, mostly."

"Ah, come on. Totally your thing. You're a dude."

"Indeed, a dude I am."

"Well have fun. I'll catch you later. Let's do something before I go back to school."

"Give me a call."

"Awesome," she said, leaning in to kiss my cheek. "And happy new year."

"Yeah," I squeezed her arm. "Happy new year."

She smiled, then turned to leave, and I watched her as she did so.

"She's certainly a beautiful young woman," came from my right a voice with a burr so deep it could have worn its own kilt, and I turned.

Anthony Hopkins.

That was my first thought the very first time I saw Angus. I'm certain the resemblance was superficial—and probably should since this is a novel and all resemblance of any character to any single person either living or dead must be entirely coincidental—but I also must note, knowing what I later learned, from Angus and otherwise, that nothing Angus did was entirely coincidental. Instead, I will say up front: Angus wasn't Anthony Hopkins, but could have passed for the great Welsh actor's brother—the same clear, blue eyes; the same neat, white hair; the same wide, puckish grin. He had that charming way that transforms wrinkles into laugh lines, and they were crinkling then. "But it's not just that, is it? Pretty, certainly, but there's a lot more to that special young lady. I can see why you like her so much."

"Excuse me? Do I—?"

"Know me? Not at all. You've never seen me before in your life."

"That's what I thought," I said. I sipped the beer I was nursing.

He had before him a highball of something amber on the rocks. His fingers circled the glass' rim, and he wore a silver pinky ring with a dark blue stone that twinkled ambient light like a tiny star.

"So how—?"

"Did I know? Besides that you wear your infatuation for her like a heart on your sleeve, I always notice. My ability to sense in the cheeks of youth the first blushes of attraction is merely but one speciality among many," he said, and then he winked at me, and here's where I started paying closer attention, because . . . okay, you know the creepy guy in the bar? That guy on the end over-age drinking, his salt-and-pepper hair slicked back but just a little too long, like he's gone one too many weeks without a proper trim? He wears his mustache unironically and trims it a touch too precisely, and that's never mind the fact that he's overdressed in a double-breasted blazer over a dark shirt, the collar and buttons of which are open enough to reveal the gold coin he wears as a pendant in a cushy bed of white chest hair. You've seen that guy, throwing around his money like he's trying to impress someone, and on his arm he usually has a woman ten years younger but no better for her wear, a peroxide blonde like a bird of prey, an *objet d'artifice*. You've probably smelled that guy, who wears too much Polo but can't hide the reek of old desperation.

You know that guy? Because Angus?

The opposite.

Classy. He had a dark suit on, but it was European cut and he wore it like it had been tailored just the week before, over a black shirt whose collar was open but not ostentatiously so. Besides the Anthony Hopkins resemblance, he had that sort of movie star ease about him.

"Specialities," I said.

"Oh my yes. Myriad specialities of various and sundry nature. A long and diverse list of skills and talents the likes of which it would take any man several lifetimes to acquire and several times that to master."

"You must be pretty old, then."

"Only to the pretty young. And you are pretty. Young," he smiled.

"Wait, are you—?" I stopped short of asking if he was hitting on me. It didn't feel like he was—just that he was a charming older gentleman—but neither was I completely certain he wasn't.

"An old man sitting at a bar, meeting a new acquaintance after having listened to a rather splendid band? Indeed I am."

"They are good."

"Splendid," he corrected. "And yes, indeed they are. Friends of yours, I take it?"

"You're quick."

"I figured that's the only reason you'd be sitting at the bar while they stowed away their instruments, instead of chatting up one of the numerous and rather splendid examples of young ladies currently in the room. I'd say I'm rather surprised you're not keeping one of them company, rather than some unfamiliar old man. Then again, the only one you've had your eye on has only just departed, and I'd wager you've had your eye on her for far longer than this single evening, pleasant as it may be."

I looked at the beer I was drinking, as though captivated by the way light shone off the green glass neck of the bottle. "That's not a wager I'd win, that's for sure," and with that, I slugged down the remainder in one long, slow draw. It had already warmed to the room, and it went down as bubbles without any taste. I set the empty down on the bar and started to signal to the tender, but Angus stopped me.

"Why don't you let me get your next round?"

"You want to buy me a beer?" I was a little less certain he wasn't hitting on me. I wasn't yet sure what it felt like, only that it didn't feel like that.

"Don't be vulgar. I might as well just piss in the bottle you just finished. No, my boy, I would much rather indulge you in one of the finer things in life," he told me, and before I could say anything, he called over the tender, a tall, muscular blonde with sparkling blue eyes and cleavage I'm sure the band could have enjoyed from the stage twenty feet away. "Good evening young lady, and might I first compliment you on your choice of tee shirt for the evening? Your splendid body has made an old man think back wistfully on the days of his youth, and I don't mind telling you that, though I never wanted for female companionship, very rarely did I find myself accompanied by a lass so lovely as yourself, and I hope you won't mind my saying so."

Like I said: from anyone else? Fucking creepy. From this guy?

I watched the girl blush. I'm sure she was used to hearing a hundred lines like that every night. She carried herself like she knew she was attractive, too—not like she was stuck-up about it, but like she was aware of it, which I'm sure she must have been, because otherwise I would have had to fault her for having been in deep denial. Even still, her lovely cheeks reddened on their high bones. "Not even a little. Thank you," she said, chuckling as she tucked a strand of hair back behind her ear. "So can I get you boys something?"

"Well, yes, my dear, I'm certain you can, in fact, get us something, as I'm sure your employment here is based only secondarily on your fine features and primarily on your ability to procure refreshment. I say this merely to point out that 'can' is solely indicative of one's ability, whereas 'may' indicates an actual action, and so, being that I am certain you have the ability to pour for my new acquaintance and me, should we require the whetting of our respective whistles, the beverage of our choice, I will tell you that what you may do is pour for each of us your very finest Scotch. And by Scotch I mean real Scotch, and by finest I mean the sort you keep on the shelf so high you will require a stepping stool to retrieve it from its perch of honor, if only so that my acquaintance and I might at the same time enjoy the sight of you reaching for it."

She considered the order a moment, then leaned forward, as if conspiratorially, and also as if she didn't realize she was displaying what was, at that point, anyway, her very finest attribute: cleavage so deep it shorted what few circuits my brain ever actually has. "I'd normally tell you a Johnnie Black—," she said.

"In a pinch, I suppose, if it's your finest—."

"But I think we have a Johnnie Blue hidden away somewhere. I'll have to ask our manager—."

"I would most certainly make any trouble to which you ventured worth your every while."

"It's not my whiles I'm worried about, and it wouldn't be trouble, although it might take a few minutes."

"Ah, but anything worth enjoying is worth waiting for," Angus said, then looked at me. "What do you say, my boy? Have you some time in your youth to spare?"

I looked back to the stage, where Tom and the guys were still dissembling the drumkit and packing away instruments and cables and pedals. After which they'd have to walk around, mingle, thank everyone for coming—"Yeah, it looks like I've got a few minutes."

The bartender nodded and headed away.

"Ever had a fine Scotch?"

"I had my very first taste of Scotch a few weeks ago. My old boss gave it to me as a sort of Christmas bonus."

"May I presume that by calling him your old boss, you're saying that in addition to being your Christmas bonus, it became your severance package as well? Or are you, in fact, referring to the poor man's age?"

"No, you're right. I was working up at the New Yorker. But I was temping."

"So interesting how the verbification of the word conceals its true nature."

"I think I might've been starting to realize that. But I'd been there for, like, a year? I guess a little more. Anyway, I asked if I could come on full-time, but it turned out they hadn't even realized I was there, and they decided they could save twenty or thirty thousand bucks by cutting the budget that paid me. Can't say they were wrong. My boss gave me the Scotch as a holiday bonus slash severance package slash parting gift."

"And was it a fine Scotch, or are we insulting my homeland?"

"Can't tell you for sure. What little I drank I mixed with Sprite—."

"My dear boy, that's blasphemy, pure and simple. I presume, at least, it was not the Johnnie I've just ordered for us . . ."

I shook my head. "I think it was a Glen. Glenlivvey? Glengoin—?"

He held his hand up. "Really, my boy, you must stop talking. The pain you've done me so far I can attribute to blissful ignorance, but I'm not sure I'll be able to forgive your adding further insult to current injury. Tell me at the very least that there was a celebratory occasion for the consumption, and that you weren't attempting to drown your sorrows over your lost—."

"Oh, no. I actually was celebrating. I'd just finished a novel I'd—."

"So you're a writer," he said. "I straightaway sensed some creative energy about you. I thought you might be musically inclined, but then realized that you would probably have been on stage earlier. I briefly thought you might be an actor—you've got the looks, not to mention the charisma—but you don't exactly seem to crave attention. I'm not saying you mind attention, don't mistake me, but you seem comfortable enough without it. Which leaves few other options. Painting, perhaps, or sculpting—."

"Believe me, you don't want me around sharp tools."

"Exactly why writing seemed most likely, though if you don't mind my saying so, you're certainly in better shape than most writers I've known. The very act tends to lend itself to a sedentary existence, but you?" he said squeezed my upper arm to emphasize; his grip punctuation-quick. "Exactly. Trim and fit as an Olympic swimmer, and I'll bet you're not just any writer but a good one. I've got an eye for talent. Which brings us to the most important question one can pose to a writer, namely with what topics and subjects said writers concern themselves with. So tell me, dear boy," he said, shaking his wrist to slip his watch from the cuff, "In five words or ten seconds, whichever comes first, what is your novel about?"

"Time travel," I replied.

He raised his eyebrows. "You still have three words. Or nine seconds."

I shrugged. "Don't need 'em. I mean, sure, it's more complicated. It's a hundred thousand words. But you want five, and it's about time travel and what to do with it. Or at least, what the characters I was writing about did with it."

"And what did they do with it?"

"You'll have to read it and find out, won't you?"

Angus laughed and did a little circular hand gesture as if in concession, and that was when a guy in a blue blazer over a tee-shirt showed up. His jeans showed signs of wear—contrast wrinkles and fraying—he hadn't earned, but he carried with him a bottle. "Heard you boys ordered some Johnnie Blue. We don't get many orders for the good stuff, so I thought I'd deliver it to you myself," he told us, setting down before us two small glasses, then unstopping the bottle.

"May I conjecture by your personal visit that you're the owner of this fine establishment I might call a tavern were it not so magnificent?"

The man smiled as he sploshed into each of the glasses a vital measure of amber liquid I could smell even where I sat, sweet heft with hooks. "I am. You like it?"

"Oh, aye," Angus said as the man finished pouring. I reached for my glass, but Angus stayed my hand. "Not yet, not yet," he said, then to the owner: "Might we in addition request a small glass of water?"

"No problem," the man said as he turned to fill another glass.

Angus said: "Have you owned this fine establishment very long?"

"It hasn't been here very long," I said. "It used to be around the corner, on a side street. Actually on Grape Street. But it got so popular—."

"Actually, they closed it. I've owned the actual building for a decade or so," he said. "We used to be more of a dance club. But I partnered with the guys over at Grape Street when their lease ran out, and we took out a loan to renovate the place."

"Which you've done spectacularly," Angus told him. "The acoustics alone—."

The man smiled. "That was kinda my pet. Trying to get the room to sound perfect no matter what sort of music was playing. Wasn't cheap, let me tell you," he said, as he slid the water onto the bar.

"Ah, thank you," Angus said, and with that he dipped two fingers into the water, then flickered a few droplets of water into his glass, at the same time tracing in the air a pattern that would have looked like a priest's signing of the cross if the cross were both ornate and Arthurian. "Just a few drops of water breaks up the surface tension of the Scotch and allows more of that delicious aroma to escape, which, need I tell you, renders a fine drink yet finer."

The owner smiled. "You know how to drink your Scotch."

Angus looked at me expectantly, and so I dipped two finger tips into the water and then flicked the drops into my own glass. "Your lack of subtlety makes up for your lack of finesse. But we can work on the latter easily enough," he said, picking up his glass and holding it up just above the bar, toward me. I picked up my own and clinked his glass.

"To the New Year," Angus said.

"Agreed." He was right about the aroma; even as I sipped it, it seemed those hard edges had become sharp hooks. That scent could have easily become addictive. The Scotch itself went down smooth and easy, and I wasn't sure, exactly, what I tasted in it: Oak? Peat? Smoke? The flavor seemed iridescent, one color at first that slipped into others like a chameleon on a roller-coaster, or perhaps holographic, moving around and capturing a tiny story in a single image. I couldn't decide if I liked it, though I tried. It was too elusive. All I knew was I wanted to chase it.

Angus and I both set our glasses down after that first sip. Like there was something in the Scotch that demanded it be enjoyed slowly. "Now that, my good sir, is a Scotch as fine as fine can be. I haven't had a drink that good in many, many years. Nor an evening this enjoyable. I must commend you on knowing how to host a party. You can rest assured I will let my friends know about your fine establishment."

"I appreciate that," the owner said. "We'd be honored to have more fine connoisseurs like yourselves. In fact, why don't you let me make this a double, on the house, simply in honor of the fact that you appreciate the finer things in life."

Angus looked at me. "What do you think, dear boy?"

"Isn't it, like, against the law to decline such an offer on such an evening?" I asked, and I smiled at the owner. "I think it might be a personal insult, in fact, and I would never insult you. We would be much obliged, and well honored by your hospitality."

The owner laughed. "You sound like him," he said as he added another splash of that wonderful amber liquid to our glasses. I swear I might have become intoxicated by the scent alone if I hadn't already been there. "You guys related? Uncle or something?"

"Actually, don't tell my new young friend yet, but I am a businessman about to make him the proverbial offer I'm hoping he will be unable to refuse."

Which confirmed that he had not, in fact, been trying to flirt with me; his old world charm aimed at persuasion, a subtlety that removed from his business pitch both the business and the pitch, at least superficially, and which I can't say wasn't effective. I've read articles in books and magazines that the most effective way to pick up women is to remove the idea of the pick up from the situation; that the key to effective effort is no effort whatsoever. Take me, for example: if Angus had opened with his pitch—which even then I wasn't yet sure of, keep in mind—I probably would have shut down. I tend to when I think people are trying to convince me of something, or even worse, sell it to me. I would rather do my own research and make decisions for myself, after careful consideration, which means that I am always inherently suspicious of salesmen. Not like I think they're going to steal my wallet, but I know they want me to do something, and wanting me to do something is often the surest way to convince me not to.

But Angus had made me genuinely curious. Wouldn't you be? Heck, aren't you?

"Ah. Well, then, I'll leave you two to business. Thank you again for your patronage," the owner said, and with that disappeared with his bottle.

I took a sip of my Scotch, waiting for Angus to begin whatever pitch he had, but he did not. I said, "I didn't think you were hitting on me."

Angus laughed. "Even were I interested in the male form, and even if I hadn't seen the way you looked after the young lady to whom you were speaking before we made our acquaintance, it's easy enough to discern that I would have been barking up the proverbial incorrect tree, as it were."

"You realize I'm probably not interested in whatever business proposition you're going to pitch me."

"I don't know how you can be sure of that, especially considering you haven't heard what I have to say, or even what I might be able to offer."

"Unless you're a literary agent, I don't see how you're going to help me any."

"Surely you don't believe that the only endeavor with which you might require the expertise of an outside source is in matters of literature and publishing? Given that you know neither the scope nor the range of my specialities, I'd request that you not be so quick to dismiss them out of their turn," Angus told me as he reached into the inner breast pocket of his blazer, pulling from it a brushed-silver business-card holder from which he withdrew a card. He set it down on the bar and slid it toward me. I noticed, as he said it, though, he didn't explicitly say he wasn't a literary agent. "On the other hand, I would not expect you to trust me so quickly and easily, but if you take this card, and keep it with you, and call upon my services when the mood thereupon strikes . . . well, certainly, you have nothing to lose by accepting the card."

I picked it up and scanned it. Just off-white, with black type embossed enough it shone, however vaguely, in the dim light. A handful of words: *Angus Silver, Proprietor, Futures Trading,* and then a phone number. "Angus Silver."

"That's me," Angus told me, extending his hand. "At both your service and disposal."

"Futures Trading?" I accepted his hand. "Like oil and steel and stock market futures?"

"My areas of speciality are diverse in nature and nearly exponential in number, but suffice to say that the nature of my business covers just about everything."

"Sounds lucrative."

"There is more than money to be found in the future, and that, dear boy, is where I come in."

"Still, I don't—."

"Have a current position with any company? Really know what your own future is going to hold?"

Whatever protestation I had been about to make died on my tongue.

"I'm not asking you to commit to any business here and now. I'm merely asking that you put the card away, slip it into your wallet, and perhaps give me a call should you wish for some certainty."

I considered the card. I figured I didn't have much to lose even if I wasn't exactly sure of anything I might gain, so I took out the cigarette case I use as a wallet and slipped the card between the cash and the plastic, and with that effectively ended the scene, because that's all that needs establishing. Every scene should either reveal something about character or advance the plot, and now the plot is advanced; I took Angus' card and set the story moving forward again. I mean, sure, we spoke a bit longer as we finished the Scotch, and then I excused myself, as Tom and the guys had finished packing the gear and I usually helped them carry it out to the van, which I did again that evening. After which we piled ourselves into the cars and drove to the afterparty, none of the fun of which can be adequately described here, so I say we just move on to the next chapter, which fast forwards a few days, and which will reveal Angus' function in this story:

Chapter Nine, which is the one you've been waiting for, isn't it?

*B*ecause of course I got in touch with Angus. I mean, as much as I've built up his presence in this story? But first: I needed a job and had no idea what to do. I was lucky that my crummy Hoboken apartment was really just a room in the three-bedroom unit/ground floor of a house I shared with two other guys, which meant that my rent was ridiculous by most standards and positively ludicrous by those associated with Manhattan and its outer satellites. Still, I had a several hundred dollar rent bill due on the first of February, and while I had some money saved up, I'd still need a couple hundred besides.

I thought about calling my temp agency, Force One Entertainment, but decided to go to their office, instead; I liked everyone who worked there and was tired of spending time in my apartment. January might be cold, but walking in Manhattan tends to get one's temperature up, and there are few more awesome places to be. So I took PATH up to Herald Square, where HMV gave way to the progress that is Victoria's Secret, and headed uptown. Past glitzy-electronic shops with pocket calculator-sized laptops next to only slightly larger cell phones modified for web-surfing and e-mail receipt, because who needs a desk in the digital age? Up past Virgin Megastore, likely the last remaining on the entire island, then a few blocks East, to a building I only call non-descript because it was in the center of a Manhattan blockful of buildings nearly identical.

Elevator up to the fourth floor, with its two doors: directly opposite the elevator was the bookbinder, with a sweetsmell of glue and a sharper one of leather, then right to Force One.

I loved Force One, but didn't often have occasion to visit their office, nor even to call it until very (then) recently; why would I, considering my long-term gig at the *New Yorker*? I got there in the middle of the afternoon, when it was full of both new graduates and the recently career-displaced, the former of whom wore, like their professional business attire, anxiety like puppies hoping for a treat. The latter tended to possess a more deliberate demeanor, their nerves less result of worry of not finding a job but rather the right job.

That first room looked as much like a doctor's office as one associated with an employment agency: the same bad prints on the wall, the same particle-board furniture on which sat semi-recent *Entertainment Weekly*s and a few copies of the latest *Village Voice*, the same half-wall beyond which the receptionist, Joanne (Jo to her friends) sat at a desk to accept incoming candidates and juggle seven or eight different phone lines. I approached that half-wall, ready to greet Jo (who had become my friend shortly after I had broken up with my fiancée, when we went out for obligatory, post-break-up drinks), but I stopped up short and surprised.

I remembered Jo as a pretty girl fresh out of college, sometimes with the same air as the recently-graduated interviewees, with a professional demeanor she was still growing into and which consequently sometimes bordered on terse. She was always chipper and humorous, teasing and halfway to flirtatious, and last I'd spoken to her had been just after what I had taken to calling the Great *New Yorker* Debacle of 2007, moreso because I thought it was funny and less because I thought it was true, but I realized it had been a while since I'd actually seen her.

In a little over a year, Jo had blossomed from fresh, new, somewhat over-eager and brand-new employment agency receptionist into confident, professional gal who could as easily have been the face of Force One Entertainment as its voice. She'd chopped her brown hair down into an uptown bob she'd dyed six or seven shades darker than I'd ever seen it, which was a few shades darker than her new glasses. She might have done something with her mascara or her eye shadow or something, I don't know, but boyhow were they blue, hued to match the shimmery, tight turtleneck she wore. Instead of clutching the phone between her chin and her neck, she wore a headpiece like a hairband, with a slender silver microphone like a swipe across her right cheek, and she stared at a computer screen while she spoke and typed simultaneously.

"Jo?" I said, unable to keep my voice from sounding surprised bordering on jubilant.

She squinted as if trying to place me. I wondered, then, how I might have changed since last she'd seen me; time-lapse personal evolution is a side effect of

Manhattan living. When working in the great big City, walking its streets every day, it often starts to—I was going to say rub off on you, but that's not quite the meaning I want. In some ways it's like a perfect spice that complements already extant flavors rather than contributing its own, but in more ways it's like . . . modern society has corrupted the word "glamour," which has come to mean the title of a magazine every bit as much as it's become synonymous with either cosmetics or old-time movie stars like Mae West or Marilyn Monroe, but glamour originally meant a sort of magic with which one could disguise oneself, and when living in Manhattan, one can't help get a dusting of glamour as conspicuous as, and perfectly opposite of, dandruff on the collar. If comic book characters and science fiction heroes often have evil-villain twins distinguished solely by their goatees, there should in addition exist the Manhattan twin, street-smart and City-hip, MacGuyver without his mullet, Patrick Bateman without his psychosis, Sam Beckett without the time machine.

When Jo recognized-slash-remembered me, she told whomever she was speaking to to hold, please, pulled her headset off, retreated to the office door so that she could step around, and gave me a gigantic hug giddy on both sides.

"Jesus, you look great," I told her. "How are you?"

"I'm great! How are you?"

"I'm doing decidedly all right. What's there to complain about after spending the holidays with family, right?"

"Somebody else might argue with you, but I won't. You had a good Christmas, then?"

"Totally. And an even better New Year's."

"Some lucky girl get a midnight kiss?"

"Went to see some friends play a gig down near Philadelphia. Great times. You?"

"Trip back home, lots of food, breaking resolutions quick as I could make them, breaking up with boyfriends—."

"Oh, I'm sorry."

"Oh, it's fine. Better off, anyway. Now I can concentrate on acting."

Jo is a terrific actress; I'd once seen her in a production of the *Vagina Monologues*, and she'd been fantastic. "How's that going?"

"More time for auditions," she said, which didn't totally answer the question I'd asked, but she delivered it with enough enthusiasm that it seemed she was happy, and sometimes that's all you can appreciate. Sometimes, when dealing with pursuits like acting and writing and painting, you have to set aside success in the result—getting on stage, publishing a book, getting a gallery show—in favor of the process, the technique, the practice of whatever spooky magic you're engaged in. Sometimes, when the going gets tough, it's less a matter of the tough needing to get going but rather realizing why you're going in the first place.

"Which can only be good in the long run."

"Exactly," she said, paused a moment, then, "So what brings you to our neck of the woods today? Didn't come just to see me, did you?"

"Well, not that I need more reason than that, but I actually did come hoping you guys might hook me up with another assignment—."

"Oh, that's right," she retreated around her corner, back into her office, while I leaned on the ledge in front of her computer. "You were at—was it an ad agency?"

"*The New Yorker.*"

"Ooh, look at you, Mister Magazine. Eat your heart out, Messers Condé and Nast. You were there for a while, too."

"More than a year."

"Which might as well be permanent in this—dammit. I—let me finish up this call really quick," she said, pulled her headset back on and began talking into it to set up an appointment with whoever was on the other end after she apologized for having put them on hold for so long. After she hung up, she tucked her mic down. "Okay, so. New Yorker. Mostly administrative, yeah?"

I nodded. "Advertising sales."

"How'd ya like that?"

I hesitated.

"Which I'm going to take as a not-much-at-all. Between you and me, I don't blame you. Sales is so hard. High-intensity. Let's see . . ." she scanned her computer. She went quiet a moment, frowned, then gestured me forward, lowering her voice to say: "Listen, I'm going to level with you, we don't have much right now. I think pretty much everything we have is going to be a paycut for you. Can you hold out a couple of days?"

"I think so, but not for much longer than that."

"We'll bump you to the top of the list. All the stuff available right now is for banks and consulting firms, but if you wait a few days—," she lowered her voice further—"I heard John say we might be getting an order from the Weinstein Company later in the week, and he's been talking to a couple of ad agencies, too—."

"More sales?"

"No, the actual agencies. That make the ads."

"Oh! Well, that'd be neat."

"I know, right? So, yeah, give us a few days. Still at the same number?"

"Always," I told her. "Awesome. Thanks so much, Jo."

"Hey, no probs. Now get on out of here and stop wasting valuable writing time."

I laughed and told her I hoped the rest of her day was as bright as she had just made mine, and she might have blushed, just a little, as I walked out that door.

***

Outside, January was cold, but I wasn't yet ready for home, so I headed west to the subway, which I took down to Union Square. I thought I'd kill a couple hours in Barnes & Noble, but instead headed south another couple blocks to the Strand—eight miles of used books!—and shopped the racks for a while. Couldn't spend much, but I found a few books priced at a quarter each and went to the counter to pay. When the clerk rang me up, I pulled out my case, withdrew from it a couple of bucks, then took the books as I stowed the case and started to leave.

At which point I felt a light grip on my elbow: guy behind me, holding out a business card. "You dropped this."

Angus' card must have fallen out of my case when I took the money from it. I thanked the man and continued out of the store, where I paused to replace the card in my wallet, but stopped. The silver embossed text had caught the January afternoon sunlight so it shimmered like it had weight.

Angus had mentioned a business proposition. While I wasn't sure how he might help me, nor even with what, we had discussed writing and publishing . . . I wondered if he was involved, somehow, in the entertainment industry. I couldn't figure out "Futures Trading," but figured if he was involved in the entertainment industry, he might have connections that could help me out from my current situations. I could always perhaps find freelance work, contract positions that didn't involve sitting in cubicles so much as banging out articles for corporate marketing—

Under most circumstances, I would have been suspicious. After the introduction of cell phones, Craigslist, and inexpensive office space in the business equivalent of broom closets, just about anyone— reputable or otherwise—could set up business in Manhattan, and many did. Many were shady but often shared something in common because of those cell phones; newer Manhattan area codes related in addition to other boroughs, and most were either 917 or 718.

Angus' 212 wasn't the area code you'd find for a new business; 212 is Manhattan. It's New York when being New York meant something: when it was the City that never slept, when making it there meant you could make it anywhere, when all its rats wore tuxes and swilled martinis and doffed fedoras while running in packs. It's New York like a sepia photograph of the Empire State Building, an old-fashioned picture of tomorrow.

I pulled out my cell—area code 917 on that, even though I'd signed up for it back during my freshman year of college, 2001—and dialed the number on the business card. Two rings before someone answered, and then another moment before someone spoke: "Futures Trading, this is Brigid. How can I help you today?"—

a sudden image in my head: copper-colored hair and pale skin. Green, green eyes behind tortoise-shell glasses, and a business suit the charcoal of etchings with a blouse the white of paper, all behind a glass-topped desk. Long fingers poised above a keyboard. On her desk, a nameplate—otherwise I would have thought: Bridget, or Bridgid. But no: Brigid.

More than that, too: sunlight like fine gauze, clear and bright but cold as January, and the intimation of the world around her, just fuzzy enough to be unclear, all washed out enough to be more a vivid impression than an explicit picture—

"Hello?" Brigid said, making me realize that impression had caught me suddenly enough it had surprised me with its intensity.

"Um. Hi. I'm looking for Angus Silver? He gave me his card a few days ago—."

"Ah, yes, we've been expecting your call and hoping for your visit. May we expect one?"

The way she said it, the cheerful hope in her voice . . . I didn't want to let her down. "Sure," I told her.

"Wonderful," she told me, and then she relayed to me an address not far from where I was even then standing, and again that sudden mental flash—

a brownstone in sepia, sun-drenched black-and-white. Fire escapes and a turret—

"See you soon, then," she told me, and with that I flip-closed my cell as I started a few blocks south and then cut east, into the heart of the Village, along St. Mark's Place—8th street between 3rd Avenue and Avenue A for those keeping score by way of Google Maps—punk-rock antiquity and rock-and-roll royalty, where artists dreamed less of the gallery than of the gutter, where it was better to burn out than to fade, where artistic integrity had more value than fame though neither ever really had any meaning, anyway.

Who lived here? Lenny Bruce—

Let me tell you the truth. The truth is, what is. And what should be is a fantasy, a terrible terrible lie that someone gave to the people long ago.—

and W.H. Auden—

All wishes, whatever their apparent content, have the same and unvarying meaning: "I refuse to be what I am."—

to name but two of its most notable alumnae.

It's where the cover for Led Zeppelin's *Physical Graffiti* was photographed as an impossible album cover, and it's where there used to exist a small café called Sin-E, where many bands, including but not limited to P.J. Harvey, Ben Folds, David Gray, and Jeff Buckley—

The only way to really make it—anywhere—is to put every bit of your being into the thing that only you can provide. The only angle is the art that you choose, that only you can provide. And to do that, you have to be quiet for a long time and find out what you bring forth. You have to know what's in yourself—all your eccentricities, all your banalities, the full flavor of your woe and your joy. What does it look like? What does it feel like? What makes it different from everybody else's? It's totally subjective. You're just given the task of bringing it up.—

played long before they were ever really discovered, much less famous.

All that aside, what matters for the moment is that it was then the neighborhood I traversed to discover, not far from Tompkins Square Park, precisely the turreted brownstone whose image had popped unbidden into my head, a building at once both conspicuous and unremarkable, a dichotomy that can exist only in Manhattan. Anywhere else, that building would have stood out to passersby as a place where one could expect great things to occur, great business to transact, great art to be committed, but right there it looked—even if it didn't look at all like any other building in the world—completely routine. That's the paradox of Manhattan, with everything so vibrant and spectacular vying simultaneously for attention, so that even a place so extraordinary as the Cloisters never actually stands out. How can you stand out, among the Metropolitan Museum or Opera House, take your pick; among cathedrals dedicated to Saint Patrick and Saint Peter; in a place whose Christmas tree seems a hundred feet tall?

I realized as I approached that brownstone that I didn't need to check the address, as well as that there was something more at work there. Not just that I'd been pulled toward that place since the moment I'd dialed the number on the card and heard Brigid's voice, but even that something unconscious had tugged me downtown from Force One's uptown offices—otherwise, there really was no reason for me to be in the Village, and Lord knows that even a quarter for new books was money I might have been better off not spending. I think realizing that broke the spell to some degree as I climbed the stoop stairs to the front door, but then I stumbled on the top step and tripped through the front door, which seemed heavier than it should have and crashed shut behind me—

I might have been first introduced to the idea of a tesseract, or the next dimension on top of an already three-dimensional cube, by Madeline L'Engle's *A Wrinkle in Time*; her idea for interspatial travel related to interstitial travel—that the titular wrinkle in time was quite literally an extra dimensional fold that placed more closely together two spatial points that had previously been separated by some great distance. Which I always thought was rather ingenious, as it could bypass the problem of crossing lightyears simply by moving destination closer to origination even if only on a plane beyond the dimensions we're used to.

Such ideas have always cropped up all over science fiction. Consider Doctor Who's TARDIS, a phone-booth time machine bigger on the inside than it appears from the outside, where people see it as a police box.

I bring those up because—

Tripping across that threshold . . . in some ways, it was similar to passing through that beaded curtain into that red-haired woman's inner sanctum of cosmology and interpretation, but extended far beyond that scale. My first thought after that brief memory of that grand Jersey hall, was that whoever owned Futures Trading had bought the brownstone whose steps I had ascended as well as several neighboring, and knocking out the walls had been merely the first step in renovating, which had subsequently included replacing carpets and hardwood floors with smooth, gorgeous grey-green marble. The room seemed cavernous and impossibly tall; if that brownstone had had three stories, they had knocked out two floors in favor of going straight from the ground to the roof thirty feet up, where sunlight streamed through a skylight and dazzled that marble dizzy. To say it looked enchanted would be to take the easy way out; the sunshine blazed through its golden veins to make it shimmer like fabled old money and the promise of new wealth.

Behind me, the door through which I had just entered was the only actually visible part of something I can't call a wall for all the water cascading down it; the anterior interior wall was a waterfall I assume was synthetic because how else would one get one inside, besides by building it there? A lip kept the water from falling over the doorway, but besides that, I could see nothing else of that wall. Where windows might or might not have been there existed only large rectangles, shiny silver against the clear shimmer of the water.

To the left, a large stone fountain the color of bones, water proud and loud enough that, though I might like to use a word like susurrus for the poetry of it alone, it cannot apply; this wasn't whisper so much as a loud plobbling—hey, onomatopoeia!—that matched in both tone and intensity the freely flowing cascades of the wall behind me. It came in jets from the mouths of mermaids, as if the tinkle of water on water were the call of the siren, beyond the appreciation of mortal men save in its irresistibility.

Directly in front of me: Brigid. Her desk before me matched to the detail the vivid image that had jumped into my head, though there was some difference in person, if only in vibrance and intensity. Her hair wasn't just copper-colored but the tawny orange of a disappearing tabby cat, while her eyes were a green you'd think every field in Ireland would be if it didn't rain there so often.

Beyond her left shoulder: two enormous, mahogany French doors, ornately carved and with visible hinges as big as two of my hands together.

"You must be the pleasant young man to whom I spoke only a few moments ago," she told me. Her voice was bright and airy as the room around us, sparkled here and there with inflection and cheer like the veins in the marble I crossed to approach her desk. It would have made me want to have been that pleasant young man even had I not been.

"This place is fantastic," I told her, my voice more an amazed whisper than an attempt at communication.

"I suppose that depends on your fantasies," she said, but so matter-of-factly I couldn't decide if she meant innuendo.

Either way . . . well. I'd like to say I found myself still too positively gobsmacked to respond either in kind or in flirt, but that would imply I spend any time in my life not gobsmacked, which I rarely do. Regardless, I was still taking in the room, because seriously, I couldn't believe what they'd done with the place.

The doors behind her opened before I had to worry too much about responding, and if the flapping wings of a Central Park butterfly can so completely change the world by causing stampedes several continents away, I hesitate to consider the impact of those large, heavy doors. Even just the sound they made—first the massive, solid chunk of a hard metal latch, and then the quiet but substantive movement of that cavernous room's air displaced by those enormous slabs of wood—if the world would only make a sound when it knows your life is about to change, it would be that one, and it would come as well with that open and empty feeling you get in your gut when you know you're about to make a decision that might not change the whole world but is certainly going to change yours.

Beyond those doors: nothing, at first, but light, though of that there was enough I thought I might have tanned just standing there. I felt my eyebrows rise and my arm followed suit, even, as I started to shade my eyes, but then the intensity faded abruptly to allow into visibility the sharp-cut suited silhouette who could only be Angus himself.

"My boy," he said, stepping forward, through the doors, sweeping into the lobby a great rush of charcoal and animation, a quick-sketch of business and the way it's meant to be conducted. He looked nearly the same as he had the night I'd met him, the dark suit that might have been a Hermés and the sharp eyes, but he seemed more vibrant, more alive, as if the room around him leant to him a power he in turn could conduct at will. "So glad you took the time to swing by my humble offices," he told me, and if he had a smile like doing business, he shook my hand like he'd already closed it.

"I'm not sure 'humble' is the first word I would have thought of."

"Please," he said, ushering me through those giant doors without my realizing I was moving at all. "You do me great kindness, my boy," he said, and he tossed a quick, "Brigid, would you do me the great favor of holding all calls while I speak to my bright young acquaintance here?"

"Absolutely, Mr. Silver," Brigid's response followed us through the doors, which Angus closed behind me, and if their opening had sounded like the possibility inherent in a posed proposition, their closing must have, conversely, approximated choices made and decisions decided.

And inside?

Angus' office was decorated mainly in grey and chrome and glass, not as if retro were clashing with futuristic but rather as though the past and the future had collaborated to form a more beautiful present. The first impression was of space, not because of the sheer size of the room, though it did seem as gigantic as the lobby had, but rather because the wall opposite the massive entryway was all windows, floor to ceiling and one wall to its opposite, and beyond them—

is problematic, for reasons which will in a moment become apparent, but for now know that beyond them was a beachscape like Malibu or Big Sur, quick sand and brief cliffs before the enormous beauty of an ocean all the way to the horizon as far as I could see, as though Angus' offices were on beachfront property.

Gaggling at the view gave way to appreciating the final details of the room, the afore-mentioned grey and glass and retro. Angus' desk in the center, back close to the view—I wasn't yet ready to commit to either window or screen, even if I knew it was impossible it was a window, because I was in the middle of the Village, and how could it have been? I think the closest body of water was the East River—while the side walls were mainly shelves full of books of varying shapes and colors, along with a few trinkets, masks and small sculptures and odd, stringed things and a Rubik's cube. The shelves on the right side occupied the entire wall, while those on the left were cut around a stone hearth in front of which sat two leather sofas and a coffee table between them. That furniture was set on a black-and-white bear-skin rug.

Best way I can put it: remember those awesome receptors I mentioned to Veronica? My own had remained intact in that awesomely gorgeous lobby, which I know only because, standing in Angus' office, they finally gave out.

"Is that—?" I started to ask, but along with losing my awesome receptors, my intelligibility seemed to follow. Thoughts like quick butterflies or, perhaps more accurately, the sub-atomic afterbursts of hyper-particle collisions, and me the confused lepidopterist, or theoretical physicist, depending on which metaphor we're going with, jump-swiping my net at leptons or trying to fine-tune my instruments to measure moths, which only jumbles up my metaphors, doesn't it?

"My view," Angus said. "Certainly is one of a kind."

"Is it—?" but I stopped there, because my brain couldn't decide whether it meant to ask whether it was high-definition or real, and I honestly wasn't certain it mattered. I abandoned that question for another: "This is all yours?"

Angus laughed. "As much as any man can call any thing his own. I've used this building as a place to conduct my business for many years, and it has always served well my purposes."

In front of Angus' desk: two chairs, both leather with silver chrome accents. They looked comfortable.

"Quite a collection of books you have."

Angus laughed, looking around at the shelves as if he were seeing them and their contents for the first time. "Don't I though? I've been lucky to find myself acquainted with many fine writers, many of whom have become my clients, and many of whom gave to me all the books you see as gifts."

"Clients? So you do work in publishing, then?"

"Please, let's not discuss business straight off. I always find business is more a pleasure when conducted in a more meandering manner. The services I might provide might be better discovered than offered, if you catch my meaning, and being the brilliant young man you are, I bet you do."

"I don't know about that," was my pretty much automatic response.

"I do. I would not have invited you here were you not. But here you are, because I will perhaps immodestly claim to possess an eye for these sorts of things, and I've never been wrong, not so long as I've been in the game."

"I'm flattered."

"I'm not complimenting you, merely stating the observedly obvious."

"So did you invite me here just to butter me up? I mean, don't get me wrong, I appreciate the kind words—."

"The honest words."

"Okay, the honest words, but—."

"No, no. Don't just say it unless you mean it."

"Sorry?"

"Few things are more offensive than false modesty. You are immensely talented, and the right person—such as myself—can sense that talent a mile away. Don't rephrase merely because you believe different words are what I want to hear. There is, you'll agree, a difference between arrogance and confidence, but the difference between them is delusion in the former case and self-awareness in the latter, which brings me ultimately to the point that self-awareness is perhaps the most desired trait of all. So don't just agree with my assessment of your talent; if you're going to do anything at all, own it, my boy."

I scanned the ocean to the horizon, and I said: "I don't know much about brilliance or talent, but I like stories, and I like writing. I hope I write them better more often than not." I don't know why I felt the urge for candor, but I know it was the truth as I said and felt it. Which I record here for the very reason I've been so committed to telling you the truth: some days, I think it's less about doing it well or badly than it is about doing it honestly, sometimes brutally so, sometimes vulnerably so.

"Well met. I can't say it was the reaction I expected if only because that would imply I expected one in the first place; I keep always in mind that the best of all business is conducted without expectation, only knowledge."

"I might agree, except I've never been much use when it comes down to business."

"Why don't you have a seat?" Angus gestured me to one of the chairs in front of his desk. As I approached it, he moved around the side of the desk, and as he did so, I realized the view must have been a high-definition screen when I found myself suddenly looking at what appeared to be moonlight on the Sphinx. Its busted-nose face was familiar enough, while behind it loomed the Great Pyramid, colored the hue of bone.

My expression must have betrayed my confusion, though, because Angus smiled.

"Ah, yes. Perhaps one of the most demonstrable cases of penis envy in the history of the world."

"The Sphinx?"

"Both monuments, to some degree. Which is all each is: monuments men now long dead, who would otherwise also be long forgotten, built for themselves. I would remark upon the measures to which many, men and women alike, have gone to distinguish themselves in history, but alas, history would render me little more than a redundant old man telling you stories of which you are already aware."

"If only they'd built them for the women they'd loved."

"Indeed, everyone likes a good love story."

"And a tragic one is even better," I said.

Angus laughed. "My boy, you got a thing for stories. It's like it's instinctual, and believe you me, I've seen my fair share of talents and instincts."

I considered the books in those giant bookcases. "It certainly looks that way," I told him. Some of the books looked expensive and rare, with mottled leather spines embossed with gold leaf letters, but many more had dust jackets, indistinguishable from some you might find on the shelves at your local Barnes & Noble (or even better, the ones just off to your right, there, easy distance from your reaching hand).

"I have indeed. I've been doing this for a long time indeed, and hope for many continued years in a similar capacity. But for now, a more important issue: what can I offer you to drink? And by drink, let us be clear that I don't mean cola, as I'm quite reasonably certain you didn't drive to my offices. Before you say anything in decision, can I perhaps offer an ale? I have recently procured from a rather noted Belgian brewery a beer so fine calling it one is nearly an insult. It's rather dark and complex——."

"I try not to ever decline a drink," I said. Life's way too short to pass up a drink; you never know what one, or its company, may bring to you.

Angus pressed a button on the phone on his desk. "Brigid, would you please bring two large glasses of the Rochefort 10 shipment we recently received?"

"Certainly, Mister Silver," her voice crackled over the phone, and Angus clicked the button again as he settled into the seat opposite me. "I must admit to you I'm extraordinarily pleased you made use of the card I gave you."

"I just stopped by my temp agency. Kinda hoping they might find me some work. Got to pay rent in a few weeks."

Angus smiled. "Something tells me you won't have any trouble with that."

"Not if I get a job within the next week, probably not."

"But they didn't have any right now?"

"They said they'd probably have something in the next couple days," I said, just as I heard the massive latch on the doors give way and felt the doors themselves open. Brigid wheeled forward a room-service metal cart, on it two large goblets and two bottles whose exteriors had already accumulated a thin, frosty film.

"Ah, thank you, Brigid," Angus said as he moved around the desk to take the cart, and Brigid nodded, ducked away, closing the doors behind her. Angus took a silver opener and popped both bottles, then poured them: merlot dark, with a creamy head just a hint of tanned where it met the liquid below it. I got a whiff even from where I sat, and it smelled like chocolate (which only made me realize how strong it was about to be).

Angus handed me one, then started around his desk.

I brought my glass to my lips, but Angus blurted: "Oh, my boy, one of the few but greatest sins of indulgence is partaking of a libation before it has been properly christened with a toast. Besides all manner of bad luck, not to mention bad etiquette, there's simply no telling the consequences of an action so base and crude."

"Sorry," I said. Feeling my face get warm.

"Quite fine, quite fine, I'm sure even the aroma itself was tempting," he said, and he was right: that hint of chocolate, with side scents of caramel and perhaps even a fruit, or maybe licorice? I'm not sure, to be honest, but I know the fragrance was strong enough I felt like I could already taste the beer. "While it may be a mere formality, business requires even such mere formalities for its conduct. And so in the spirit of business and new acquaintance, I propose a toast to your future, dear boy, to your future."

He extended his glass, which I clinked with my own; the nape of my neck prickled, fine hairs shivery.

"To my future," I said.

The beer was better than I had ever known beer to taste, full and enormous. Its flavors—of licorice and chocolate and perhaps that fruit I had smelled earlier—were not dense; it seemed there was too much room in it for that, and every flavor in it had plenty of elbow room, plenty of space to make the most of, and each one did. Some bitterness on the floor, but then all that sweetness waltzing to smooth finish that made me want to take another sip. Which I did. And again.

Which made Angus laugh. "I do believe our young lad likes it."

"It's very good. Stronger than I'm used to—."

"Oh, indeed. So much so it's very nearly a barley wine."

"Belgian you said?"

"Brewed by Trappist monks."

"Those monks sure do know their beers. You know, I had an Austrian one, only ever brewed on Christmas—."

"Samichlaus. Another one nearly a wine."

"Strongest beer in the world," I said, taking another sip. As I did so, the view behind Angus changed again: a time-bleached London skyline like Dickens must have known, smudged grey with smokecloud and overall tinged the color of old pennies. "Wow. Looks like hard times."

Angus chuckled when he glanced over his shoulder. "Best and worst of them, I would wager."

"Except that was a tale of two cities, and we're only looking at one."

"You know your Dickens."

I shrugged as I took another long pull of my beer. I could have easily gotten used to it. It was really good. "Only of him. I tried reading a couple of his books, but I never got all that far. Always struck me you could tell right away he was getting paid by the word."

"Surely you don't fault him for being loquacious."

"I always fault writers for being loquacious."

"Brevity is the soul of wit."

"Exactly. See? And Shakespeare, too, arguably the greatest writer ever, though never for the reason anyone ever says. Everyone's all Hamlet-subtext this and problem plays that and Marlowe-how's-your-mother, and I always think it spectacularly misses the point," I took another sip. I was getting lubed up. But beer and books? Try shutting me up: "Like, even the language, right? The so-called poetry of the plays? Of course he wrote to rhythm and unique turns of phrase. He was writing for actors, who had to memorize the damned things in a few days and perform them in a week. And then people read the plays and analyze them, as if anyone ever meant for them to be read by anyone besides the actors performing them. You want to appreciate Shakespeare, you need to go see it, and you need to see it acted well."

"You're a fan?"

"Love watching them. Well acted, anyway. And *Shakespeare in Love* is my favorite movie, which isn't technically Shakespeare but has him in it."

"Tragic love story," Angus pointed out.

"See? Told you."

"Indeed you did. You know your stories well, being such a fine writer of them."

"Maybe on my better days."

"On your better days, you're one of the greats."

"I hope so," I said, taking another drink. You may at this point assume I continued to drink, just as I continued to lose my inhibitions. "But then again it's not really up to me, is it? I just do the best I can, and whether that's good or bad or even great is up to somebody else to decide."

"You don't really believe that. You would leave the works of art into which you so wholeheartedly pour yourself, into which you so heavily invest yourself, to the critics? The same people who debate not even just what Shakespeare actually meant with his words but whether he even wrote the plays we attribute to him? You'd leave your work to them?" he asked me. His eyes were mischievous, and I got the distinct impression he was goading me, like he wasn't so interested in the answer to his question but rather in getting my answer to it.

But that was okay. I was enjoying my beer and didn't mind some goading. "Of course not. I'd leave my work to readers."

He laughed again. "My, but you are quick."

"Not really."

"I would beg to differ."

"Then you can't choose."

"I suppose not. But tell me: have you been published?"

I shook my head. "Not yet. I'm—working on it. I think I mentioned my novel the other night, and I just sent it out to an agent. I'm hoping she'll represent it."

"To publishers."

"To editors. Who might buy it. And then we can all make it into a real book, and then people can read it."

"People don't already?"

"Some friends, maybe."

"You say that like they're not enough."

"I've got a handful of friends I ask for advice when I finish something, but that's it. But just a handful of people—that's not why I do it. I get these ideas, and I want to share them with everyone. Like, everyone everyone. Like, speaking of Dickens before, I want people to line up, just waiting for the trucks delivering my books into stores."

"Something tells me you won't have to worry much about that."

"Something tells me I shouldn't. So I try not to."

"Is that what you want?"

I hesitated, but I smiled as I did so. Such a simple question, but the kind that requires an entire book—maybe sort of like this one, to be not-so-subtle about it—to answer. "Some days I think I just want to write full time, but I have a feeling I might drive myself well and batshit if I ever had that much time to myself. Some days I think I just want a book deal, but then I'd probably just pay off my student loans and write some more. Some days I think I just want everyone I see to be carrying my book, but I'd probably wonder what they thought of it, and knowing me, I'd probably ask them all. I guess—I want to write stories I love, and I want them to find people to love them. And you know, if I get anything else, I think it sort has to follow that, or spring from it. And I worry that might sound a little trite, but then again, this is some really good beer."

"And if I told you I thought you were well on your way to getting pretty much precisely what you described?"

"I'd say it's tough be certain of anything, because life is what happens when we're making other plans, and besides that, you've never read any of my stories."

"Poor Mister Lennon. Still a young man, too."

"Tragic," I agreed.

"As you said, that's the best kind of story there is."

"That wasn't a story. That was a life. Cut tragically short, considering what he left behind."

"Yes, his poor wife and their children."

His response made me hesitate, because: "I hate to say I was thinking of his songs."

"You shouldn't hate to say anything, because of course you did. I note you quite conspicuously left out any mention of legacy when you described what you wanted."

I shrugged. "I'm not sure that's something one should really want, or can. What am I supposed to say, that I want my work to go down in history as great? That I want my stories to be held in the same esteem as Shakespeare's plays?"

"You don't?"

He had me there. Hell, if I've been telling you that the whole point of recording this story is honesty, it's time to go full-on: "Higher."

Angus laughed. "You know you can have that."

"That's why I keep writing."

He nodded. "But my question is whether that's really all you want."

"Everything we just mentioned? If it's not a completely comprehensive list, I think it's a reasonably fair start to one."

"But it's all stories this and reading that and writing down the other. Not to put too fine a point on it, but don't you fear all work and no play might make you rather dull?"

I thought back to all those Foolish evenings, dancing with Veronica, and to the myriad evenings I'd spent there in that grand City, with my friends, carousing and generally upholding the reputation many before me had so righteously earned. I laughed. "I know how to have a good time."

"I wasn't implying you did not. I was merely wondering if such pleasure had any bearing on what you wanted. Because all you mentioned related to your writing."

"That's all we were talking about."

"That's not all I was talking about. I asked if something was what you wanted, and you responded by enumerating several other desires, none of which were anything not related to your writing and your work."

"I wasn't thinking about anything else."

"You should."

"What do you want me to say? Maybe I stuck to writing because besides that, I haven't got the first clue. Long-term? I mean, if I say I just want a good life, what would that even mean? Victorian house with a white picket fence and two and a half kids?"

"I'd presume you'd share those things with a wife."

"I'm not even dating anyone."

"But you'd like to be, wouldn't you? Say, for example, that beautiful young girl to whom you were speaking on the night we met?"

"Veronica? I don't think—does that—look, not to be rude, but I was under the impression this was about business. And work. Which might be why I focused so much on writing and my books when I answered. So if you don't mind, can we concentrate on that instead of my personal life? I don't even know what your business is yet."

"Of course you do. I'm in futures. I trade them."

"So, like the stock market?"

"Of course not. I mean *futures*, my boy. Not random slips of paper, nor shares in companies that may or may not fail depending on the vagaries of supply and demand. Nor gold nor oil nor anything of the sort. If I tell you that the future is my business, I mean the future. Tomorrow. And tomorrow and tomorrow, at that. You'd be amazed what you can accomplish with the right guy in your corner, and I'm the right guy. You're not here to invest in the stock market, my boy. The only future you're here to discuss is yours."

"My own?" I said. I'd say I couldn't keep the skepticism out of my voice, but it wasn't as though I tried very hard. Because, honestly, what do you say to something like that? Even if I took him seriously, where would that get me? In the course of ultimately finding Force One, I'd been on more job interviews than I could count, because they all eventually blur together. Someone in a suit, behind a desk, reading over a single sheet of paper that's supposed to summarize your best attributes as a worker, nevermind that the best measure of any worker, the only measure, in fact, that counts, is the work itself.

"You're skeptical," Angus said, but, then, it wasn't as though I'd tried to hide it.

"Can you blame me? I'm not even sure what you're talking about yet," I told him, thinking of a few of those other interviews I'd been to: the debt consolidation firm where some guy whose position and function were never clear spoke like a working-class Hitler-by-way-of-Anthony Robbins about how he had been sick and tired of being sick and tired. The younger-than-me CEO who had asked me, after I'd given him several professional articles, if I had any "relevant" writing samples, and who was proud his company had created a Facebook application to pass a virtual beer to your friends.

"Of course not," he rose and went to the bookcase to my right. "Truth be told, I'm happier showing you. I've always gotten spectacular results, and it's just going to make my offer to you that much more intriguing."

"I still don't know—."

"Patience, my boy, patience," he said, as his fingers danced over bookspines. He chose two, one a small pamphlet and one a sort of journal, before he returned to his desk, where he sat, then passed the one that looked like a journal across to me.

It looked like an old newspaper. It might have been an old newspaper, in fact. At the top—

New York Mirror—

with a subtitle

(*A Journal of Literature, Music, and the Fine Arts*)

I liked if only for its order of priorities.

It was dated January 29, 1845.

I looked at Angus. "It's old."

"More than a hundred and fifty years."

"And you just keep it in your bookcase?"

"Best place for books. Have a glance through it."

I shrugged as I started to leaf through it. It was slim, so there wasn't much leafing to be done, but I stopped even before I had seen the whole thing, because I noticed text blocked out in rhythmic lines, the first of which caught my eye—

Once upon a midnight dreary—

I didn't mean to whisper, "While I pondered, weak and weary," though the quaint and curious volume of lore I held was quite the opposite of forgotten.

I considered the cover again. "Are you—Seriously? This has to be the earliest publication I've ever seen."

"It was the first."

I looked up at him. "Are you kidding me? It must have cost a small fortune."

"What's it say? Three dollars a year?"

"Surely you paid more than that."

"I paid nothing for it. It was a gift from one of my clients," he told me. "As was this."

With that, he passed across the other book he had chosen, which was, again, more a pamphlet, really: half-folded sheets of paper only barely bound by small pieces of string punched through the fold. The first page was blank, while the second read: *The Tragedie of Hamlet, Prince of Denmark*, by Wilm Shekspere. The third was a list of dramatis personae, and then the fourth—

Bernardo: Who's there?

Francisco: Nay, answer me. Stand and unfold yourself.—

all on pages the ecru of country eggs on a summer morning, and all written in a spidery scrawl clearly written by hand and almost certainly penned using a quill.

"What—what is this?"

"One of the finest plays in the history of literature."

"I've never seen a copy like this."

"Few have. Do you let people see your rough drafts?"

"Well, no, but I—wait. Are you—a rough draft? Of *Hamlet*?"

"In so far as young Will ever wrote rough drafts, of course. Considering the schedule he so often worked under, rough drafts were rare. As you noted, he composed mainly on the fly—."

"Because he and his actors only had a few weeks to rehearse."

"Precisely."

"So this is—what, exactly? It looks hand written."

"By the bard himself."

I nearly fucking dropped it. "Excuse me?"

"Shakespeare. Will. The bard of Stratford-on-Avon. He wrote that himself. That's the copy the actors used to copy their lines from."

I set it on the desk. Carefully, even though I wasn't entirely certain I believed him. "Another gift from a client, I take it. You must have rich clients."

"Not when I start working with them, usually."

"So, what, you make people rich, and they buy you expensive books bec—?"

"Buy me? Of course not. Neither of those books was bought for me."

"But you just said—."

"I said they were gifts. Which they were. One from a young poet in Philadelphia, the other from a young playwright in England."

"You said they were clients."

Angus said nothing, just held my eyes, and nodded his head once.

I stared at the books on the desk. I thought I understood pretty clearly what he was telling me, and I was only starting to get around to whether I believed it.

"Your clients," I said. I didn't realize how soft my voice would be, nor that there might be awe in it, until I heard it. I set my beer down.

Angus smiled but again said nothing.

And yes, there was a side of me that considered simply getting up and walking away without another word spoken, but the moment I acknowledged that part of me, I also acknowledged it as a rather unexciting part of me. Maybe it's silly or idealistic, but a bigger part of me had grown up reading stories of boy wizards and tales of high intrigue, then had graduated on to reading about American gods and Anansi's boys. That bigger part might have been the same part of Jack that had traded the cow for those beans, the same part of Alice that had taken off after the White Rabbit.

I had long ago given up on flying, but that part of me that would have traded his cow for beans or followed after Alice and her rabbit wondered if the simple act of belief was even more powerful a magic than flight. I wasn't sure, but finding out . . . I didn't necessarily have to believe him to just sit there and listen a while longer, and why not?

Besides, I hadn't yet finished my beer.

Angus smiled when I picked it up. "I realize it will be difficult at first to believe, but really it is no different from the idea of Gods and gardens and men walking up mountains to return with constitutions. What I'm telling you, in fact, is a lot less myth and a lot more truth."

His words reminded of Pilate confronting Jesus behind the closed doors of the Roman consulate, the voice of the crowd so loud it surpassed the stones: "What is truth?"

Angus laughed. "The truth is simple. The truth is that I helped each of those men get what they wanted, and that I can do the same for you. The truth is that Shakespeare wanted his plays about love and madness and death to transcend time and age, and he gave up a happy marriage to his dear Anne to have it. The truth is that Poe wanted to write poetry to shed further light upon the darkest of truths, and so he gave up his own mental health and the health of his beloved Virginia to do so," Angus told me.

Me? I sipped my beer as he spoke, and it gave me a warm feeling to counteract one of darkness and of depth: the feeling that comes when deciding whether to trust the moment. You know the one I mean—that sense that just deciding to be open to possibility could change your entire life. That was what I felt right then.

Angus snapped his fingers, and suddenly: what starts the fourth movement, the famous Ode to Joy, of Beethoven's final symphony? I'm reasonably sure it's the strings section, but those opening notes seem too deep and full to come from violin; I'm thinking a cello, something big and proud enough you have to spread your legs to play it, and my God can those notes catch you there, in the groin, less in lust than in purely physical love. I mean, if falling in love at first sight came with a soundtrack, it would have to be that, wouldn't it, with that great highness like euphoria, the strings trilling and wriggling up and down scales like water over rocks?

I don't know what Angus did for those acoustics, but it sounded like I was sitting beside the cellist. I could hear each individual string.

Is there anything in the world like Beethoven to open you? I mentioned that feeling of possibility, of decision, but Jesus, the Ninth Symphony is like a key to what makes us human, not just unlocking those parts of us we have secreted away but convincing us to open ourselves to the possibility of life. It's like you listen and you feel like someone else gets it, all the pain and all the joy, all the sorrow and all the kindness, all the sadness and all the happiness inherent in every moment you've ever been alive. Listening to it is as much like falling in love with music as it is like trusting the world, because for those fifteen or twenty minutes of that final movement, what possible harm could befall you?

Angus made as if to speak, but I stopped him. Maybe it was the buzz I had going from the beer. Or maybe just those fantastic acoustics. Whatever it was, the moment I heard those opening notes I wanted to listen to the rest of them. I knew my eyes might film with tears as the music played, but I discovered I couldn't care. And so he sat back, and for the next ten or so minutes, we listened to Beethoven's final symphony and greatest masterpiece.

Silence for a moment when it had finished. When Angus spoke, his voice was quiet in reverence. "He came to me when they still called him Luigi. He wanted to write songs that would touch the heart of anyone who heard them. I asked if he'd mind never hearing them himself."

I swallowed but didn't say anything. I don't think I trusted myself to.

"Without me, Shakespeare would have had a happy marriage and we'd never know what people dream on a midsummer's night. Without me, Poe would have been healthy until the end, but he never would have hallucinated the raven that would become the subject of the world's most famous poem. Without me, Beethoven would have passed away listening to his daughter play the piano, and we would never have learned what a sonata full of moonlight sounds like."

"So, what, without you, I'm going to pass away into obscurity? No one will ever read my books, or at least not on the scale I hope for?" I asked, and even as I did so, I felt the defiance rise in my gut. I know it's how I am: if Angus wanted to tell me I wouldn't be able to do it without him, I was going to turn my hat backwards and sit my ass down and try anyway. "I don't believe that."

"Believe as you will, but you mark my words, my talented young friend, you have it in you to be great."

"So then I don't see what I'm doing here. Not that I didn't enjoy the beer and the Beethoven."

"Ah, but as we have established, what you want has only partly to do with writing and your work, does it not?"

Maybe I didn't want to believe I knew what he was saying, or that he was saying it, but I found I suddenly couldn't pretend. I felt it, dense in the pit of my stomach, as sudden knowledge that something is about to go wrong. Part fear, part denial, part something else entirely and entirely unidentifiable, that same terrible feeling you get when you witness tragedy like you never imagined occur.

Even just the thought hurt, but I gave it voice: "Veronica."

Angus smiled, but he did me the mercy of allowing some sadness into it. "Precisely her. Because the reason I talked to you, the reason I gave you my card, is not just that it's plainly and obviously clear how very much in love with her you truly are but also that you will never know her love in return."

There was only a sipful of beer left in my glass, and I swallowed it gratefully, mouth gone dry. "Without you," I said, placing the glass on the desk between us.

Angus said nothing, just a small gesture that somehow managed to include his entire body for participation: yes.

It felt like getting punched in the stomach. It felt like one of those vertigo-inducing shots for which Martin Scorsese is so well known: as if I had to zoom in and hold close to a world from which I had suddenly discovered myself totally detached. When I asked, "Are you—are you the devil?" my voice sounded a long way off.

Angus laughed, perhaps with a bit too much glee. "My boy, I cannot tell you the last time I was mistaken for Old Scratch. But alas, I'm just an old man who knows a thing or two about futures and chance, and who has in his time discovered a way to help certain talented individuals choose what they want in life when they otherwise might not receive such an opportunity. Surely there can be no harm in that."

"So what happens now?"

"Oh, but I can't tell you that, my boy. Now you must make a choice. Decide between one or the other."

"But is it—can I be blind instead, or—," but I stopped, because Angus was already shaking his head. I breathed out, and my voice, when it came again, was more reedy and panicked than I liked. "I can't have both."

"You ever hear that old expression about having your cake and eating it too?"

I nodded.

"I'm sorry to say it's true."

"But what if—?"

"You stopped dealing in 'what if's the moment you walked through my door, my boy. We're dealing with the future here, and now you must choose your own. Would you write and have your words received as you've always wanted? Or would you have the love of a certain young lady with whom you've been in love very nearly all your life, and certainly as far back as matters? Do you want your books translated into more languages than you could ever learn? Or do you want to be with Veronica, and know her love?"

"And that's it?"

"Does anything else matter? It's simple really," Angus told me, glancing, as he did so, at his watch. "Now, mind you, I don't expect you to decide here and now and upon the spot in which you currently sit, but I must note that I am a busy man; there are many people with futures—and even more without them—and I'm the man they talk to. So the deal is simple: all you have to decide is whether Veronica's love means more to you than telling stories, and you must do so within the next forty-eight hours. After that, this offer expires, and neither of us will be any good to the other."

I'd like to say I considered what he was telling me, but I'm honestly not certain I could; there were too many thoughts misfiring across my alcohol-lubricated brain, so many flashing out of existence before I could fully discern them. One came fully, though: "Would I be trading just the fame?" Because maybe I'd just continue doing exactly what I'm doing right now, just writing all this down in a little room, and maybe I'd still be writing this for someone like you but you just wouldn't exist, or I would never know you did. I'll be honest and note that, even were that the case, I still wasn't sure I could live with it, but still I had to ask.

Angus, however, merely shook his head.

"Either way, I'll always wonder, won't I?"

Angus smiled, but it seemed sad. "That's just human nature, wouldn't you say? You'll try not to. You choose the writing, the work, the gift and the fame, I'd wager you'd convince yourself it was the right thing to do. You'll think of her, but every time you do you'll remind yourself there will be another girl along, because you know there are plenty out there."

I didn't say anything.

"You won't, on the other hand, tell yourself none of them are her, because that minor bit of knowledge won't make it any easier. That could destroy you, in fact, and so you'll ignore it," Angus told me, paused, then: "I had a young Jewish kid come in here once. Nervous little guy, stammered a lot. I made him much the same offer I'm making you now, a chance to be with the girl he was in love with. And he listened to my offer, but when he came back, he respectfully declined it. Said he'd thought a lot about it, but he kept thinking of his grandfather, who had once told him that women are like trolley cars, and there's always another one coming along. Told me he'd just wait for the next one to stop at his platform."

"So he turned you down."

Angus nodded. "I'm not a salesman trying to convince you to buy something you don't want. I'm just a guy offering some options."

"So what happened to him?"

"The Jewish kid? My business associates are confidential, but let's just say he went on to build a very successful film career on being nervous," Angus said, paused again, then: "Look, a lot of choices have been made by people sitting in the very chair you're sitting in now, and I'm not going to tell you they were all good. I'm not going to tell you every client I've ever worked with has been happy with the decision he or she made. Statistically, perhaps, I can say that I have a high rate of successful business happily done, but what that would neglect is that none were statistics. Every person has been real, with real dreams and real talents and real lives, and every one has chosen a real future, for whatever that's worth. Some got exactly what they needed, and some took what they wanted, and some ultimately ended up with neither, but what I'm trying to get at is this: not every choice made in that chair has been made happily, or with excitement, but every choice had to made. Now it's your turn. You've got two roads in front of you, here, both less traveled, and now you have to decide which one is yours. Either way, though, whichever road you choose, you have to make a choice, and you have to move forward, and you have to do it now."

"Why can't I just wait to see what happens?"

"Because it doesn't move you forward, and because when it comes to what happens next, you're about to find out," he said, rising. I did, too, almost more out of instinct than anything else. He offered his hand, and I shook it again as he ushered me toward those giant doors. "You have a lot to think about over the next couple of days. Don't make this decision lightly."

"I won't," I told him as he opened those doors. "I won't. I won't," I said twice more, as though was trying to convince him, but more likely I was trying to convince myself.

"Given how much you liked that beer, I'll have Brigid send you off with a bottle for the road," Angus said as our handshake broke, and then I was moving through the lobby, back toward the door in the waterfall. Brigid thrust into my dumb hand another bottle of that fine ale, and then, nearly before I knew it, I was back on the Village street, the sounds and scents and taste of the City dancing all around me, assuming me quickly into it, spinning me right round like a record baby, my head full of dancing and my heart scared of decisions as I found my way back to the subway, back to the PATH, back home . . .

Chapter Ten, in which certain things,
which may or may not already have been obvious,
are, if not revealed, at least made explicit

*W*here I found waiting for me a letter. The envelope addressed to me in my own writing.

Crash course: back when the events of this story took place time, aspiring writers would query their aspiring manuscripts (whose dreams are to be bound into real, honest-to-goodness books that will be shipped to real, honest-to-goodness bookstores, where they will be placed on real, honest-to-goodness shelves from which they will one lucky day by plucked by real, honest-to-goodness readers) to prospective agents by mail. As I record this at this very moment, many agents have switched to using e-mail, and who knows what tomorrow will bring (hopefully this very story will have something to do with whatever happens next)? The first time I wrote all this, nobody'd ever heard of Kindle or digital distribution.

Nowadays, I can read books on my Android-powered smartphone.

Back then, however, was different. Back then, writers had to use the good ole' United States Postal Service to send literary agents query letters, and given that many agencies received hundreds, if not thousands, of queries *every week*, they simply couldn't possibly keep up with the price of return postage, so writers had to include self-addressed stamped envelopes with their paper queries.

(Quicker crash: a literary agent acts on behalf of authors to negotiate publishing contracts with publishing houses.)

I mention all this so you understand why I was so excited to receive a letter addressed to me in my own handwriting; I'd included that very same envelope in the query I'd sent to Merrilee Heiftetz only a week or so before.

It may not be possible to open one of those letters calmly. Too many of us writers associate too much of our identity with our words and the possibility of the publication, and each new letter brings with it the blackjack rush of a gambling high: not the euphoria of winning but rather the uncertain glee of going all-in on a straight flush. That gut-clenching, icy feeling of knowing how much rides on the current hand.

Me, my hands have always shaken. Every time I have one of those moments—which don't come often—I try to remain calm but never succeed. I know they shook, then, as I withdrew from the envelope a single, twice-folded sheet of high quality paper, thick and off-white. Fountain pen letter head, business address, and, below—

A sidenote: I've gotten many rejections. All writers do. Rejection is part of the process, and ultimately, it often becomes a game of numbers and chance—what editors are looking for what type of story when, and how does yours fit?

I was lucky that my first ever rejection came as a personal letter from one of the most reputable agents in the entire industry, a note I received because my creative writing professor was a personal friend. I got it when I was a sophomore in college, and over the years have received hundreds more.

Besides that first letter, I've gotten mainly form letters addressed to someone named "Author," as if that is my name, and often not signed at all. When from a literary magazine, they are often so generic as to be attributed not to any single person in particular but rather "the Editors," as if their staff is some nameless, faceless—on my worst days I'd like to believe soulless—entity that exists for no other reason than to dash the dreams of the hopeful. I imagine every office of every editor and every agent in the world has a stack of prepared letters ready to send out to authors who submit work to them, and to be candid, that proposition can't be far off from the truth. Like I said, they get hundreds of queries per week, often thousands per month.

I like to think they don't like sending rejections. I like to believe there's still a part of every agent and editor that yearns only for that next great read by an as-yet-undiscovered writer.

I've gotten forms from lots of places. I've even gotten personal notes from some of the best: Mike Curtis told me he liked my story and was sorry to say it wasn't for the *Atlantic Monthly*. Same I heard from one of the editors at the *Magazine of Fantasy and Science Fiction*—

Whereas on that day, I opened that envelope to discover that Ms. Heifetz, for her part, complimented the sample chapter I had sent her and requested the first fifty pages of my manuscript. This is known in the industry vernacular as a 'partial.' This is a very good thing. Awesome, in fact. If the moment of opening the letter was the equivalent of that precariously uncertain moment of yanking the arm and watching the cherries spin, that letter was hitting for a hundred bucks. Though I probably should have said the jackpot, if the whole point here to redeem my actions through honesty, the truth is I wouldn't have called anything less than the promise of a publishing contract a jackpot. Yes, sometimes I'm fucked up like that.

As for that decision and my actions—

We'll get there. Are you dying to know what I told Angus? Because standing there, with the beer Brigid had given me in one hand and that letter in the other, I certainly wondered.

As I put the beer in the fridge, I pulled out my cell to call Veronica with the news, but hesitated. Talking to Angus, hearing his offer . . . I'd become self-conscious about a relationship I'd had all my life. I was still thinking about what he had told me, and I may have been trying to ignore his proposition, because I didn't know how to take it seriously, or what it would mean if I did. Then again, in ways, I had attempted to ignore my feelings for Veronica under the assumption that shelving them and continuing to talk to her as though nothing had changed might keep everything from changing.

Still, a large part of me didn't consider my novel solely my own because it felt such great debt to the inspiration and encouragement that had carried me through to completion, and so I stopped hesitating and dialed the number of the girl with whom I had fallen in love, the girl to whom I had written that perfect letter—

(the girl who did not love me in return, a fact I bring up because it's about to become extraordinarily relevant)—

Veronica Sawyer, who answered, slightly out of breath, after the third ring. "Hey, what's going on?"

I couldn't keep the excitement out of my voice; it pitched high as I told her the news.

"So does that mean you're a client now?"

"Not yet. Just that she wants to read some more, which I get to send her now," I said, and that was the moment I realized I didn't want to just send it off. Getting a request for a partial manuscript is not an enormous deal, not a deal as big as selling a manuscript to a publisher, but it's not a small thing, either, given that it's not the usual way of things. Its not being the usual way of things, I decided then and there I wanted to do something to make it special, and I wanted Veronica's help. "How busy are you tomorrow?"

"Not very. School's a few weeks off, so I'm kind of climbing up the walls."

"I want to send it off, and I want to take you to dinner. Tomorrow. Can you do that? Make a day of it with me?"

"Sounds like fun."

"Awesome. Mind picking me up at the train station?"

"Call me when you're here and I'll swing by."

And then I hung up and started revising.

***

Neither revising nor polishing is simple. The common aphorism—

Great art is never finished, only abandoned.—

makes many novels lonely as broken-down cars left by the side of the road, defeated orange flags fixed to their antennae. Most are hiccups in your afternoon commute, barely worth attention on the way home.

Even the most accomplished novel has a busted headlight or a loose belt—

A novel is merely a long work of fiction with flaws.—

and while writing is about cobbling together some strange form of transportation using every spare part at your disposal, revision is more nebulous; it's about seeing what you just built and figuring out how to make it run better. You know it's never going to run perfectly—what you begin with is less a Lamborghini than a go-cart made from a cardboard box and a couple of wheels cast off a shopping cart—so you pick up an entirely different set of tools, rev the engine, and grease up the parts you want to run more smoothly, tighten the belts that squeal, add air to a tire lacking pressure.

You do the best you can with what you've got. You know the first five pages are most crucial, while the importance of the first paragraph can't be overstated and the first twenty pages are critical; an opening reveals a lot about how a book handles. To extend the metaphor, if the first five pages determine whether the car even starts, the first twenty are getting used to the clutch, setting the radio to the proper station, and adjusting the seat.

One reason for short stories' appeal is they're like a test drive. I think agents ask for the first fifty because that's when you know whether you want to go anywhere. By then, your seat's adjusted. The radio's tuned, the mirrors set. Only two simple decisions are left: are you going to fill up the tank, and where is that tank going to take you?

A brilliant novel presents the same simple question Microsoft posed: where do you want to go today?

The most difficult part is that revising isn't nearly so straightforward as any diagnostic a mechanic might run on a car. It's not like you can kick the tire or hook the computer up to the muffler to check the emissions. It's instinctual.

So I sat down with those first 50 pages, which was roughly the first act of my 100,000-word novel, and I polished them up as best I could. I tried to forget that I had built the car I was looking at and tried to decide how best it might provide a better ride for whoever chose to drive it. Some changes were minor—a comma here, semi-colon there—but others were more significant—puzzling over the chapter order, or whether to combine certain scenes, whether to keep certain characters or . . .

I printed it out, then composed a simple note to Ms. Heifetz, thanking her for the opportunity to send it to her, and then I set those pages carefully atop my printer, where they waited until the following morning, at which point I tucked them into a manila folder and hopped a bus hometown-bound for Veronica and queries.

***

Jersey January is cold and colorless, spindle treetrunks bare and shivery in the freezing wind, which comes often and sharp as a morning shave and leaves behind a windraw world like shorn skin. That was all I saw beyond the bus windows, and all the while I saw it I thought of that magical office in the Village and the offer I'd found there. I was still, in ways, trying to decide if I believed the proposition Angus had presented me; listening was one thing, and didn't require commitment, but actually acknowledging it might in fact be true—if you've seen the third installment of the Indiana Jones trilogy and recall the moment when, during the final act, Indy stood upon the precipice of a yawning cavern, closed his eyes, held his father's journal over his heart, and stepped forward to make literal the oft-mentioned metaphorical leap of faith, you will have some idea of how I felt.

I didn't know if I wanted to well and truly believe my Grail awaited me on the other side of a stone bridge I couldn't actually see but could easily traverse. Not least of all because the very idea of its existence terrified me.

Because, in all honesty: part of me thought believing might be a minor miracle, but there was another part of me, too, and it cowered in weakness. That weaker part of me perhaps understood that, were it true, I wouldn't have the strength to resist the urge to drink from the cup.

I thought of Veronica the whole way, too. I knew I was putting her on a pedestal; I'd never been on a date with her, but somehow I had worked up in my head the idea that she was not just my ideal mate but a woman for whom I would have dropped everything to be with. If Veronica had asked me then and there to marry her, I would have answered in the affirmative under the confidence that I could spend the rest of my life working out the little details. Nothing to me mattered so much as the idea of the commitment, the fantasy of the romance: I could even imagine the ceremony, out of doors and among the trees, full of green and lace and

Vivaldi, with a kindly old preacher who would smile at each of us before pronouncing us husband and wife and permitting me to kiss my radiant new bride.

I know how that sounds, but remember I had known Veronica all my life. Tom would probably be the best man at my wedding regardless of whom I married, and the fact that I could so clearly imagine her in a white wedding dress with a veil like revelation might well have been simply because it was remarkably similar to the dress I'd seen her wear to her first holy Communion. Given that we had grown up together, and the fact that our families had remained, if not exactly close, certainly friendly . . . well, the idea didn't seem so incredible. We were close enough, in fact, that had we eloped as a frivolous adventure during a sudden and drunken trip to Atlantic City, our families would have probably accepted the news easily enough and still thrown us a terrific reception.

I realized, too, I wasn't sure if I was going to tell Veronica about my visit with Angus and what he had offered me. I think I felt I should know whether I believed him or not, first. That wasn't going to be an easy thing to decide.

***

I wish for you a moment as exceptional and sublime as the moment I stepped off the train to find Veronica Sawyer—her thunderstorm coat, her cloud-fluffy grey scarf, her obsidian turtleneck and blue jeans and thick, black, Inuit boots—waiting for me. Her smile made the trip worthwhile; even if my novel was ultimately rejected, even if nothing else came of the trip, that smile would have been enough.

Nevermind her hug: I can't describe what she smelled like except to compare her scent to those old cartoons in which some magical fragrance tendril-hooks some unsuspecting character's nose to literally lift said character off his feet and pull him through the air. I took a deep breath of Veronica Sawyer and would have followed her anywhere. Anywhere then was to her old Toyota Camry, where I waited while she got in and unlocked the passenger side door. I settled into the seat, buckling up with my manila folder of manuscript pages on my lap.

"Is that the precious cargo?"

"It's the first part of my novel."

"Are you excited?"

I was, but I was also distracted by thoughts of Angus inspired by the sight of the beautiful girl beside me. I swallowed. "Yeah. Totally."

***

One of the few great things about small towns is that everything's relatively nearby; the post office was basically down the block and around the corner, clerked by a sweet blonde woman with a quick nose and a hint of a drawl even as far north as we were. Veronica knew her better than I did—they attended mass together sometimes—and so they chatted while I addressed the envelope to a Manhattan office I probably could have gotten to, leaving from my apartment, inside of an hour.

Veronica's voice over my shoulder: "You're shaking," and then her light touch on my forearm. Veronica's fingers: long and slender, pianist's hands in want of ivory, and still, too—a subtle but nonetheless distinct contrast to my own trembling grasp. The fingers in which I held my pen: shivering, while my palm sweated like a prom. My own jitters worse than any first-date nerves I've ever had, but then again I'd never been on a first date with Veronica.

"You shouldn't be so nervous. You know it's good."

I shrugged. "Easy to say. Less to believe. What if she doesn't want it?"

"You give up. If this woman doesn't want it, nobody's going to."

"Um. What?"

"Exactly. Even just the idea is so foreign you don't really know how to process it. If this woman—whoever she is—rejects what you send her, you send it to the next person on whatever list you've made. And if you don't have a list yet, you make one. Because not a single agent is the only one out there, so you keep sending them letters until you find one who wants to read it all and then falls in love with it and then wants to represent it, because one of them is going to. And in the meantime, you go up to the counter and you pay to send this particular one what she wanted."

Which is what I did, and then we returned to Veronica's car. I waited while she unlocked my door, and then, as she started the car, I took a deep breath while buckling my safety belt. My breath stayed for a moment, filling my lungs and my head and my heart, before it came out, hanging in the air great and hopeful.

Veronica smiled. "You needed that."

I stared straight ahead at the brick-wall exterior of the Post Office. "You realize I might never have to do that again? She might ask for the whole manuscript, and then represent it, and then even sell it." I'm pretty sure I meant it to come out happy, but I wouldn't have called it that had I heard it, which surprised me a little.

Veronica let that statement stick around for a moment like a surreptitious cat, then: "Do you really want that?"

I looked at her. "To sell it? Well, yeah. Of c—."

"No, wait. Stop. Before you answer like I know you want to, would you just take a look at yourself for a second? I don't know if I'd ever have used the word 'giddy' to describe someone, but you earn it. You're shaking with something electric coming off you in waves, and think about that. You get published, you get famous, you get what you always wanted, and I hope that will be everything you ever wanted, but just for a minute appreciate this delicious, if uncertain, excitement, would you? If you never have to do it again, if she calls you tomorrow and sells it the next day, will you ever feel this excitement again?"

She put her hand on mine. I watched her delicate fingers touch my wrist, and as soon as I felt their feather-light caress my hand wanted to grasp, to hold hers—

Man's reach should exceed his grasp, else what's a Heaven for?—

and I don't know how I kept from doing so. I don't know how I controlled my hands and my body, every cell of which suddenly ached for the girl sitting beside me.

"I know how hard it is, because I know how seriously you take it. I know you just want it to happen. But you know . . . regardless of what happens with this woman, or any agent or editor or whatever for that matter, you know you're going to be okay, right?"

If you had asked me, before that moment, if I ever planned to tell Veronica how I felt, the idea of doing so in the parking lot of our local Post Office wouldn't have crossed my mind. I'm not sure I would have known how it might occur: a fancy dinner, perhaps, or a day at the park or the beach or the boardwalk. Given how special I thought Veronica was, I'm sure I would have imagined equally special circumstances, but as is so very often the case, life is what happens when you're making other plans. Perhaps the romantic in me might have made a dinner reservation in some candlelit restaurant, or planned out a picnic before which I might practice several times in front of the mirror the monologue by which I would reveal to her my innermost feelings.

Hell, given that we had already made plans to have dinner, the romantic in me might have waited another hour or so, drinking his courage and eloquence.

Instead:

My fingers closed on her hand without my meaning them to, and I looked at her. Sunlight through the window shone her eyes bright, and I said: "Do you know I love you?" like I legitimately believed she might not, my voice pitched slightly strained, almost as if sad. Maybe it was: even just uttering those words made something immutable concrete.

I wish I could describe how her expression changed. The smile never left her lips, the support her face. Not a single one of her fine features moved, but still, something about it became different from one second to the next, even if it was only her straining to keep it from changing.

"I mean, you must, right? All these years? That time I gave you those poems I don't even know you still have? Because I've gotta be honest; for a while there, even I didn't know. It was like, I was just so busy being young and going out and dancing with you in dim bars that I didn't pay attention to the fact that I was falling in love with you all over again. Which is what it was, if only because for a while there—," I stopped, though, because—well.

Honesty: her expression might not have changed in any measurable way, but there are other ways more important. When I spoke, my voice was level and precise, using no more sound than absolutely necessary and certainly not allowing emotion. "I shouldn't hav—."

"No, don't—," Veronica said. Her fingers squeezed my hand. "I'm just—I'm sorry. I'm so sorry."

"Sorry? For what?"

"You asked if I knew like I might not, but did you really think—how could I have possibly not known? It's not like you hide it well. I was so happy when you got engaged. I thought maybe you were over me, that maybe you had found what you deserved. Truth is, I don't know if I ever led you on, but I should have told you a long time ago that—,"she paused, then, and when she did so, she seemed to realize her hand was still grasping mine. She withdrew it to her lap, stared ahead at the wall in front of us as if searching its bricks for words.

I put my hands in my own lap. I didn't know what else to do with them.

"It's not that I don't love you," she said, turning to look at me again. "You know I love you. You're one of the most amazing people I know, and one of my best friends."

"But that's all."

"But that's exactly my point; it's not enough. You deserve more than that."

"Not more than you. Don't say more than you."

"More than how I feel about you. I'll always love you. I'll talk to you about Ionesco and Beckett and drama and teaching and writing, and all like I can't talk to anyone else. But you know that feeling you get when someone you like texts you? That swimmy feeling that makes you want to grin so hard you feel your own dimple? Don't you deserve someone you make grin like that? Don't you deserve someone who's just as in love with you as you are with them? Because you know I love you, but I'm—."

"Please don't say you're not in love with me. Could this conversation be any more of a cliché?"

"Could it be any more true? Maybe we needed some cliché in our relationship, finally, because we've been keeping things from each other for a while, haven't we?"

"I haven't kept anything from you."

"Except the fact that you were in love with me."

"Which you've apparently always known."

"But not because you told me. Isn't that the whole point?"

"I don't know what the point is anymore. I just know—I wrote it for you. When I wasn't sure I could go on, the thought of you helped me through it."

"You don't seriously think you wouldn't have finished it if not for me?"

I hesitated. Shrugged. "I never had to find out."

"Don't put that on me," Veronica said. Somewhat shortly, like she didn't want to leave room for argument. "I don't deserve that. You wrote a book. Big, thick stack of paper with words—."

"All for you."

"Even without me, you would have written it."

"Maybe not the same way."

"The way it needed to be written. You wrote something that should make you happy, regardless of me or anybody else. Because what if that agent rejects it? And then the next one, and the next—."

"But you just said, I keep sending it."

"Because you believe in it. Not because you wrote it for me, or you think that's what I want. Because you believe in the words you put down. You can't do it for any other reason than that, and certainly not for me."

"But it was your support—."

"Then maybe you need to do it without my support."

"What? What're you—are you breaking up with me? We're not even dating."

"But there are feelings. And if we're going to have an honest relationship, we're going to need to sort those out, right? Especially if we mean to get past them."

"Who says I want to move past them?"

"Then how can we possibly have a good friendship? With you pining away after me—."

"I'm not exactly pining."

"You know what I mean. It's not fair to either of us. It's not fair for me to lead you on, and it's not fair for you to put me in that position."

"And what position is that?"

"I don't know, but I don't want to be in it."

"So what, then?"

"Just . . . we give each other some space. We can get through this. We get through everything. We'll figure it out."

"And if we don't? Because I'll be honest here: I don't really know what we mean. Am I supposed to avoid Tom's shows now? Are you going to not go? What're we—?"

"No, I just mean—look, I'm going back to school soon anyway, and Lord knows I've got enough on my plate I should probably just stick around there on weekends as it is. And like I said, it's not like I don't love you. I do. You really are one of my best friends.

And I've always thought the best thing about friendship is the fact that it's always there to come back to. Real friendships never change. They're always right where you left them, to pick up where you left off."

"So we should not be friends for a while," I said. I hated myself for saying it, the tone of my words, the way I half-spat the question at her. Because on another level, on a very reasonable level, I knew that what she was saying made sense, that what she was suggesting might well be not only the most reasonable option for both of us, but also the best. She was right, too, that maybe I needed to get past this idea that I had written for her, or because of her. Especially given my experience in Angus' office . . . just the fact that I had considered his offer worried me.

"Don't do that to me," she told me.

"Do what?" Mock-defensive. I knew what I'd done. I knew what I was doing, too, and I couldn't help it. I'm not proud of that moment. But: warts and all, right?

"Don't turn this on me. It's not—I don't—I didn't mean for this to happen, and if you've had feelings for me all this time, have I ever encouraged them? Have I ever led you on to believe I wanted anything more from you than friendship? Because I never have. Not once. I've never held your hand. I've never drunkenly kissed you while we've danced in a dark bar. You can't blame me for feelings I don't have unless I've misled you, and I don't think I have."

I said nothing. I had nothing left. Just breath, and even then only barely.

"I should take you back."

I hesitated, then nodded. "Dinner's probably not the best idea."

"I think we can work through this, given some time."

"But how much?"

"I don't want this to end our friendship. Maybe we can be even better friends now that we got this out in the open."

"I hope so," I told her.

"I'm sure of it. I'm sure we'll hug each other again. I'm sure we'll laugh together again. I'm even sure we'll dance together again. One day."

"But not today."

"No, today I'll take you back to the bus station, and you can go back up to your apartment, and you can work on some story that will have nothing whatsoever to do with me. You can put one word in front of the other, because more than anything else in the world, including me, that's what you love. We'll take a rain check on dinner."

I hesitated, then nodded, because what else was I going to do? We drove off under the promise of a rain check, but I noticed through the windshield there wasn't a single cloud in the sky.

***

I just passed the novel mark there, in that scene. Sometime through there, we hit 50,000 words. I think it was sometime between the moment I told Veronica I loved her and the moment she told me she didn't love me in return, which is probably appropriate, at least in a dramatic sense. I can't tell you how many times I've written and rewritten this story, how many false starts I have on this and various other hard drives. I think I'm happiest right now that I might finally be getting it right.

Maybe there's something to be said for telling the truth.

For example, I'm really not sure about the last line of that previous scene, mentioning the lack of a single cloud in the sky, but then again, I remember that moment. I remember thinking rain check was such an odd term, and that the January day was bright enough I could believe spring was on its way; it was one of those days so bright it's surreal, the kind of bright that makes you think everything should have a halo, and that everyone should be happy.

It stayed that way the whole way back to the bus station, where Veronica dropped me off to catch the next Greyhound back—I almost wrote "home," there. Back to Manhattan, back to the trains that would take me to my crummy Hoboken apartment. I told her she didn't need to wait with me while I waited for the next bus, as I wasn't too worried about getting stolen, and she gave me an obligatory chuckle, and then a hug that felt that way, too, and she told me to take care, that everything was going to be fine, and she knew it in her bones.

I wished I had as much confidence as she did. I didn't tell her that.

I didn't tell her any more at all, in fact. I couldn't think of anything else I might; I'd already told her the biggest thing I possibly could, after all. We've seen how that went down.

Except—

The fact that I was in love with her, that I had been for as long as I could remember, that wasn't the biggest thing I could have told her, I realized, riding that bus back north to the City and my apartment. I could, after all, have told her about Angus, and Futures Trading.

So much for that, I thought, staring out the window as the sun set down to blaze the sky orange through charblack tree branches and clouds like antique shawls. So much for Angus and his offer, but then, I had to admit I didn't mind that so much. I had to admit it was just about a relief I no longer had to decide, that I could visit his office for only the amount of time necessary to thank him for finally motivating me to talk to Veronica, who had conclusively rendered his offer completely moot.

I guessed I was no longer a candidate for whatever futures Angus might trade, but that was okay, considering the other option. The not-Veronica option. The stories.

I didn't mind that idea, truthfully. Because I felt, in some way, like . . . remember Schrodinger and his cat in its safe? I felt like I'd opened that safe and made the observation. I felt like there was no longer a quantum state, no longer a possibility. All that was left was certainty and decision. All that was left was a dead cat and a puddle of poison and a half-bit of radioactive decay.

I dozed through most of the ride, then walked to the connecting station to catch the train back to my own stop. Down the hill to the corner church, another couple blocks left, and then I turned the key in the lock and let myself into an apartment that might as well have been empty. Light like a welcome mat from under one of my roommate's doors, a muffled television through the wall. I opened my own bedroom door to throw my coat on my bed, then went to the kitchen, headed for anything in the fridge, trying to remember if I'd ordered anything recently.

Nothing, really, save the beer Angus had given me on my way out of his office. I remembered its heady aroma and its deep, dense taste, so expansive it had felt like it shouldn't have fit in my mouth. I popped the cap and reached for a tumbler before I decided against it, brought the bottle to my lips and took a long, slow pull of it. Heavy enough to be a meal on its own, and I remembered how it had affected me nearly right away, and I thought maybe that wouldn't be so bad. Maybe that would take my mind off of . . .

Well. Everything, really.

Chapter Twelve, in which we skip ahead.

*T*he astute among you will notice that we're skipping chapter eleven (and the not-so-astute, of course, know it now). I debated how to convey the action that occurs therein, in fact—do I skip it without mentioning it? Do I include it and release all the tension?—and decided I was best off acknowledging the skip and noting the intention to return to it later, at which point I am reasonably certain that my reasons for skipping it will become clear. For that you will have to take my word.

For now to the following morning (so it's not really a large jump, just a handful of hours), to my crummy apartment. I can't quite explain why I suddenly want to block this scene like I would a movie, but I do, and so I'm going to, which means I'm going present-tense for a moment: no lights are on, but the sun shines through the windows and lights up the hardwood floor. The hard-drive on the XBOX360 spins next to the old, beat-up television in front of the slightly newer but no less beat-up couch (it was there when I moved in, but I assume somebody bought it fourth-hand if they didn't simply pick it off the curb).

The doorbell rings.

Nothing moves besides that hard-drive, which continues to spin with a tiny electronic whir.

Cut to my bedroom. White walls and all, old bed. My sleeping form huddled beneath my Calvin Klein comforter.

The door bell rings again. Nothing continues to move.

I snore. When the doorbell rings a third time, I shift and pull the covers over my head, but the movement might be more subconscious than anything else.

Now: a quiet few seconds. Not too long, of course, because you can't hold your movie audience hostage. That wouldn't be nice at all. Just a beat.

Close on my cell phone as it rings, as its display lights up, but not close enough to see the caller ID.

I groan. Shift again. This time pulling the covers down. I reach for my phone, which I pull to my face and squint at, because I haven't put on my glasses yet. And now you get to read the caller ID: VERONICA.

I drop the damned thing when I flip it open. I pat the comforter until my fingers find it, and then I pull it to my ear and croak into it. And not a real croak either: this is the croak of a deaf frog who's never actually heard a croak and so can only produce a reasonable facsimile.

Now here's a dilemma: do we want to stay inside, with me on the phone, and hear Veronica that way, or do we cut to the stoop of my apartment building, where she is even now standing, out there on a chilly Saturday morning? Movie-wise and drama-wise, it might be better to hold that revelation, but then again, given that her first words are, "Are you awake? Are you in bed? Can you get up and open your door?" it's not like the dramatic tension would exist very long anyway. And yes, that's what she said.

Which was the verbal equivalent of mainlining a double-shot espresso. Not that I know what that's like, but I was trying to think of what would make a double-shot espresso more powerful than drinking it.

We can go back to past tense now, because I only wanted the movie thing for those moments I wasn't actually awake (look, I told you at the start I was going to pull out every trick I knew, so you shouldn't exactly be surprised if I make some up on the fly, should you? But hey, you trust me—

really? Why?—

right?), because once I awoke, I stumbled out of bed, pulling on a pair of jeans I was even still buttoning as I padded across that same hardwood floor to the door of my apartment. Which I opened onto the little vestibule, then the lobby door, and finally the outer door of my apartment building, beyond which I found Veronica and her storm-black hair and her storm-blue eyes and her storm-grey coat. Or at least I was reasonably sure it was Veronica; I realized as I opened the door that I had left my glasses on my night table, so I started squinting like Mister Magoo, except with more hair.

"Um. Hi," I said. I don't think I was awake enough to be confused, but I gave it the old college try, anyway, and pulled a C+. Obviously the espresso I mainlined took its time kicking in.

"Hi. I'm sorry. I didn't mean to get here so early. The train went faster than I thought it would."

"Yeah. I—," I stopped, then, because I realized how terrible my tongue tasted. And also that my hair was all over the place when I scratched my head. "You took the train in?"

"I wanted to talk to you. Can I come in?"

"What? Oh, sure," I said, moving aside to allow her entrance in a rushle of wool and perfume. Her scent was what finally kickstarted my brain, bridging gaps between cotton-coated neurons that still wanted to pull the covers back over their heads, which was about when I became self-conscious if not conscious of everything else just yet, and realized I should wonder, given the abysmal taste of my tongue, how it probably smelled, too. And so, for the rest of the conversation, I basically mumbled in her general direction. "Can I get you something?" I asked as I closed and locked the apartment doors behind me.

"I'm okay," she said, following me into my apartment itself.

"No, really. Let me met get you something. Water at least. Because I really did just wake up, and you said you wanted to talk, but I won't be in any condition for the next few seconds. I at least need my glasses."

"Water's good," she said, and so I led her into my kitchen, where I filled a tumbler from the Brita pitcher, before I stumbled sleepily away to the bathroom.

Which was good. Because I needed a moment. The moment consciousness started to kick in, it brought memory with it, the big one being my conversation with Veronica the day before. And so, while I brushed my teeth and scraped my tongue and then put my contacts in and ran my wet fingers through my disgruntled hair, I wondered what she wanted to talk about. I don't know if I imagined it could possibly be good.

I walked out of the bathroom to find her on the couch with the television on. "Hey."

"Better?"

I nodded. "Never been good at getting out of bed."

"Who is?" Veronica said.

"True," I agreed, sitting down next to her, and then there was one of those moments so pregnant I might have considered names. "So what's up?"

"I'm sorry about yesterday."

I chuckled, but without much in the way of humor. "Yeah. Well. My fault, really. I have to admit I'm glad I finally said something, but I might wish I hadn't. I just—I don't—I mean, I know you love me like a brother, and really, if that's all I ge—."

My throat closed up on me then. Not choking on a thought or unsure of the next one, but rather with surprise.

Because that was when I felt her take my hand. I looked down at our fingers as if to confirm that she had actually done so, and: she had. Her fingers were on mine.

"That's not what I meant."

"Okay," I said.

"I did a lot of thinking last night, after I dropped you off. Kept me up through most of it. I was worried we couldn't be friends again, until I realized maybe we couldn't be, maybe we shouldn't be—."

"Right. We said some time apart might be good."

"Will you stop talking a minute? Please? It's funny, I went over and over in my head what I wanted to say on the way here, but then it all flew out of my brain the second you opened your door. So stop interrupting?"

I thought that responding at all might count as interrupting, so I just let myself fall silent.

"I was laying there last night wondering if we could be friends again, and then I realized I wasn't sure I wanted to be friends with you, anymore. I remembered how I told you that I wasn't in love with you, but then I started to wonder if I didn't think of you like that solely because I never had. You've always been like part of my family, and I realized maybe I just hadn't thought of you any other way. And then I . . .," she looked down at her hands on mine. "I started thinking about you. And your smile. And those baby blues of yours. Certainly, physically, a girl could do worse—."

I smiled. "I'm all right some days."

"And I wondered if you're such a great guy—."

"With such brashing good looks."

"Why didn't I have feelings for you?"

"It's not uncommon, if that's any consolation. You wouldn't believe how many gals have not had feelings for me. Or maybe you would."

She looked at me. "Maybe I do."

"Believe it? You should. Like I—."

"No. Maybe I do have feelings for you."

I'd like to think that if I'd been awake for more than a handful of minutes by then, I would have been able to follow the conversation more easily, or at least have been a better participant in it. As it was, I feel even still rather like I sucked at it, and I certainly didn't know what to say then. I swallowed. A part of me wanted to be hopeful about where the conversation was about to go, but after the one the previous night? My heart wasn't sure what it could handle, but it knew false hope wasn't on its list. I wasn't sure what to say, so I went with: "Maybe?"

"I don't—we have fun together. And we might not get to see each other as often as we'd like, but we always make it count when we do. We have so much in common, and we're always honest, and—aren't those all what's really important?"

"Maybe," I said, because all, to some degree, are, "But what's more important is how you feel."

"How we feel, you mean."

"No. How you feel. We know how I feel. I told you that yesterday."

"You love me," she said.

I felt my heart shrink back like a frightened puppy from her seeking hands. It wouldn't have bitten, I'm sure, but it would have trembled at being held, and it might not have stopped for a while. "I do."

She was looking into my eyes as if for something, but I'm not sure she found it. "How long have you felt that way?"

I shrugged. You know, of course, but I hadn't told her. "I don't remember not feeling it," I told her, because I was sure shrugging wasn't reassuring. "I'm sure the romantic thing would be for me to be able to recall the first moment I saw you, but I don't. All I know is that I've felt this way for as long as I can remember, mainly because I feel like I've known you for as long as I remember."

"It's been a long time, then."

I wondered if I could make her understand. I thought of grade school and church, of Catholicism and eternity. "You know how Christians believe Heaven lasts forever? Because I don't know about forever, but Heaven is as long as I've been in love with you."

"And given that we've known each other so long— We'd have a good foundation. Which is important."

"No, what's important," I said, "Is how you feel. Having a lot in common is great. So is being good together, and laughing together, and having families that get along. Those are all things you hope for. But what's important, the only thing, in fact, that's important, is how you feel."

"I feel scared."

"Scared."

"Scared," she said, looking at our hands. "Of this. Of you and me, of trying to be together and of it not working out and of breaking up. Of ruining one of the most important relationships in my life. Wouldn't you be?"

"I'm always scared around you. I was so scared of how you'd react if you knew how I felt, but then I was also scared that I'd get old and meet another girl and settle down and the only reason that girl wouldn't be you would be because I'd never told you how I felt. I never knew how to act, or what to say or do, and so I never did anything. I just put my head down and kept going, and it might've been a really sucky way to live, but it taught me you can't let the fear stop you. Didn't some philosopher guy say that the man who fears nothing is the man who loves nothing? And you know the only thing I was scared of besides you? Mediocrity. I'm scared to death this writing thing is going to go nowhere, of becoming one of those sob stories about pathetic, used-up never-wases, and you know how I fight the fear? I sit down and I do what I'm scared of as best I can. I could give up writing easily, I'm sure, settle in to a decent job and live a good life, and no one would fault me for it, but I can't, because that'd be giving up, and that's the easy way to deal with the fear. That would only let it fester into something that would just catch up to me when I finally ran out of live to outrun it in, and then it'd all have been wasted."

Veronica was quiet a moment, which was okay: I felt like I'd stripped down and then opened up, and there were things I had said I only realized as I was saying them, which may be why they stand out so well in my memory.

Finally, though, she said: "It wasn't a philosopher. It was Sean Connery."

Of all the ways she could have responded, that might have been dead last only because I couldn't think of any others. "What?"

"What you said. About the man who fears nothing. It's from that movie where Richard Gere plays Lancelot—."

"Oh. *First Knight.* I knew someone had said it."

"Which is fine for Hollywood, but what about here and now and Hoboken, when it's real people, and there's no director who's going to call cut and all the lines aren't already written? Because I don't get another take, and I'm scared of doing what scares me."

I considered that. "You're right, of course."

"Easier said than done."

I nodded. It really is easier to say that you should do what scares you than it is to actually do it. No arguing that.

So I didn't. I just considered the single action that scared me more than any other, and then I cleared every thought from my head as I reached my left hand to Veronica's cheek and pulled her lips to mine and kissed her. I kissed her like I'd always wanted to, and I put everything I had into it, like I'd been in love with her all my life, because most days it feels like I have been. I kissed her like she was everything I'd ever wanted, because right then she very much was, and I kissed her like I might never get the chance to again, because I wasn't sure I would, and in fact, I knew in my heart I would never kiss her like that again, would never again kiss that girl for the first time.

The first thought I finally had, in fact, as that kiss fulfilled, was that I was glad I had brushed my teeth. I would have searched her eyes, then, but they were closed, and so I waited until they opened as if she were waking from a dream. She seemed a little stunned, but I couldn't blame her for that, because I felt much the same way.

"I hope—."

I never got to tell her what I hoped, because then we were kissing again. I'm not sure, now, who leaned in, if I did or she did, but all that mattered was our lips pressing together, my fingers on her check, her fingers in my hair like spring wind after too long a winter.

***

Part of me wishes that were the end of the story. Of course it's not; I'm sure I built up Angus's presence in the story enough that you realize he wasn't just a catalyst for change. Another story might work with that set up and its pay-off: there's something to be said for finally having the balls to do what scares you most, that it might just pay off. We could cast Topher Grace and Natalie Portman for the movie and fade out there, and it might not be the most satisfying resolution, but it might be okay, and besides that, you'd have popcorn and Cherry Coke and why would you care?

It would probably never get to the multi-plex, , so maybe you'd just swallow that last gulp of wine as you set aside the book. You'd consider yourself amused if not actually satisfied, and then you'd forget about it.

Like I said, though: of course it's not.

Wrong book.

Unfortunately, I have to keep going to see this through to the end. As with so many other aspects of this story, I've got no choice. I'm not sure I'd blame you if you wanted to stop here, with that story and that resolution, and you probably wouldn't blame me for doing so, either, but let's be honest with each other at this point. Because we're in this together at this point, aren't we? And you know as well as I do that there's more. There has to be, right?

Chapter Thirteen: Kissing Veronica Sawyer

*V*eronica kissed with the sort of slow-burning smolder that lends itself to lasting a while, and we spent the rest of that morning making out on the sofa. I don't think we meant to, but kissing her was something I'd always hoped to do, and I wasn't going to quit if I didn't have to.

At first, that was all we did. You might think that all those years we had known each other would careen through our systems like a subway through our veins, that we'd loose our clothing in a third-rail rush of full-charged electricity, but once we started to kiss, once I felt her lips on mine, I only wanted to take my time. It was a new sensation I'd hoped for and dreamt about for years, and I was content just to relish its novelty. Her lips were soft but firm, and her quick tongue darted at times playfully and at times searchingly, and I sucked on her lower lip until she bit mine, gently. The soft pliability of her mouth, her body against mine, in my arms, her scent in my head every time I took a breath . . . it was a heady enough experience without going any farther than lips on lips.

In other words: kissing Veronica Sawyer?

Rad.

I had always had feelings for Veronica, and I'd thought I'd always been in love with her, but her actual tangibility? I could feel her in my abs, and it wasn't just her hand on my stomach. I wanted to laugh giddily that I was actually making out, on my old couch, with Veronica Sawyer. Kissing Veronica was like Manhattan and flying and hitting a home run. Kissing Veronica was a long, slow pull from a glass of ice-cold water on a hot, thirsty day; that moment in a concert when the lights go out so all you can see are thousands of people holding up their cell phones, and then the singer decides to let them carry the words, too; twisting the gas-cap closed and starting the engine and then gunning the accelerator, getting on that highway and knowing you can drive to the horizon and beyond.

Kissing Veronica Sawyer was positively stupendous, stupefyingly amazing, ridiculously awesome.

Kissing Veronica Sawyer, in fact, deserves its own chapter, so let us move on to:

Chapter Fourteen, in which I go on a date with Veronica Sawyer

I would say we made out like teenagers, but that would be a lie; there was no dry humping, no awkward fumbling at bra straps and belt buckles. This was partly because it was too confident, too comfortable, but also because it never quite got that far; at some point, my cell phone went off in my bedroom, blasting "Sweet Child o'Mine" through the paper-thin walls. I didn't leap to get it, because, hey, priorities, but I paused.

"Do you need to get that?"

I laughed. "Nothing in the world could convince me to leave this couch right now."

She laughed. "Be serious."

"I was."

"We can't spend the whole day making out on your couch."

"Really? Why not?"

"If nothing else, we're going to have to eat."

"Fair point."

"Go see who called. Might've been your agency."

So I stood and went into the bedroom to get my phone, which I flipped open and dialed to my voicemail. "Hey, it's Jo from Force One. Listen, call me back as soon as you can."

"You were right," I called to Veronica.

"So what'd they say?"

"To call them back."

"And you're waiting for what, exactly?"

"Nothing," I told her, because the phone was already ringing at my ear, and I greeted Jo.

"Just wanted to find out if you're available for tomorrow."

"Worth getting out of bed for?"

"That depends on whether you want to work for Harvey Weinstein."

"Harvey Weinstein? Seriously?"

"I told you we might get an assignment from the Weinstein Company, and you're the first one we're offering it to. You want it?"

"That's not a gig I can turn down."

"So don't! Take it. Ready for the address?" she asked, and I jotted it down. "Ten tomorrow morning. Day of training before regular office hours next week. Sound good?"

"I'm seven different kinds of there."

"Awesome. I'll let them know. Rock on!" she said, disconnecting the call. I shut my phone as I returned to the living room.

"Well, there's that problem down," I said. I was still smiling, and it was still sinking in.

"Interview?"

I sat down, shook my head. "No. Job."

"Oh, great. Whereabouts this time? Still in publishing?"

I smiled. "The Weinstein Company."

"Weinstein? Why do I know that name?"

"Bob and Harvey. Two of the most powerful guys in Hollywood."

"So you're moving?"

"No, their offices are here."

"And they're the most popular guys in Hollywood? That's pretty far away. They must be pretty powerful."

"Very."

"And wait, they're a movie studio? And you're going to work for them? Seriously?"

"I know, right?"

"What're you going to be doing?"

I shrugged. "Probably just admin stuff for now, but that's where it always starts. Even Harvey himself probably started in a mailroom or something. Regardless of what the actual function or title of the position will be, it will be at the Weinstein Company, which any way you look at it must be a step up from selling ads for the *New Yorker*."

"So that's pretty terrific then."

"I think it's safe to say today is pretty definitely coming up me," I laughed. I was, by that point, positively giddy.

"We should celebrate."

"We should totally celebrate. We should, in fact, do something the sort of special that would make other people say, wow, they must have had a good day. And I think that the only way this day could possibly get any better is if I took you out on a date. A real date. What do you say, Veronica? Will you go out with me?" I asked her, and even as I did so, I was planning potential destination, secret spots in the secluded places, or at least the closest you can come to secluded in a city like Manhattan, which is really not so secluded at all. It's the illusion of seclusion, the happy myth that maybe, just maybe, everything's all yours.

"Sounds like fun."

"And we'll catch the proverbial picture show, and then—," I paused, because I realized I already knew where I wanted to take her. A place called Candela, my favorite in the City, just off Union Square . . .

"We're going to do this up right," I told her.

***

I remembered Angus' offer and our appointment as I showered, but calling to cancel sank immediately to the bottom of my list of priorities. With Veronica Sawyer in the living room, I figured it could wait, and so wait it would, while I shaved and got ready to go, casual-dressy, jeans and a decent shirt and my leather jacket, and then I left my apartment, arm in arm with Veronica Sawyer. January nights fall early on Manhattan and promise their presence hours before, lending to the late afternoon into which we descended a surreal, golden quality like halos around new pennies, ready to be spent.

PATH to 23rd Street and then a quick jaunt to Chelsea Cinemas, where we had a difficult time deciding what to see once we saw the marquee, full as it was of flicks studios had crammed into the final weeks of December for Oscar contention. We knew to avoid *Bloodrayne* because, though medieval vampires are probably a lot of fun, it was not the movie I wanted to take Veronica to on our first date.

Which was a little weird. We'd been to movies before, probably dozens of them. Perhaps it was the formality that made this one different . . .

No, we're being honest, and I'll tell you what made this outing in particular different: the potential. The sudden crackle of tension between us, charged as static electricity and with its own field of depth and intensity. I don't think it was merely that we had kissed, though I'm sure that small fact didn't hurt; I think it was rather the acknowledgement of something big and powerful and exciting between us, our own personal storm with lightning-lust and thunder-attraction and a slow, constant rain of happiness.

Of all the choices on the marquee that weekend, we chose *Little Miss Sunshine*, which was probably the perfect combination of funny and poignant for a first date. We left that theater grinning, and I'm not sure anything really counts for more than that.

A handful of blocks south, to Union Square, awash in neon and street lights, a wintered park an island between the downtown Virgin Megastore and the Barnes & Noble Union Square where I had twice seen Neil Gaiman read and once heard David Sedaris do his Billie Holiday. Cut down 16th toward Irving Plaza—

I am always at a loss to know how much to believe of my own stories.—

around the corner from the W Hotel, where I led Veronica to a simple, wooden door that belongs in medieval Europe, clean and unassuming and the sort of heavy that you can't open by accident. Candela wears sincerely its romance and sensuality; it's like stepping away from the City and into old anywhere else, not just a different century but a different age in which things might be both simpler and more luxurious—part of its magic is that it reminds you that simple and luxury are not mutually exclusive.

Look: deep tones like mocha and cappuccino, lit by candle chandeliers. Booths to the right, soft leather with dark curtains hung to the high, high ceiling. Behind the booths were mirrors, in front of each a cluster centerpiece of white roses, as well as artfully arranged twigs and leaves, Autumn all the year round. Their menu was both comprehensive and indulgent but neither overly so, with a steak worth doing time for and a crème brulee best when shared.

Eating there with Veronica . . . a quick-rush of patter about restaurants and plans and comments about the menu and the City and the evening. We talked about the movie and her upcoming semester and my upcoming gig, about what we hoped to do wherever we hoped to go. We drank the whole bottle of cabernet sauvignon, then sipped Sicilian coffee, complete with Amaretto Di'Sarrono and Kahlua, when we best-shared our crème brulee, and by the time we left that restaurant, still arm-in-arm, we shared the intimate warmth of a happy buzz. It was already dark, though not exactly what one might call late.

As we walked, I felt her head on my shoulder. I could feel her contentment. I liked it. I know I've wished for you many moments already, but to those I add a moment like walking through Union Square Park, blissfully inebriated and arm in arm with someone you love. There's nothing quite like it.

The day had begun so surreally, continued with such conviction, and hovered all its hours in a magical balance. The kind of day that seemed to have existed solely for us, like the whole rest of the world had been cast with extras and lit solely for our habitation. So magical was it, in fact, that I hesitated to intrude upon it with questions of practicality and pragmatism . . .

"Do you—you don't need to go back tonight, do you?" Even as I asked it, I clenched my stomach in the same sort of tension that fills your body when you wish on a star, or when you pray to a higher power: the kind of moment you want to say "Please."

"Don't you have to work tomorrow?"

"Not until ten. So I have to get up early, but I'll be taking the train in anyway . . ."

"And so you can say goodbye to me then."

"If I have to."

"I have to go back eventually. Degree to finish and all."

"Right. There's that."

"Still, I'm having a wonderful time. And I'd hate for the evening to end now."

"So let's not let it, then. Not until tomorrow. Let's keep it for ourselves."

"Let's," she said, and though I'd drunk a half a bottle of wine and then strongly liquered coffee on top, still that single word in the golden darkness cut through my inebriation and made me instantly sober, so cold and quick it took my breath away. I kissed her there, on the corner of Union Square Park, right across from Virgin Megastore, a flush of neon in a City like motion, while stories above us a display of numbers counted down on one end and up on the other with no seeming meaning to either.

***

How to describe that evening? If kissing Veronica got its own chapter, loving her would be a novel, and of course it quite literally is, but even still there's more. Knowing her would require a lifetime.

Then again, some experiences are a lifetime. Some you wait for all your life because you know Heaven would be incomplete without them. Some you hope for knowing that your memory will seem too empty when you look back on your life.

Some last all your life because they are too powerful to be constrained by time or space. Some experiences are so tactile, so intense, they pierce your skin and your body and your heart and your soul and become, immediately, part of who you are. Part of your DNA, part of your being.

That evening, Veronica and I rode the PATH back home, and I don't know, can't know, what she felt, how sharply or strongly or sweetly, but I wonder . . . I wonder if she was as aware of that train ride as I was, if she noticed the cracks in the seat, if every new event etched into her memory because she knew they would all become important later, after it was already over, when we wanted to revisit it again. I don't know if she was giddy, if she was nervous, if she was excited or timid or anxious, if she ached for me as I ached for her, to hold her.

Just the idea of the evening loomed at me in a way I'd never expected it to, and I realized I had idealized my love for Veronica Sawyer as I had idealized Veronica Sawyer herself. Though I had hoped for and dreamt for and maybe even wished and prayed for that very evening, I had done so in a generalized sort of way; riding that train through the darkness, I realized I had only ever wanted Veronica Sawyer to love me, without ever really considering what that love would mean. Not in the sense of consequences, but rather in the sense of actions. I had always wanted Veronica to hold my hand without considering her fingers and her palms and her grasp. I had always wanted to kiss Veronica without ever considering her lips and her mouth and her tongue.

I had, I realized, always wanted to love Veronica without actually considering the girl and her body and her heart and her soul.

If her saying "Let's," had sobered me, the possibility, the potential, of what was to come—or even what might come, because who knew? I've never been one to presume such things—made me self-conscious. Not anxious or nervous, exactly, though those, too, were present in ways, but rather conscious of the evening and aware of what it might bring.

We'd gotten off the train and passed a CVS and a few blocks of Washington, headed back toward my apartment, when Veronica spoke. "You're nervous."

I chuckled. "That obvious?"

"You shouldn't be."

"You're not?"

"I trust you."

I remember our footsteps up the stairs of the stoop, the sound and feel of the key in the lock, the darkness of the outer vestibule before we got into my apartment. The dim nightlight cast our amber way to my bedroom, where we closed the door, where I locked it behind me, where I put my iPod in its dock to play a list I had made to listen to while I'd written the more romantic scenes in my novel.

Our arms were around each other, our bodies close and our lips together, her fingers through the hair just at the back of my neck. Sensation everywhere—everywhere—arms and hands and lips and tongues, so many it didn't feel like more than two bodies so much as it felt like that was all there was, just Veronica and me. I gave up, I gave away, I let go, and she became my world. She had already been all I'd ever wanted, so it didn't feel like so far a leap.

Sink into the bed with Veronica Sawyer. Sink into it—sinking with her, this girl I wasn't sure I had ever expected to be there, in that moment, with. For all the being in love with her I had ever mustered I had neglected the visceral lust she could stir in me in favor of the way my heart had longed for her. I had romanticized her as I had romanticized my feelings for her, and that Platonic love had concealed my own primal desire for her. I felt her on me and around me, and as I disrobed her I reveled in quiet revelation like falling in love all over again, because that's very much what it was. First her sweater, to reveal her dark bra over her firm, white skin, and I realized I couldn't get over the fact that I had just removed Veronica's sweater.

It wasn't self-conscious so much as realization. This is Veronica Sawyer. This is her skin beneath my lips. This is her belly contracting beneath my fingertips. Those are her arms around me, her hands holding me and clutching me; this is her body arching toward me as her back lifts from my bed, her fingers slipping the buttons on my shirt as my own slipped the clasp of her bra, which loosened like a sigh. The warmth of her neck under my mouth, the sharp gasps and rush of hot breath next to my ear as I slid her bra from her.

Her breasts full and round, her nipples tight beneath my fingers and then beneath my mouth and my tongue. I caught one between my teeth as I sucked, gently, flickering my tongue back and forth over it even as my hands moved downdowndown—Veronica Sawyer's stomach, flat, tight—to the seam of her jeans, the snap and the zip of denim in the darkness . . .

If there is such a thing as divine revelation, it can be no more wondrous than Veronica's body in the darkness. I realized, as I unbuttoned that denim waistband, as I slid my hand down and in, cotton beneath my fingertips and hard zipper against my knuckles, that never had I fantasized about slipping my hand into Veronica Sawyer's pants.

Never had I imagined pulling those jeans down, and never had I considered nibbling her thighs. Never had I imagined the elastic of her panties beneath my teeth. Her quick hips, brief and angular, and then the softness of her, the give of her beneath my lips as I pressed my face to her, her firm scent in my nostrils. The lift of her bottom, the epiphany of Veronica nude, the sight of Veronica open, the image of her knees and legs and thighs and then that glorious swipe of hair to which I pressed my lips to taste her, to taste Veronica Sawyer, to feel her beneath my tongue, her texture and movement and arousal. Her gasp as my lips found her, as my fingers sought her nipples, her excited exhalations as I realized her, as a person, as a woman, as a lover.

Her reality. Veronica Sawyer was not a fantasy, not an idealization. She was not just a girl I had fallen in love with as a child and grown to love all my life. She was a girl; a solid, tangible girl in my bed; a girl whose pleasure I sought and whose support I cherished; a girl I didn't love in the way of poetry and musing and romance but rather in the way of life and the world.

And when her body clenched to mine, when her thighs tightened, when she moaned as I slid between her legs first one finger and then another, when she cried out my name into the darkness, it was like an answered prayer. When she whispered how good it felt, and then when her breathless utterances sidestepped speech in favor of approval, when she shuddered and groaned and called the name of God like rapture . . . I'm not sure I've lived a greater moment than that.

When she had relaxed, when her muscles had let go, when her body had ceased shuddering to tremble instead, I kissed her thighs and hips, her navel and then her chest, her collarbone and her neck, and then her lips met mine.

Without words, almost without pause, she was rolling, her mouth and her lips and her tongue and breath just totally fucking everywhere, like she was hungry, on my neck and my chest even as I felt her hands on my waist, her fingers uncatching my button and zipper, for which I was grateful; I was aroused enough to strain painfully against the denim, which came down, along with my boxers, in the brief rush that was Veronica releasing me into the darkness and freedom, and all I could feel were her hands and her fingertips, the fullness of her breasts against my thighs, the whisp of her hair against my hips and then her mouth, her lips—

oh my heaven her lips around me, her tongue a quick swirl, her mouth up and down and up and down and wet and hot and dark. My hips rose of their own volition, my hands in her hair as her head moved over me, and I groaned and shuddered and harshly whispered her name—

before she stopped and then was above me, her body against mine, her breasts against my chest and I felt myself against her, there, against Veronica, felt another warmth against me, and I whispered that I had condoms in the dresser but she whispered that she was on the pill and she trusted me, and then I was insideindsideinside of Veronica Sawyer, and though I had idealized her before, though I had romanticized her, in that moment we formed each other, made each other real; in that moment of darkness and glory we called to each other by name across the universe, our cries a summons less to each other than love in the world, acts of defiance against fantasy and romance, truths lighting each other our ways to ourselves.

We clutched each other, there in the darkness, solid and tangible and there in a world so often too quick to rend asunder, and afterward, Veronica and I rolled sideways, her bottom pressed to my stomach, and I kissed the back of her shoulder as I found in the nuzzle of her neck the space in which I might find rest. The morning after crept closer toward us, but in the meantime the darkness and the joy of deep, peaceful slumber interrupted only by cherished moments of bed.

Chapter Fifteen, in which I see Veronica off before I attempt unsuccessfully to cancel one appointment on my way to a second

Whenever I have an important appointment, my body tends to anticipate it to such an extent that it sets its own internal alarm clock; given a day I'm looking forward to, I tend to beat the alarm by a solid ten minutes. Usually, I spend those ten minutes in quiet contemplation of the excitement to come, but that morning I discovered an even better way to use them by having a pre-dawn quickie love-fest with Veronica, all lips and breasts and ass, morning breath and bedhead, reveling in the feel of the City and the previous night and sleep on our skin like nebulous grit. Dry tongue collision and the soft-hard angles of intersection and penetration, wet waking dream of full-on arousal and incredible execution.

If there's a better way to wake up, I have not experienced it.

The morning: a high-comic trapeze act of routine and preparation, a quick together-shower before we engaged in a domesticated dance of jean-pulling and tooth-brushing and hair-doing. Veronica let me take priority given that I was leaving for the office while she was just taking the train home, and by the time we closed my apartment door behind us, we were a little breathless and a little flushed but totally ready for the day. Our fingers found each other as we descended the stoop to the street, blocks to the PATH station, where we waited on a platform.

"You go back to school soon, don't you?"

"Next weekend. But I was thinking—maybe I could come back tomorrow night? We could spend the weekend together?"

Was I really going to turn that down?

We got on the first 33rd Street train; she was headed for Penn Station and points West after I got off at Christopher Street, smack in the middle of the gayborhood and just a few blocks north of my destination. I stopped at a corner breakfast truck to buy a large coffee (dark as night, sweet as sin) and a cranberry-orange muffin, then continued slightly South along Hudson to the Weinstein headquarters. I can't say the City was waking up all around me—because it never does sleep, after all—but it was certainly coming to vibrant, winter morning life, early-morning sunlight glittering like topaz off windows and highlighting the hard angles of corners and rooftops.

That was when I remembered Angus. I nearly cursed but didn't care enough to do so; by then I planned on calling solely to cancel, which I did then and there, clutching my muffin bag against my coffee cup as I retrieved my cell and found his number in my dialed history. I pressed the send button as I pulled the phone to my ear, ready to wait for the ring Brigid would answer, but it never came. Instead, just the three-note sequence of disconnection, so familiar I hung up before the robot-operator could explain my call could not be completed as dialed.

I frowned. I hung up, and tried again, but heard again those same three notes.

I thought about fishing the card from my wallet, checking the number for certainty, but by then I could already see the building that housed the Weinstein offices. I clipped my phone shut as I crossed Hudson to enter, elevator up to the indicated floors . . .

***

I don't know if you've ever worked a temporary administrative job the contract for which you obtained through an agency specializing in such, but they're all pretty much the same. You arrive early by, say, ten minutes or so. Sometimes you wait in the lobby for your liaison; other times, the receptionist places a quick call and another assistant comes to show you the way into the offices, leading you to a small cube with the same computer and fiberboard desk you'll find anywhere else. That first day accumulates minor tasks like Post-Its on a computer monitor, which is largely the best way to accomplish things if only because plucking that sticky paper and crumpling it in your fist before you toss it in the can offers a quick, if minor, sense of achievement.

That was how it was at the Weinstein Company that first day: all downtown-hip, hardwood floors and glass walls with frost-etched lettering. A constantly busy lobby with continuous traffic and a phone whose every trill sounded the kind of urgent that makes or breaks Hollywood careers, the receptionist a brisk, efficient girl with brisk, efficient blonde hair razor chopped and held in place by a wireless phone headset like a Bluetooth boom mike, silver spaghetti looped around her ear and hovering just at the corner of her lip like it hung on her every word. She asked me if I wanted anything to drink and to have a seat all in the same breath even as she finger-pressed a button on her phone like she was gesturing at it.

I declined, happy enough with my coffee, and sat for thirty seconds before a guy strode through the office-way, crossed the lobby hand already extended. Crisp blue open-collar shirt over graphite slacks, smiling my name and informing me he was Ben even as I stood to shake his hand. If Angus had shaken my hand like closing a deal, Ben shook it like he looked forward to working with me, and I very much agreed.

That first day was very much as I described. I could tell you more details—the flat panel monitors, the exposed brick walls, the boutique atmosphere and the casual environment that not only realized but downright embraced the fact that it didn't need a tie to conduct its business; I hadn't gone fifteen minutes before I'd loosed my tie to stow in my desk drawer. I kept my blazer, tailored as it was, and my smile, genuine as it was, and I enjoyed that first day like I've enjoyed few other days in my life, of course excepting the one most immediately previous.

Feet light as I descended the building's steps to the street, sun setting down on rooftops and in tree branches, City in a magic hour, and damned if I didn't want to skip as I hiked back to the Christopher Street station, where I caught the train home to Hoboken.

***

As I ascended the steps of the Hoboken PATH

station, my cell dinged that I had a message. Veronica had called to see how my first day had gone, and I'm certain when I called her back I couldn't keep the excitement from my voice mainly because I didn't think to try. It had been the sort of first day you dream of, and the next day continued the same trend. I liked the people, the environment, the offices, even the commute. I was doing light administrative work, nothing major, some coordination, calls here and there, a spreadsheet how's-the-numbers, chores not exactly challenging or demanding but somehow lent some satisfaction by the environment. Everyone and everything buzzed with energy and enthusiasm for what they were doing, and we were constantly reminded of what we were doing by the movie posters on the walls: *The Libertine* and *Hoodwink'd*, *The Matador*, *Clerks II*, all flicks in the can or in the process of canning and many already in general distribution. It was nice to work in a place with range and diversity, a place as comfortable with a CG-animated children's cartoon as with the possibly Oscar-worthy turn Johnny Depp had delivered as the licentious Earl of bawdy Rochester. Whereas the *New Yorker* had steadfastly kept its tie straight and even with a perfectly set dimple, the Weinstein company seemed more happy to eschew the neckwear altogether.

I felt comfortable right away, and the feeling didn't go away. By the time Friday afternoon hit, I was already looking forward to Monday morning. And of course I knew that might not last, that the proverbial honeymoon might end, but still it lent to that weekend a buoyant quality part surreal and all fantastic.

Veronica could see it immediately when I picked her and her luggage up at Penn Station. "Don't you look like the cat that ate the canary?"

"Do I? I've never caught said cat canary-mouthed," I told her as I took her bag and hefted it over my shoulder.

"Thank you. And you don't want to. Rather gruesome. But I'm guessing today was as good as yesterday."

"Even better."

"And yesterday was awesome."

"It was indeed," I told her as we followed signs and corridors in the labyrinth that is so many Manhattan subway stations, and certainly Penn Stations; across the platform and up above ground for a block and a half before descending again into the PATH station to HOB. All the while I chatted about work, about my new colleagues and my new boss and my new breakfast truck and my new jobborhood, my new digs in my new office in my new building. The movies they were producing and distributing and marketing and promoting, the constant rush of posters and reels and contracts, in and out and through, messengers with orange bags and mailroom delivery guys who carried thick bundles rubber-banded together and dropped them on the corner of my desk to distribute to my principals. I was working in the production department as assistant to a handful of producers whose days were spent viewing casting tapes and coordinating budgets and making Hollywood shoots happen from several thousand miles away, and I loved it.

And even better: they had extended my contract. They had told Force One that they'd like to keep me for the foreseeable future.

"Which could be a long time," Veronica said as we ascended the Hoboken stairs onto Washington Street, the air brisk and sharp and so full with the scent of food you could taste it, Indian and Thai and Italian, burgers and fries and chili dogs from Johnny Rockets.

I smiled. The sun had set and evening had fallen and the night was tinged orange by the streetlights and alive with the bustle of post-commute restaurant-goers and happy-hour revelers, some buzzing with the excitement of the night ahead and some already full swing into it. The evening was alive and Veronica's hand in mine hummed. "Totally," I said.

"Then it's going to be."

We continued back to my apartment, where we set Veronica's bag next to my bed before turning on our collective heels and striding back out into that same sublime darkness. "What're you in the mood for?" I asked her.

"What's around?"

"Here? Pretty much six of the seven continents, and that's only because there's nothing to eat in Antarctica. Within a few blocks we've got Chinese, Japanese, Vietnamese, Thai, Indian, Middle Eastern, French, Italian, English, Mexican, Spanish—which are not the same thing, mind—Brazilian, not to mention, like, seven different kinds of American, including barbecue, steakhouse, and burger. And that's not even mentioning the fusion, which is like they all had sex and made happy babies. But edible."

"Unlike babies."

"I've heard baby flesh is soft and succulent."

"I'm totally going to pretend you didn't say that. And you're leaving this up to me?"

"I'm good wherever."

"Awesome. Then you're going to lead me to the Italian place, where we're going to order calamari and bruschetta and heaping plates of pasta we're going to consume with a fine bottle of wine, and I am going to treat you to said meal—."

"Oh, you don't have to do that—."

"In celebration of your brand new job you so obviously love, and I will harbor no arguments about it."

"Well, if you're not going to harbor any, I'm not going to offer one," I told her.

We found a quaint place right on Washington, where we waited for one of fifteen tables in a small dining room with exposed brick walls, and which smelled like my grandmother's homemade meatballs and marinara. We started with the crisp give of fresh calamari, drizzled sharp with lemon juice and tangy with balsamic vinegar, dipped in hefty, still-steaming marinara. Crunchy, just-from-the-oven garlic bread slices topped with diced onions and tomatoes, pure olive oil, dashed with basil that might have, judging by the taste and scent, been picked only a few moments before from the owner's backyard herb garden.

Our entrees came on plates steaming so thick and hearty we could have eaten the vapor, the sauce light and complementing—rather than overwhelming—pasta so distinctively cooked it could only have been handmade and only hours before, just the right combination of doughy and light, tiny tortellini pressed like their little-ear namesakes around chicken and artichoke, long linguine perfectly al dente. We consumed between us one of the best cabernet sauvignons I've ever drunk before we split a perfect tiramisu.

By the time we left we were warm and happy and tipsy. We walked out into that still-cold evening so close and comfortable we projected our own private bubble of intimacy, sealed off from the rest of the world by giggles and held hands and slurred chatting.

We found ourselves near the PATH station, across from which we stumbled into a quaint bar with a comfortable vibe and a DJ spinning a delirious remix of old-school Motown as filtered through guys like Z-Trip and Fatboy Slim, exuberant without being loud, vibrant without being intrusive. We weaved through to the bar, paused just a moment considering an order until the dude with the headphones and the turntable spun those singular, oh-so-recognizable notes that begin "Let's Get It On," and then Veronica's hand was pulling mine. She led me onto the hardwood dance floor under the dim but multi-colored lights, spinning like a disco ball-produced laser-light show, and then she was up against me, her body so close, her whole body, and my whole body wanted her feeling of love. I wasn't pushing, but come on, and we danced like electrons in a bond, barely touching but sharing nearly the same space, held together by ab-clenching, barroom gravitation, our bodies colliding and bumping and deflecting like hyper-charged particles in a super-collider. It was like we were building up potential energy, and I could only imagine the kinetic motion it would become.

But not then. Then we danced. Then the DJ spun and spun again, songs like meteors in an asteroid belt, slipping in and out of their orbits, teasing with a beat or a melody before another swooped in to take its place for a tantalizing moment before again retreating much as Veronica's body against my own, hips slithering like the offer of an apple, a promise worth falling for.

As if I hadn't already.

So we danced as the music spun and burst through moods like chemical reactions, changing moods almost as easily as the songs changed notes, through Motown and into funk before it went 180 into full-on Def Leppard rock and roll with a chorus the whole bar shouted, at which point Veronica pulled my close, elbow crooked hard around the back of my neck, and spoke, clearly and surely, into my ear:

"Take me home."

Which I did.

Chapter Sixteen, in which we montage for a moment.

*B*ecause I think that would be appropriate here. We could start with that weekend: a movie would depict Veronica and I at the Cloisters and the Met, burgers and beer at Chumley's on Belvedere and Barrow, and we would be laughing like we were having way too much fun because we very much were. That weekend was an even balance of fun outside and fun inside, because we got our City on before we got it on ourselves, shagging like it was the most urgent and important thing in the world, because isn't it always? I saw her off at Penn Station, worked for a week, and then went back to Penn Station to catch the train back home the following weekend, helping Veronica pack and relax before she left for school again.

The first night, we decided to stay in and watch a movie. It had just ended when Veronica excused herself, and Tom came home while I waited for Veronica to return.

"Dude," Tom said. "What's going on?"

"Just finished watching a movie with your sister. You?"

"Just some practice. We're working out a few new covers, playing with some new stuff. Next gig'll be comin' up pretty soon."

"You know I'll be there."

"You always are. So what, Ronnie duck out for a minute?"

"Refreshing our drinks."

"Oh, good. So you got a minute," he set down his guitar and sat next to me.

"Sure. What's up."

"You've got a sister, right?"

"What?" Tom knows my family, including my siblings, pretty well.

"Your sister."

"What about her?"

"Just hypothetically, let me ask, what would you say if your sister and I started dating?"

"You and—are you? She didn't—."

"I said 'hypothetically.' Which tends to mean not actually occurring but as a possibility."

"So you're not?"

"No. But pretend, for a moment, we were."

"Okay?"

"How would you feel about that?"

I thought about it a moment, and I said, "Well, I'd be happy for you, first, because she's my sister and you're my best friend, and that'd be pretty cool. I'd probably put the whole physical thing out of my head. But I'd kick your ass if you hurt her."

Tom listened, nodded. "Good. As long as we understand each other. So, since you're my best friend, and you're now dating my sister, how about we just pretend I just said all that to you and we'll leave it there, shall we?"

I chuckled. I'd just given myself the big brother speech, and I'd gotten off easily compared to some of the ones I'd delivered. One of my sister's potential suitors met my brother, a born-again Christian, before he met me. When I met the young man in question, he mentioned that; I told him, "Oh, good. Just remember, my brother might pray for your immortal soul, but I'll just kill you." I was joking, of course. Mostly. He understood that. "Fair enough," I told Tom.

Veronica returned, then, wearing loose pajama pants and an old tee shirt and carrying two glasses of wine.

Tom stood. "Hey, sis."

"Hey big brother. What's going on?"

"Just having a man-to-man with my best friend here."

"Sorry to interrupt."

"Oh no," Tom said. "We were finished. But speaking of my best friend here, I'm happy for you guys, but you remember I found him before you did. You break his heart, you've got me to answer to."

Veronica laughed. "Understood."

"Right then. I'm going to leave you two kids alone," he said, picking up his guitar and heading down the hallway.

Veronica handed me a wine glass and resumed her spot on the couch next to me, and we started another movie I can't tell you the title of because we never really got around to watching it. Which is how we spent most of the weekend.

***

All that could have been covered by the first verse of whatever pop song our imaginary movie played during our fantasy montage, while the bridge would sync to my opening my apartment door for Veronica and the first chorus might be Valentine's day: candlelight and chocolate-dipped strawberries and a fine pinot grigio that made us tipsy enough to eschew our dinner reservations in favor of the kind of evening in bed that might make Hallmark finally admit its fraud, because it might sell cards about love and romance but dammitall had absolutely nothing on Veronica and me.

I wouldn't mind montaging February, of which I have a phobia. Not in the sense I fear February like someone with agoraphobia avoids crowds, but rather in that a phobia is an intense and irrational aversion and I've always been intensely and irrationally averse to February, because man, the second month of the year is a doozy. It doesn't have the initial bounce of January, ringing in a brand new year, the hope of resolutions and change; by the beginning of February, most resolutions are either broken or on the verge of breaking, and most people are resigned to the fact that any change they hope for isn't coming this year. Neither does it have the hope for warmth and summer that March starts to suggest.

No, it's cold and dreary and everything is still frozen and wet like a hard grey shell over the whole world. The world feels saturated with it, hopeless down to the bone.

That month, however, was terrific. Looking back on that time, that first blush of an actual romance . . . what could be more perfect? It was brand new but lacked any of the uncertainty that usually comes during with such brand-new-ness; I never wondered if she wanted me to call. I never analyzed her text messages. It was like holding hands with her; that first time holding hands with someone is a combination of hope and possibility and not a little bit of uncertainty, a hesitant dance of fingertips and an eager turn of the wrist, neither hand sure of holding the other until they come together, but when Veronica and I held hands, it was comfortable.

She felt like home. Being with her was like letting go. Like acceptance.

Being with her was good. So good.

Life was good, in fact. I was in a relationship with a girl I'd been in love with for always, I was working for a company I actually liked, I had a primo apartment in a hip spot just outside an amazing City . . . I couldn't imagine it getting better, until

***

The final Friday of February.

My supervisor, a striking woman named Claire who signed my timesheets with a half-swoop like a Nike swish, called me into her office. She told me to close the door behind me, which is generally a bad sign. Closed doors in the workplace? Might as well play a Bach fugue. I wondered if I was getting let go on a Friday afternoon.

"You like it here," she said, her voice not rising enough, there at the end, to make it a question.

"I love it here."

"We're glad to have you on our team."

"I'm glad to be on it," I said, but I was wondering by then if she'd asked me to close her door so that we could have some smalltalk. I had expected more.

Which she then hit me with: "We'd like to offer you a more permanent position on it."

"You mean—?"

"The position would only come with a slight raise, but you'd get full benefits. You'd continue at your current position—your principals love working with you, particularly Roseanne and Eric. And you'd get a little more responsibility. It might mean a little more time, some hours here and there. But the important thing is there's room for growth—."

"Totally. I'll take it."

She smiled. "We'd hoped you would. We have to work it through payroll and HR to make the offer completely official, but I wanted to tell you now. We can finalize it on Monday?"

"Yeah we can," I told her.

"Terrific. Well, why don't you get an early jump on the weekend? We can't retroact your pay, but we can give you the afternoon off."

Which was cool by me. It might have been the final weekend of February, but there was a hint of promise in the air, bright sunlight over an otherwise cold afternoon, like the world was trying on spring and seeing how it looked, how it walked, before it committed to laying down the plastic and the variable interest to come. Which is very much what spring is, really, the most bipolar of all seasons in the places that have them, sunny and warm to start a week that brings snow by the end.

Still, I was buoyant on the promise of work I enjoyed, not to mention that Veronica and I had made plans for the weekend. She had midterms coming up, just before spring break, and so she was bringing a few books and her thesis with her to visit me for a weekend we planned to spend mostly inside. I had told her that every study session required multiple breaks and that shagging could be precisely the right sort of cleanse for the mental palate, and she'd laughed half-giddily as she'd bought the train tickets to New York.

We had planned that I would meet her at the station, but I called her to find out if she could make her way to my apartment on her own.

"Everything okay?"

"Way better than that. I'll tell you all about it when you get here. I thought I might cook."

"You cook?"

"I can. And I would like to."

"That sounds fine to me. I think I remember how to get there. I'll call you if I ever find myself unsure."

I hung up. I made my way north to Christopher Street, stopping on my way at a small, organic market. I picked up some chicken breasts and some pasta, some marsala wine and some mushrooms. Fresh-baked baguette, and a couple of bottles of wine, figuring that we had all weekend to finish them. Everything fit in a big, canvas bag I shuffled home, glad to have an early-afternoon commute mostly to myself if only because it meant there were fewer people to jostle and crowd. I even found a seat.

I smiled. I was elated to work with the Weinstein company and anxious to see Veronica. It seemed like a terrific day. I couldn't imagine how it might get better.

And I was right. It didn't.

Chapter Seventeen, in which it doesn't

*I*t started even before I walked into my apartment
            It wasn't sudden or terrible or dramatic. Life, real life, so rarely is, which is why those moments of high drama become, ultimately, the stories you tell years later all over again. No, when life starts to unravel, when great things start to go bad, it happens in small measures, tiny details. It's like losing hair or putting on weight: the loss of a strand here or the gain of a pound there. Nobody goes bald or fat overnight, and it often happens so slowly, so gradually, and over a long enough time that we don't realize it as it's occurring. It's only when we see our pate or our jeans don't fit one day that we finally realize it has already happened, that the process began a while before and we simply didn't notice.

        Maybe that's just me. Maybe I'm just the unobservant one. Maybe you're all masters of self-introspection and keep a constant catalogue of strengths and weaknesses you can see objectively. If so, that's very nice for you. I'm not so lucky.

It began with a letter.

I opened the outer door of my apartment building to find on the immediate vestibule floor a quick-band of a stack of mail for me and my roommates, and I picked them up as I executed the semi-complicated dance of unlocking and relocking doors that was entering my pad. I strode into an apartment quiet with the peculiar stillness that occurs in the early afternoon when the rest of the world is still working, interrupted here and there by the quiet growl of car engines and industry sounds, set the bag on the counter, and then started thumbing through the mail.

Much of it was junk. A packet of coupons for local eateries and small grocery stores my roommates and I might pass a hundred times but never once enter. The sort of local weekly shopper guide that crosses a newspaper with ads so that you're never certain where articles end and selling begins, if indeed either occurs. A utilities bill and a Comcast offer, and then—

The sight of the envelope, the sight of my address in my own writing, stopped me. It always does. Those letters bypass reason and mailboxes and seem to be delivered straight to your psyche; just receiving one, you can't help, for just a moment, opening yourself to possibility.

Most times, anyway. The only reason I'm not going to tell you my hands were detached when I opened it is that doing so makes it sound like I was in morbid need of emergency surgery. Instead, I'll just tell they didn't shake as I tore up the flap and slipped the letter out, unfolding it.

It was addressed, specifically, to me. Not to an author, not to silly maybe-future-writer-wannabe-guy, which is how getting letters addressed to author has always made me feel. It addressed me by name and referred to my novel by its then-soap opera-esque tentative title, before—

Thank you for writing. So nice to encounter a young writer inspired by a client.

Thank you, too, for allowing me to read your sample. You are a good writer, and it is a good idea, but I'm afraid I must decline representation at this time. I have to be selective about choosing to represent only those about whom I am most enthusiastic, and while you are talented, the market for time travel is notoriously difficult.

Please keep in mind that this is only one opinion, and other agents may not feel the same. I wish you all the best luck in your future career.—

it very politely, very professionally, very personally rejected my novel. Not me, but my novel. Not my writing; that was good. Just the novel, the market for which—

If you build it, they will come.—

was apparently not just difficult but rather even notoriously so. Which I think surprised me in a way, at least given that I had grown up on time travel, *Quantum Leap* and *Superman*, for two, nevermind that one of the *Harry Potter* novels—was it the third?—used time travel as a plot device. Nevermind Dean Koontz and Michael Crichton.

I admit now, I was trying unsuccessfully not to be bitter. I was trying to silence the thoughts of vampire-series clones and all the sad young literary novels I had ever read ten pages of only to close them again in boredom, tucking a stack into my backpack to sell to the

Strand for lunch money. I was trying not to go to the artistic versus commercial argument, trying not to let the thought that marketing and the ability to easily sell something could be such a determinant to literary success as to irritate the living Hell out of me.

I was, quite obviously, unsuccessful in those attempts.

I crumpled the letter in my hand and let it drop unceremoniously to the table. I turned my back on it and began to unpack the food and prepare to cook, and all the while I considered how badly I really wanted it. Did I really want to base my life, or even build it, around a career that didn't just desire the validation of other people but in fact required it?

I said I've gotten hundreds of those letters. Some more consolatory than others, but what they all had in common was:

no.

What they all come down to was a single negative. No matter how they phrased it, no matter the words they used, no matter delicate and gratuitous lengths to which so many went to pretend otherwise, they all said precisely the same simple thing:

No.

The only word in the entire English language I dislike more than "no" is "can't," because at least "no" isn't a coward about it. When people say they "can't" do something, they generally just mean they won't; when people say "no," it can mean nothing more.

And where had all those "no"s, all those rejections, gotten me? I stood there in my kitchen, cutting up mushrooms and preparing for some sauté magic, and all I could think was that everything good in my life, right then, at that moment, had precisely nothing to do with writing. All I could think was how much I was looking forward to seeing Veronica, and how much I was looking forward to work on Monday morning. All I could think was that I didn't much care about the letter, because I had enough other things going well in my life that it didn't really matter so much.

I tried like Hell to be scared of that line of thinking but found I couldn't be bothered. I found I couldn't think of a single wonderful thing writing had brought me. I was in my mid-twenties and had, up to that point, earned a couple of degrees and worked a temporary job that had basically boiled down to organizing my supervisor's rolodex, but things in the past few weeks had taken a solid turn for the better, and all that better had come during weeks when I really hadn't been writing much at all. I had been reading during my commutes to work, scribbling stray ideas in a notebook I keep in my back pocket, but had, overall, become intent enough on Veronica and the Weinstein company that, I realized right then, I really hadn't written anything since the day I'd revised my novel to send it out the month before.

I thought of my job, of working for the Weinsteins. Of how much I enjoyed it, of Claire and Ben, of the posters on the brick walls and the flat-panel monitors on the desks. Of steady work at a place I enjoyed.

I continued to think of those things as I cooked, but there was little in the way of sadness about the letter. My thoughts instead focused almost entirely on how good my life was, which, I regretfully admit right now, is not something I often either realize or appreciate. Life was good, and I had nothing to complain about. Some agent hadn't wanted my novel? It wasn't like my happiness depended on it.

My cell phone went off in my pocket, but my fingers were filmed with raw chicken juice. I tried to wash them quickly so that I could still catch the call, but by the time I had dried my hands and pulled the phone from my pocket, I'd long missed it. The ID showed Veronica's number, and so I dialed her straightaway.

"I'm just walking down your street. If you open your door right now, I'll be there by the time you do."

So I crossed my apartment and unlocked those few doors and then she was in my arms, smelling like citrus and summer, lips like vanilla and body like a dream come true. Cliché, perhaps, but that is, after all, why they were invented.

"How was your trip? Found it okay on your own?"

"I'm here, aren't I? I did get propositioned by a hooker near the bus station—."

"You didn't bring her back?"

"She's waiting outside. I told her I had to run it by you."

"Come here," I told her, peeling her jacket down her arms and setting it on the couch as I led her to the kitchen.

"Smells good."

"Told you I can cook. Why don't you crack the wine?"

"Don't you have an opener?"

"Smart ass."

"Maybe. But awesome."

"No arguments here," I told her, handing her the opener I'd fished out of our utensil drawer.

"So, good day?" she asked as she twisted the opener down and pulled the cork.

"Mostly, yeah. In fact, it was mostly better than good. So I'm sitting at my desk, right? And my supervisor, I've told you about Claire, calls me into her office. She asks me to close the door behind her—."

"I'm hoping this doesn't go where I think it might," she said, pouring two generous glasses of wine.

"That's what I thought! I mean, closed door, Friday afternoon? That's a clean-out-your-desk meeting. But it totally wasn't. They offered me a full-time spot. There's a really slight raise, but full benefits, and I get to be a full-time employee of the Weinstein Company. Room for growth."

"So here's to that, then," she offered me one of the glasses, which I accepted and clinked to hers before I took a sip. I'd chosen a dry white. "Oh, that's pretty terrific."

"Very. So why is that only mostly good? Did you have to sell your soul for the job?"

I chuckled, pulling from the table the still-crumpled letter and handing it to her.

"What's this?"

"Just read it," I said, turning back to stir the chicken. Which didn't really need it.

"Thank you . . . you're a good writer . . . time travel's hard . . . oh, damn. I'm sorry. I really thought you might get it. But hey, like we said in the car that day, you keep going, right?"

I thought back to that conversation. "We said a lot of things in the car that day."

She smiled. "I remember. That was when you told me you loved me."

"And I do. Because you're awesome."

"So what now, then?"

"The chicken's almost done. The pasta—."

"I meant with the writing."

"Oh," I said. I turned back to the stove. Since the chicken hadn't needed stirring, it was probably okay to move to the back, so I could start the pasta, and if you're wondering why I'm going on about the chicken and the pasta, that's totally the point. The whole time I had prepared the meal, I'd been pushing from my mind the idea of writing because I was scared of what addressing the issue might bring.

"Hey, Earth to you."

I smiled at Veronica. "Sorry. Just wanted to—."

"It's not going to burn," she said. She moved to me, taking my hands in hers. "Are you okay?"

"I'm better than okay," I told her. "I think maybe that's what scares me."

She didn't say anything, but I saw the confusion on her face. She just waited.

"I'm way better than okay. I've got a great job. I have an amazing girlfriend. I rent an awesome apartment, and I live five minutes from the most exciting city on the entire planet. I'm so terrific it's completely ridiculous, and what more do I need? I wrote a decent book I'm proud of, and I gave it to you, but now—I could pursue it more. I could send it out again and again, but what's the point?"

"Sharing it. Because somebody's going to want it. You know they're going to. They're going to line up for it," she told me, and there was such conviction in her eyes. God bless her, she believed in me not just at the moment it felt like no one else did but rather and perhaps importantly when it didn't feel like there was a whole lot to believe in.

"Doesn't mean I have to give it to them. Doesn't mean I have to put everything I have into everything I do and constantly worry about how people are going to receive it. I don't have to do that. I'm totally happy not doing that."

"But you can't just give it up."

The world swam, then. You know those moments so big you can feel them? Not just all around you but in you? The moments that make your head feel lighter, or heavier? Or maybe if you consider a super-saturated solution in a beaker and then imagine the single grain around which solute crystallizes in a hyper-intricate lattice of shimmer and strength? That was how I felt right then, like something solidified in me, like I had tipped over. "I think I already have. I haven't written pretty much anything in a while. I thought I needed some time to replenish the well, but I'm not sure that's true anymore. I'm not even sure there is a well anymore. I don't remember the last story I thought of."

"So you want to just walk away? It's what you've always wanted."

"It's what I always used to want. Maybe it's time to want other things. I told you, I'm really rather happy. I'm not sad. I'm not angry or hurt or dejected. I'm actually totally okay with it."

"So that's really it, then? You get just one letter, and you decide no more? You get one person who says not that it's not good but rather that she's not sure about marketing it, and you're done? Because really, that's not a reason to give up. It's a setback, but it's a small one. Look at the kinds of things all the great ones faced. Shakespeare had a wife and kids hundreds of miles away, but he stayed where he needed to be and wrote the greatest plays ever. Beethoven started going deaf and couldn't hear his music anymore, so you know what he did? He cut the damned legs off his piano and put it on the floor, and then he pressed his ear to the wood while he pounded the keys so he could feel the vibrations of the strings and the chords through the floorboards. You get one damned letter that says hey, sorry, you're good but I've got a bunch of clients already, and you're ready to quit?"

Part of me wanted to argue it wasn't that easy, that it wasn't just the one letter, that it's letter after letter after letter from agent after editor, but I couldn't, because the rest of me had clamped shut. The rest of me heard her mention Beethoven and Shakespeare, deafness and families, and thought of Angus Silver. I thought of walking into that surreal office, and I thought of the chance he'd offered me to be with Veronica if only I would give up writing. I had tried to cancel our appointment the morning I'd begun working for the Weinsteins, but I remembered the disconnection message—

but something stuttered there. Like a skipping record, like it wanted to think of something else, something more, but couldn't leap over the scratch.

I worked the memory like one might work a stray something caught in a back tooth, my mental tongue fidgeting and plying and coaxing. I think maybe Veronica took my sudden, somewhat stunned silence for the beginning of agreement, though, because she said, "You can't give up. It's your dream. It always has been," and finally the record cleared its throat and the memory came full and clear and terrifying, and here and now I circle back around to—

Chapter Eleven, which was skipped before

*P*opped *the cap and reached for a tumbler before I decided against it, brought the bottle to my lips and took a long, slow pull of it. Heavy enough to be a meal on its own, and I remembered how it had affected me nearly right away, and I thought maybe that wouldn't be so bad. Maybe that would take my mind off of . . .*

Well. Everything, really.

So sweet and strong, so full and bright. I don't know if I meant to chug it, but I wouldn't have been able to, the bubbles tickling my throat, but the strange thing, the odd thing, was that even after I had glugged down two, maybe three swallows and pulled the bottle from my lips, it didn't appear as though I had drained any liquid from it. It appeared freshly opened.

I drank and drank again and again, but still the liquid remained in full.

So surprised was I by this miraculous turn of events, this neverending bottle of beer, that I took out my cell to call Angus' office. I thought they should know what they had given me.

Brigid picked it up after two rings. "Good evening. How are you?"

"How am I? I'm—," I started to say great, but then I thought of my conversation with Veronica. I hiccupped. "I've seen better days, Brigid, and speaking of seeing, do you know I can see you when we talk? Very first time you picked up the phone I imagined you in my head—."

"I'm sure that's not uncommon. You're a writer, after all. You must be used to an active imagination."

"No but it was more than that. More than that. It was like—it was like I could see you. But not creepy see you, like from a hidden webcam or something. Because I'm sure you're not under surveillance or anything."

"You have put my mind at ease. And how may I help you this evening?"

"Help me? Help me. Oh, no, wait, I just wanted to tell you about this beer."

"Your beer?"

"The beer you gave me. Because," I took another long pull, then, "It's totally awesome. I've been drinking it straight from the bottle—."

"Oh dear."

"But it never—it's like I'm not drinking it at all."

"But you are."

I took another drink. "Oh, I am."

"And how much, exactly, have you drunk?"

"I've no idea! Like none at all!"

"But you've drunk some."

"Well, I've drunk some, sure. It's good. This is good beer. Have you tried this beer? It's really quite wonderful."

"I have not tried that particular beer. Mainly because you are currently drinking it."

"I'm currently enjoying it, too!"

Brigid laughed. "This I can tell."

"But it's good. I just talked to Veronica—do you know about Veronica? Angus knew about Veronica. Do you know about that?"

"I do not. Your business with Mr. Silver remains confidential."

"Oh, right, okay, but Veronica is this girl I love? I mean, she's gorgeous. So pretty. But anyway—I talked to her earlier. And after talking to her I kinda feel like maybe coming back to see you guys might be unnecessary and I wouldn't want to waste your time."

"I'm sure Mr. Silver would still like to discuss the matter with you. But if you spoke to this young lady earlier, perhaps it would behoove us to have you come in sooner, rather than later."

"What, like now?"

"No time like the present after all."

"After all," I said, taking another sip. "Well. I mean, I live in Hoboken, so it might take me a while to get there—."

"I'm sure it will be just fine. Can we expect to see you shortly?"

"That's what I mean. I'm not sure about shortly, but sure, I'm not doing anything," I told her, and even as I said it I began to cross my apartment, stumble-fidgeting over stubborn locks that didn't seem to want to cooperate with my nimble fingers, but then again they might have been too nimble right then. I managed to open the door of my apartment itself and I stepped through it to—

"Well that was faster than I would have expected," Brigid greeted me. "You can go right in. Mr. Silver is expecting you."

The office seemed brighter than it had earlier, and more surfaces shone. The light was near on glaring, in fact, and it lent to everything a strange quality as though the colors present had overstepped their boundaries and were crowding each other. The office took on a luminous but hazy quality, and as I crossed the lobby I looked up to notice a skylight I hadn't seen earlier and the sight nearly blinded me.

Those enormous doors opened like I'd stepped on a supermarket sensor. Across from them, Angus stood facing his windowspace, on the display of which a cartoon Mario flipped and jumped through space.

I took a sip of my beer. "Wow."

Angus paused the game, looked at me over his shoulder. "Ah, so nice to see you miboy. A bit sooner than I expected, admittedly."

"Brigid tole me to come."

"So she did, so she did," he said, then noticed the beer in my hand and smiled. "Ah, you are partaking of the libations I provided you upon our last meeting."

"Partaking . . ." I said, before I caught up to his meaning. "Oh! My beer. It's good."

"I remember. Why don't you have a seat? Would you like to try my game system?" he asked, holding out to me, one in each hand, two plastic controllers joined in the middle by wire like toy nunchukus.

I looked at them. They presented a problem: if I wanted to take both, I had to set down my beer. I did so reluctantly. I held them as he had while I slunk down into the leather chair.

"You do quite enjoy your beer."

I nodded, already more interested in the game. Mario smiled at me, then flipped around. I started to attempt to control him, but he immediately started gesticulating like he was having some sort of epileptic seizure, at which point I realized the controllers were as sensitive to movement as to button pressing. "What is this?"

"They're going to call it a we."

"We? Like you and me?"

"Two eyes," Angus said, then, "On second thought, maybe a game isn't the best idea," and with that he gestured his hand to sweep it way, leaving in its stead an image of Times Square. People moving to and fro, the sun set and evening encroaching.

"Izzat—real time?"

"*Perhaps we should eschew matters of temporality and physics in favor of the matter at hand, what say you to that?*"

"*Uhh,*" I said, as always eloquent. I put the game controllers down and picked up my beer again, taking a quick swig.

"*And by the matter at hand I mean your ladylove Veronica.*"

"*Ohohoh rightrightright! That's what I was telling Brigid. Because she's not my ladylove. I talked to her earlier. I basically told her everything—.*"

"*By everything I hope I don't take you to mean you told her about either me or my offer. I offer confidence, and expect it in return.*"

"*Ohnono. I mean like that I'm in love with her. That everything. Totally different everything.*"

"*Very different, yes.*"

"*Probably not the best idea.*"

"*I suppose that depends.*"

I took another sip. "*She told me I was like her brother—.*"

"*Then certainly not the best. Of that I am sorry. One of the truly tragic things about life is that you don't get to choose whom you love, but perhaps even more tragic is that you don't get to choose whom you don't, either.*"

"*Youknow I think—I think I always believed I'd end up with her, you know? Like maybe it was because I'm a romantic. Or I'm over-confident. Or maybe I'm just a damned fool. Or maybe, maybe they're all the same thing and I'm all of them at the same time and I just don't know the difference. I don't know a lot of things anymore,*" I said, taking another sip.

"*Have you considered my offer?*"

I nearly choked, which meant I couldn't answer right away.

"*But—she said . . .*"

"*Oh, believe you me, make no mistake, I know what she said.*"

"*But—how—?*"

"How do I know, or how can you be with her?"

"I don't . . ."

"I knew what she was going to say before she thought about saying it. I know what she'll keep saying. And right now, you're sitting here in my office because I can change that."

"What, like you can cast a spell or something?" I asked, relieved my tone came out a little disgusted because I wasn't certain I'd felt that way. "Like magic."

"Come now, my boy, what isn't magic? I'm only talking about what you want."

"But how . . .?" I think I was going to ask how he was going to do it, because I think I might have thought it made a difference. I'll never find out, though, because that's where my question stopped, and Angus was waving his hand anyway. It was a small gesture, not necessarily dismissal, but neither far off.

"You don't need to worry about how. You just need to make a decision and let me worry about the rest. That's it. So now tell me you want to be with her, or leave my office once and for all. What's it going to be?"

I wanted to get up. I thought I was going to. I thought I would get up and leave, find my way the few blocks back to the train, back to my apartment, backbackback timelapse subway stations and mad-rushing tracks to emerge, finally, blinkingly, into the grey pre-dawn of Hoboken proper. I'd taken that train home so many times I could have done it on autopilot, and probably had, and I wanted to, right then. I swear I thought I would.

But I didn't move.

I watched Angus as I took another drink from my beer. Who knows how much I'd drunk by then? And then I realized something. "You already know."

He smiled coyly. "I knew before you ever walked into my office. I knew before I gave you my card. Hell, you want the truth of the matter, I knew before you and Veronica ever even met."

"But how could you?"

"My boy, there are more things in Heaven and Earth than are dreamt of in your philosophy."

"You shouldn't go around underestimating people's philosophies. And how is that even fair?"

"Forgive me, I thought this was war."

"What?"

"Sorry, did I just say war? Love. I meant love. And what's fair to do with that? Is it fair you love a girl who doesn't love you in return? Is anything ever fair?"

"Sometimes."

"Perhaps. But for all the other times, there's me."

"But then what's the point?" I tried to keep the sudden anger out of my voice, but I was only mostly successful in doing so. "Why go through all this if everything's already set? What's the point if you already know what's going to happen."

Angus smiled, standing. "I would have thought you'd have put it together by now. You're so quick about everything else."

"Put what together?"

"This," Angus said, sweeping his hand to take in his whole office. "The point of it all. Why I might go to such trouble if I already know what's going to happen, which has a rather simple answer, if you consider it even briefly."

So I considered it briefly, sipping my beer as I did. Maybe the beer was why nothing came to mind. Maybe not. I don't know. I shrugged.

"The point," Angus said, "Is that while I may know what's going to happen, you do not."

Few things kill anger like confusion. "What?"

"I may know, but you don't."

"You're asking me to make—."

"I am doing no such thing," Angus said, his tone brief. Not abrupt, and neither raised, but certainly more professional than it had been. He dropped the warmth, the friendship from his tone, *like a businessman giving a presentation, or a salesman peddling his wares. "I'm merely asking you to tell me what you want. Don't you know that? There's no decision, no making choices. All there is, in fact, is one young man who loves to write and who has fallen in love with a special young lady, and all that young man has to do, all you have to do, is tell me what you want."*

"But I don't know what I want," I said. I didn't realize how desperate he had made me feel, how anxious I was, until I said that nearly in a yell, my voice high and scared. "I don't—."

"Of course you do. You've known all along what you want. You just won't admit it."

"It's not—that easy," I told him, but my voice betrayed maybe it was and I just didn't want to acknowledge it. Which scared me even more.

"No one said it would be."

"So, what, I'm supposed to give up my words, my stories, the single thing I love to do most in the world? To be with her?" I kept my voice from breaking, but only just.

Because what I felt like I was about to do terrified me.

"You're supposed to tell me what you want. That's all."

I tried to speak, but couldn't. My mouth had dried, and I could feel my Adam's apple bobbing in my throat. Every time I opened my mouth, nothing came out.

Angus put a hand on my shoulder. Comforting, perhaps, but also encouraging. Across from us, the window/display began to flash, cycling through images: the pyramids, Tokyo, the Sidney opera house, Parliament, Big Ben, Mann's Chinese Theater—

Deserts and mountains, dreamt-of towers and dreamt-of oceans in dreamt-of lands.—

Angus' voice, when he spoke, was calm. "Do you love her?"

I didn't consider the question, didn't hesitate. I nodded. "Yes."

"Then go to her," Angus said.—

Chapter Eighteen, in which I tell Veronica everything I hadn't already

*A*ll of which made me gasp there, in the kitchen, my gorge rising, and I went to the sink and retched up nothing at all. That empty, swimmy feeling in my gut did a somersault and sloshed my equilibrium into a twist that weakened my knees, and I dry-heaved again. I put on the spigot, ran the water until it went cold and then palmed it against my face, sipping the splash and spitting it back against the steel. Veronica, for her part, stayed where she was, giving me a wide berth, for which I was grateful. I held a wet hand against the back of my neck, hesitating there, staring at the water rushing down the drain.

I'm not sure that skipping that chapter to come around was the best way to tell this story, but I think it was if only because I didn't remember any of it until I stood there staring over the sink, waiting for my stomach to solidify again. Pretty much everything below my chest felt like fluid, which may have been why my heart had sunk like lead.

"You okay?" Veronica asked.

And still I hesitated. What could I say to that?

I knew I had to tell her. It's as likely that the knowledge I had to tell her made me as sick as the memory itself had. It wasn't sick disgusted or sick repulsed; it was more the sick like "Holy shit, what have I done?" crossed with the "Holy shit, this is bad."

"I'll be . . ." I trailed off. I picked up my wine glass, which I'd abandoned on the counter as I'd spun to the sink, and I drained it in a go. "I think maybe you should sit down," I told her, pouring myself another glass of wine as I said it.

"What?"

"I need to—there's something I have to tell you, and I think you're going to want to be sitting down when you hear it. I know I'd like you to be sitting down."

"What? Why? Nothing good—."

"I know. But look. Please. Just sit, okay?"

She just looked at me a moment, and then, without ever once looking away, slowly pulled a chair from the small wooden table in my kitchen, and sat.

I took the seat opposite her.

"I hope you're not going to tell me you've met someone else," she said. Her tone indicated she didn't believe it but was way too chilly to be joking.

"There's no one else," I told her, because there's not. There hasn't ever been, really, and I think some days I doubt there ever will be. This thought may be getting ahead of myself, though. "It's just—remember New Year's? And your brother's launch party?"

"Yeah. But what—oh, I hope you're not going to tell me you slept with one of the strippers."

"What? No."

"Because, I mean, we weren't seeing each other then, but ew."

"What 'ew'? Stripping's not so bad. It's not like they're prostitutes," I said, then realized what I was saying. "This isn't about strippers. It's—okay, so, maybe a minute or two after you left, this guy approached me and sat down and started talking to me. Angus. Looked like Anthony Hopkins. And we got to talking about writing and work and dating and then you—."

"You talked to Anthony Hopkins about me?"

"He wasn't actually Anthony Hopkins. He just looked like him. And just listen, okay?"

And with that, I began to tell her the whole story, everything. Beginning to end, or at least from the moment Angus had started talking to me until I had asked her to sit down so I could talk to her, there in my kitchen. I told her about Brigid, about finding the offices and how surreal they were, about the beer and the books and the bargains.

Most of all, I told her about the offer Angus had presented to me, that it might have been partly what had prompted me to talk to her, that day in her car after I'd sent off those chapters to that agent. I told her what I had just remembered, that parts of it had seemed a dream but considering everything else about Angus, who could really know, and Hell, maybe that was just how he worked, maybe that had been merely business as usual. And I told her I hadn't remembered that night until right then, in that kitchen, when she had mentioned Shakespeare and Beethoven.

"So what, you blacked out?"

"I don't know. All I know is the following morning you showed up and told me you loved me, and the following evening . . . that was the day we went to Candela, and oh! That was the morning," and when I said I got the call about the Weinstein Company, we said it together.

"So you think he was behind it all?" Veronica asked.

"I don't know. It's hard to believe. But the letter, and the job. And let's be honest, you—."

"You think I'm here because he made me be here?"

"Of course not," I told her. "But the fact is I haven't written a word since that day, and to be honest, I haven't minded it a bit. I've barely even thought about it, I've been so busy with other things. Not to mention so happy about other things."

"So maybe he did have something to do with it."

I shrugged. "Maybe?"

We both stopped. Truthfully, I didn't know what to say, much less do. I stood and went to the stove, moved the chicken again, stirred the pasta. Busy work.

"I think we should call him."

My hand hesitated in stirring the chicken. After a moment, I said: "I told you. I tried. The number didn't work."

"But you only tried it once? Maybe you misdialed."

"It was already in my phone."

"What is it?"

"What?"

"Give me his number."

I stopped pretending to stir the chicken, turned. "Why?"

"So I can call."

"You think I got it wrong?"

"I didn't say that. I just wanted to try." Her voice low and even.

"But why do you want to try?"

"Because I—because I can't handle the idea that you gave up writing to be with me, okay?"

"I didn't give it up—."

"Look, if it's the wrong number, and it stays the wrong number, fine, okay? But if there's any chance at all, no matter how small, that there's any reason we are together right now besides that we both want to be— can you really live like that? Because I can't. And you know what's more? You loved writing. You always have. You've always wanted to tell stories, and I've loved the ones you've shared with me. That novel you gave me—I loved it—."

"You did? You didn't tell my you had finished it."

"I know. I wanted to read it again. That first time, I just wanted to enjoy it. But I wanted to tell you why. I could tell how much you had put into it, and I wasn't just going to tell you I had liked it."

"But you did."

"I loved it. Which is all the more reason we have to try to make that call. I just can't take the risk you gave up something so important to you—."

"It couldn't have been so important if I was so willing to give it up. And I might be."

"And maybe you will. But not for me. I'm sorry, but not for me. I just think of Shakespeare and Beethoven, and can you imagine being the reason the world never got to see Hamlet, or hear the Moonlight sonata—?"

"I'm not that good a writer."

"Maybe not yet, but you never will be if you give it up. And maybe you really do want to give it up, and that would be fine, but you can't give it up for me. I need to know we're together just because we want to be, that you've stopped writing because you're happy. You can't ask me to be the girl you gave up something so important for."

"But I'm not—."

"Then give me the number, and we'll call him, and we'll find out once and for all."

I started to respond but stopped myself. Instead, I took out my phone, flipped it open, and searched my calls log. Which only went as far back as 30 days. When I pulled out my cardcase wallet, I realized I couldn't find Angus' card. Had I thrown it away at some point?

"Problem?"

"It's just—my phone doesn't save numbers that long, and I don't seem to have the card. But I think we can look up my phone bill online. It's probably on there."

***

Five minutes later, I read from my computer monitor the digits Veronica punched into her own phone, which she brought to her ear. She waited a moment, then, "Hi. This is Veronica Sawyer, and you did some business with a friend of mine about a month ago. I was hoping—yes, exactly. I'd love to come in to see Mr. Silver. The sooner the better. Tonight? Really? Absolutely I can make it," she said, and then she pushed the button to end the call. "All right. Let's go."

"Now?"

"They had an opening for tonight. So let's make use of what's available."

I nodded. I pulled the food from the stove, shut it off, and put the meal in the fridge, uncovered, hoping we would come back to it but not certain. I wasn't certain of anything by then besides the fact that Veronica was right, that we really did need to know what had happened, if only because otherwise it would become something too large and too overwhelming hanging over both our heads. Knowing might change our relationship, I knew, but I also knew that, if we didn't find out, not knowing would destroy it.

And so we pulled on our coats and headed out into an early evening in February. That afternoon had been balmy and mild enough I could have believed in spring, but the evening had taken a different tone, every inhalation tinged with a taste of metal and stormclouds, and the wind blew devils of dead leaves and dirty grass into spontaneous dervishes on the sidewalk. We walked together to the PATH station as darkness gathered and clouds accumulated, on our way to Angus and his offices, but to relay the events that occurred there, I think we're going to need

A Bigger Act

*B*ecause here comes the homestretch. This marks act the third, which is the one in which all the events that have so far occurred must come together in the sort of perfect storm that was gathering even as Veronica and I descended the steps of the Hoboken PATH stop. The act in which the gun you saw above the mantle in the first must now be loaded, its sights calibrated, the target spotted. This is the act in which the shot must be taken, though not, it must be pointed out, the act in which that shot is guaranteed to find its mark.

It never is, after all.

Are you excited? I am. This is where it comes together, and I think I've known since before I began that pulling it together was going to be a challenge.

So I've poured myself a drink, and I've turned my hat backward, and I'm ready for this. I'm staring at my screen and thinking less "Bring it," than "All right, let's tell this story." I've got Keane and Snow Patrol and Steve Acho performing piano covers of awesome songs, including Coldplay, and I can't be sure I'll ever write a song for a girl, but I think maybe I'm ready to finish a novel, and even were I not, I think it's a bit out of my hands now. Here I am on the verge of an ending, a third act I've already written first and second and seventh drafts of but know in my heart I can't use. They just haven't felt right, haven't felt true, and worst of all haven't felt like what happened, but I know I can do this. I feel like I've got something special in this story, with this novel, and I feel like somewhere along the way it became more than I realized, and my only hope, here and now, is that I can make good on the challenge of pulling it off.

Because there are three options here. The first is to stop now and never show this story to anyone, and while there would be nothing wrong with that, the simple fact that you have read this far demonstrates that's obviously not the way I went.

The other two are to finish it successfully or fail spectacularly in trying. Either way, how can you not read on?

Let's do this, shall we?

Yes, I think we shall.

On to:

Chapter Nineteen, in which we do this

*V*eronica and I didn't talk much as our train rushed to 9th Street, where we got off and ascended the steps into a storm that had, in what seemed like a handful of minutes but which was probably closer to half an hour, gathered up its courage to put on the kind of show that could make even jaded New Yorkers seek shelter. We looked at each other when we reached the entrance, where water slipped over the lip of the doorway and fell in streams like a bead curtain, and then she took my hand, and we took a deep breath of clean, gritty-tasting, rain-drenched Manhattan, and ducked out into the storm.

Most of the time, stories above the street, there are outcroppings and decorations that catch the rain first, so even a solid rainfall barely makes it down to the streets. But that night? The wind whipped it sideways and upward and counter-clockwise, and the City rejoiced in it. The City gleamed like sex-sweat, a hard sheen it wore like it was proud of it, like it had enjoyed working so hard for the flush. Tail-lights trailed red-streak reflections like "Just Married" limousines, and the neon shone like glamorama Heaven.

And rain like that? Hard rain in the City falls loud, echoing as it does off every available surfaces and finding so many available, and it came thick and fast, micro-waterfalling from awnings and gathering in ankle deep puddles at every handicap-accessible curb. The City is normally so full of sounds, car horns and engines, constant chatter, the micro-tremors of the footsteps of so many millions of people, but a rain like that reduces the entire City to one vibrant whisper.

All of which is to say Veronica and I were drenched before we'd gone a block. We hurried our strides as if we hoped to run between the drops, but before long we seemed to be wearing most of them, our coats and boots heavier than moments before. I could feel the cool stream down my whole body, and I shivered.

***

The rain slacked off a little as we went, and then Veronica stopped at one particular stoop.

"Is this it? I think this is it. This is the address they gave me," she said, consulting a slip of paper she had pulled from her pocket. I couldn't help noticing that the ink had run together, and I wasn't sure how she could be certain. "At least, I think it is. I'm pretty sure. Is this the place you came?"

I considered the building. It seemed familiar, somehow, but I couldn't be sure it actually was. It felt, in ways, like the familiarity that comes with dreams when you realize your house is actually your old grade school is actually your current office, the sort of vague familiarity—

You've been here before.—

you tend to go with rather than question. Looking at it, I didn't exactly recognize the building, but I didn't figure that was uncommon, not when so many Manhattan buildings look alike, not when construction changed so quickly the facades of buildings so many people paid so little attention to, anyway.

"I think so? It might be."

"Haven't you been here before?"

"Only once."

"Twice."

"Right. Twice. But I told you, that second time . . ." I trailed off, unsure how to describe it. Dreamlike? Surreal?

"Only one way to find out, then," Veronica said, and with that she started up the stoop to the door at their top. I followed just a step behind, then through the door . . .

***

into a lobby completely different from the marbles and the waterfall I had seen. Gone were the chrome accents, the leather furniture, the glass surfaces; in their place were hardwood floors and fine Persian rugs and beautiful mahogany fixtures with baroque accents, tiny wooden claws for feet, intricately hewn patterns in the wood. The basic layout may have been the same, but it looked more like the lobby of a country club than anything as hip and modern as I had seen. The details were so decisive, so well-executed; one of the walls was not only full of leather-bound books with gold-leaf titles that sparkled in the sunlight but also included a slide-ladder as if people climbed it and retrieved volumes on a consistent basis.

And yes, you read that right: sunlight. Behind us, rather than a waterfall, were windows looking out on expansive grounds more botanical garden than country club. No golf course for this place; these were well maintained lawns with finely manicured areas with themes like Shakespeare and Japanese and deciduous. It had to have been a display, right?

The desk in front of us had a surface so highly polished it reflected everything above it, including the slightly quizzical expression with which Brigid greeted us: a sincere smile still slightly abashed, still a little confused. "You must be Veronica," she said, her voice straining for professionalism and cheerful greeting. "And you've brought a guest. We didn't expect to see you again," she told me. Her smile didn't waver, but her voice did.

"Believe me, neither did I," I said. "Just here with her."

"Why don't you both have a seat, and I'll get Mr. Silver straightaway," Brigid stood and went straight for the doors behind her. The décor of the rest of the office might have changed from whatever I had seen to the country club chic it had become for Veronica, but those doors were the same: enormous, intricate, life-changing. She opened one enough to allow her to slip through, and I wouldn't have guessed a door like that could close softly until it did, behind her.

Veronica looked around, seemed to take in the books and the windows and the furniture, her expression inscrutable. "Impressive," she said, finally, but coolly, analytically, the kind of "impressive" more acknowledging impression than actually impressed. "Didn't you say something about a waterfall? And a fountain?"

"The waterfall was there," I pointed toward the windows. "And the fountain was over there," I gestured toward a spot where there was nothing but rug and wood.

"I wonder what they're trying to hide," Veronica said, as if to herself. "They sure pulled out all the stops to convince me of something."

I wasn't surprised the effort had so little effect on her, nor that she could see it for what it was even if she might not have actually been able to see through it. Not that I knew she couldn't, but I didn't think so. If she could have, she would have known what they were trying to convince her of.

There were two well-stuffed armchairs there, in the lobby, but before I'd even really considered having a seat, the doors beyond Brigid's desk opened, and Angus strode through them. He seemed confident if a little rushed, like he'd just showered and prepared on notice short enough he hadn't had a chance to shave. His hair just slightly askew; suit basic, if elegant, black on black with a black shirt, open at the collar. His eyes were the same startling blue. His appearance surprised me; I'd half-expected Angus and the futures he proposed to trade would be waiting for us when we arrived.

"A pleasure to meet you, Veronica Sawyer," Angus said, extending his hands and taking in them both of hers. "I've heard much about you, and all praise from the mouth of this young man. A fine surprise to see you, as well," he told me, shaking my hand. If he was offput to see me, he didn't let on. "I don't mind telling you this is unusual, most unusual, but don't for a moment think we're not happy to see you."

Damned if I didn't believe him. "Didn't expect to see you again, either, Mr. Silver," I told him. I don't think I had even the first time I left his office; part of me, I realized, had very much wanted to believe him, but another part of me had thought it was a fool's game, and that might have been the part of me that hadn't thought much of the disconnected phone number.

I wondered if he meant the same thing.

"And now might I inquire as to what brings you to my humble yet auspicious offices on such an evening?"

"Doesn't appear to be an evening," Veronica said, casting a glance over her shoulder. She was right; considering the view behind us, evening and darkness both seemed long ways off.

Angus smiled. "The spirit and the question, however, remain; to what do I owe the pleasure of your calling?"

"Which was difficult, considering your number wouldn't work from his phone anymore. Isn't that strange?" she asked, but as though she knew it wasn't.

"We remain difficult to reach so as to attract only the most exclusive clientele. But here you are, and I get the distinct impression that you have scheduled some time with me with deliberate purpose in mind, and so I invite you into my office, where perhaps we can discuss the matter further?" Angus said, even as he began to usher Veronica through the lobby and toward the enormous doors of his office.

I took a step, just a single step, before Angus held up his hand. "I'm sorry, but you and I have concluded our business, and you must remember how I told you all my clients are confidential. What you have shared with her is your business, but if Veronica is to become a client herself, our confidentiality begins right now." There wasn't any room in his voice for argument, so I didn't try.

"No, I'm sorry, Mister Silver, but that's not how it's going to work. Whatever business you both conducted seems to have included me, and whatever business you and I conduct will inevitably affect him. Our business is his, so he would be included in that confidentiality. So he comes, or we have no business to conduct," Veronica told him. There might not have been room for argument in his tone, but that was okay, because she just pushed everything else aside and made her own.

That, then, was the first indication that Angus wasn't in total control of everything, that maybe, just maybe, his magic didn't extend quite so far as it seemed. It was also, then, the first moment there seemed some hope, the first moment I thought maybe we could get through it.

Angus looked from Veronica to me, then sighed. "Very well, Veronica. And please, call me Angus," he said, and then he nodded to me and cocked his head toward his office.

***

We entered that bright, almost too perfect office. Whereas the lobby had changed so completely, that office was precisely as I remembered it, and I would posit that, had I recorded the titles of the books on the shelves the first time I had seen it, I would have seen them again, and in exactly the same places. Which, of course, is not altogether unusual; how often do you move the books in your bookcase? A fire crackled in the fireplace, warm and comfortable, and beyond Angus' desk, in that window-display-screen-whatever it was, a dirt road stretched ahead through autumn-hued trees before finding itself bisected before another road nearly identical.

Veronica and I sat in the two leather chairs that faced the desk.

Angus walked around to its other side. "Can I get you anything? I've a fine beer—."

"Is it true?" Veronica cut him off.

He could have easily played it off, stepped sideways to badly act the fool, but he did not. He didn't even ask her what she meant. "Must we really waste time with questions to which we already know the answers?"

"So you tricked him."

He looked at me as he shook his head. "No tricks. It was the only way I could get you to tell me what you wanted. Hell, you want the truth, it was the only way to get you to admit what you wanted, nevermind my having anything to do with it in the first place."

"But it was a dream," I said. I meant it as argument, but the protest never made it into my voice.

"What better than a dream to base love upon?"

"Don't twist this. You interfered with things you had no place in," Veronica said, her voice indignant.

Angus smiled. It was sad, but a smile nonetheless. "Anywhere there is a choice, anywhere there is potential, I have a place."

Veronica was silent a moment, then: "If that's true, I'm here because I have a choice."

"You're here because you received an invitation. But you received that invitation because you have a choice, yes."

"And I can tell you to undo it. Whatever you did, whatever you changed, I can choose for you to change it back."

"Are you certain you wish to?" Angus asked her. "You realize he loves you. Truly and deeply," he said, then looked straight at me. "Don't you?"

I started to respond, but Veronica cut me off.

"Leave him out of this. If I didn't have any say when the choice was all about me, he doesn't have one now." She said it with enough contempt I might say she spat it, except she didn't.

I didn't blame her. I don't even think I disagreed with her. I might have begun to realize the enormity of what I had done back in my apartment, but I hadn't really appreciated what it had meant, nor the emotions it would bring: the nausea of fear, the quease of guilt.

"You realize you'll never find an—."

"I swear to Christ if you say I'll never find another man like him I might just up and deck you," Veronica said, her voice straining enough it made the threat more a promise than anything. "I don't need some old man in a tailored suit to tell me that, but what's the price? That he gives up writing to be with me? Two and a half children and a mid-life crisis because he gave up what he loved? I will not be his white-picket fences. Undo it."

"You're sure," Angus said more than asked, and the way he did so gave me the impression just the act of asking was mere formality, third time the charm.

"Do I seem uncertain?"

Angus considered her, then, "All right," he said, nodding. "All right. Of course, it's not so easy as undoing it—."

"I didn't think it would be, but if you tell me it's going to require sacrificing a virgin—."

Angus laughed. "Nothing so vulgar, and who knows where you would find one nowadays? Not even the old ways ever worked like they used to, and the old ways never were mine." He opened a drawer in his desk, withdrawing from it a velvet pouch from which he slid a stack of ornate cards, their backs an intricate pattern of knots and whorls and Mobius angles. "Tell me, Veronica, do you know the Tarot?"

"I wouldn't say I'm an expert."

"But you are familiar."

"I have some experience with them."

"And do you feel comfortable with the cards?"

She seemed to consider that a moment, then: "I think anyone who would claim to feel comfortable with Tarot cards is a fool. Snake handlers should always be mindful of the fangs and venom."

Angus chuckled again. "Well put, well put," he said, placing the deck on the desk between them. "And if I suggested they might be the instrument by which you might find the resolution you seek?"

"I'd say I'm listening."

"As I said, it's not so easy as merely undoing what has been done. When first we spoke," Angus said to me, "I told you that many things were likely, and then asked you to make a choice, the very act of which borrowed some amount of certainty from some things to allow the possibility of others. What we are dealing with, then, is potential and probability, the manipulation of which, as I told a young man named Werner when he asked to contemplate his brave quantum worlds, is very nearly impossible."

"But very nearly means it isn't actually."

Angus smiled. "If you are familiar with the Tarot, with the cards currently between us, you know that those who come to them often seek guidance and reassurance. In the interpretations of cards and their readings, people find comfort, because they believe the cards either acknowledge or inspire some degree of certainty about things which are, in fact, not. Do you see where I'm going with this, Veronica?"

"I think I may," Veronica said. "We can use them for the opposite, too."

"Quite right. If people find guidance, we can use the cards for obscurity. Given the decision made, you may use the cards to decrease my influence in the matter. Unfortunate as it may be that you had so little input into a choice that affected you and your future so deeply, you may use the cards to change that."

Which reminded me of an old Stephen Wright joke—

Last night I played poker with Tarot cards. I got a full house, and four people died.—

and prompted me to speak up: "Wait, you're—you want us to gamble for our future using Tarot cards?"

"Of course not," Angus told me, which made me feel relieved until he continued: "You forfeited any claim you had the moment you made your choice. Any business hereafter conducted remains between Veronica and myself, and if indeed there is to be contract between us, you may not be part of it, just as she had no part of yours."

"If we're going to use cards, I want to use mine," Veronica said, removing from her bag the neon-pink velvet pouch that mysterious red-headed woman had given her back at the end of the first act. Sometimes, the literal gun above the mantle is just window-dressing and glamour, psychological misdirection and literary sleight of hand; the one you have to worry about is the one you never expect until the bullet's already shot through your heart.

Angus nodded, smiling at the sight of the pouch. "I can allow that, certainly," he said, putting his own deck back into the drawer he closed with the soft scratch-thunk of wood on wood.

Veronica opened the bag to slip the deck from it, fanning the cards as she set it down, their backs like Times Square at four in the morning, neon-glowing and sparkling and spectacular. "Should I shuffle them?"

Angus shook his head as he slid the cards together and pushed them across the desk toward me. "It was his decision to set his future, after all, and this is his reading," he told her, then looked at me as he withdrew his hand from the deck. "You shuffle."

I considered those cards, unsure what to do, how to proceed. I looked at Veronica, who nodded. "He's right. If you gave up part of your future, it's your future we have to get back," she told me.

I reached out, tentatively as though I thought those cards might shock me should I touch them; I'm not sure I didn't believe they might. But they were just some Tarot cards, their backs impressive but still just cardboard, and I received no shock as I picked them up. Both Angus and Veronica watched as I shuffled them, which made me self-conscious, and I thought back to how it felt to shuffle those other cards for that woman with her red-hair—

the power and energy of the cards as my fingers slipped each one past the next past the next past the next, over and over again—

and I wished I could feel that again, tried to recreate the dexterity of nimble fingers flipping those cards in a blackjack rainbow, but I couldn't. I closed my eyes and attempted to set aside everything besides those cards, attempted to feel beyond them—

It is not in the stars to hold our destiny but in ourselves.—

because I remembered that woman's words, that the cards were not about the future or even guidance or answers but rather about what you bring to them, and I wondered what that was. Was I bringing confidence and ambition, or was I bringing static happiness? I wondered what cards Angus would draw and what he would read from them, and what Veronica would feel with each successive card drawn, each face interpreted.

Would the cards show what I had given up to be with her, and how much? Or had I given up ambition for happiness? How much is too much to give up for something you want so badly? If we're to take Hollywood and romantic comedies and all our conceptions about love and romance at face value, is there any price too large? If Ryan Reynolds and Sandra Bullock, Tom Hanks and Meg Ryan, Hugh Grant and Julia Roberts have taught us anything, isn't it that love comes first, that a life without romance is not worth living, that there is no price too high?

My fingers stumbled then. My eyes still closed, and I felt my stomach clench with realization, because no, I suddenly realized.

The romantic notion might be that there is nothing so precious, so valuable, so important that it shouldn't be set aside for something like True Love.

But the real answer is nothing, if only because if love is real and true, it shouldn't require you to give up anything at all. Life may be about compromise, and reality may require choices, but real and healthy love should be nurturing, accepting, and most of all allows room to breathe and space to grow. Love can find a way.

Some moments hurt. Some moments break your heart, reminding you as they do of how big and scary life can be and how small you are in an indifferent universe. They are cold and empty and lonely, and if I am to be honest, that moment hurt doubly so; it hurt, then, to live, and it hurts now, again, to recount. That was the moment I realized I was to tell this story, and this is the moment I have realized why; it was the moment I realized that though my relationship with Veronica might continue and would certainly change, there would no longer be anything romantic about it. That was the moment I realized not only how much I loved her but also that I would never really be with her, not for real, not for true, and realized I had to write this story: in its telling there may be salvation, and in its sharing redemption.

That was the moment I let go. I could try to understand why I had to make the decision Angus prompted me, even why I made the choice I did. I could in addition continue to beat myself up over that choice, to feel guilty, but I would rather accept why and how I found myself where I was.

Where I was: sitting across from Angus and next to Veronica. No longer wondering what those cards would say: I already knew. No longer wondering if Veronica might counter them: I already knew that, too.

The cards slowed in my hands to a stop, and I set the deck on the desk. I kept my hand on top as I turned toward Veronica. "I'm sorry."

Her eyes showed intensity she hadn't yet let into her voice, and the muscles at the tops of her jaw, just in front of her ears, clenched and unclenched. "I know," she said. She placed her left hand on mine, gave it a gentle squeeze.

I wasn't sure what I was sorry for, but I guess that was okay. I might have been apologizing for any number of things, and maybe I hoped that I might cover them all if only I didn't choose any in particular.

"You may cut the cards yourself now," Angus told Veronica, and so I started to withdraw my hand, but her fingers tightened.

"No," she said. "I know he said you couldn't have any part in this, but we shared something real, and we were starting to build something, and this future is ours. I can't exclude you from it any more than I could continue to date you if we hadn't called. We'll cut the cards together."

I started to cut the deck, but she stopped me.

"Use your other hand," she said.

I had set the deck down with my right hand, and so I withdrew it as I set instead my left hand upon hers. Our fingers moved together as if in a digital tango, and we slid half the deck sideways so that there were two, both about the same size. My part finished, I sat back, my hands in my lap.

"I will use one half for the reading. The other is yours to choose now," Angus said.

Veronica considered both the halves, then chose the one that had been on the bottom. "This is mine."

"You're sure?" Angus said.

"I'm sure it doesn't matter. The point is that I counter your reading, not the content of that reading. Whatever you read and however you interpret it, I use these cards to counter what you say. Unless I've got the rules wrong."

"No, you haven't," Angus said as he reached toward the other half-deck. "You have them exactly right," he said, but in a voice like he hadn't expected Veronica to understand the game like she did. "And the final rule is simple," Angus said, looking at me. "This business is between me and Veronica. If you speak, you forfeit the game. Do you understand?"

I only nodded, worried verbal response would forfeit.

"Excellent," Angus said, and with that set down his first card, a sun, then crossed over it sideways one depicting a man and a woman facing each other and holding cups. I noticed him pause, so briefly it would have been easy to miss, but then he quickly set the third through sixth around those center two, then four to the side. There were several pentacle cards, and one devil, but then again there was a sun and a fool and an ace, and those seemed hopeful enough.

Only one, the final card he set down, was facedown. None were reversed, or in different directions to each other. Every card besides that last seemed to be set down as it should have been, and it seemed a straight-forward spread.

I remembered the reading the red-haired woman had done, with its swords and blindfolds and dilemmas, its cards sideways and reversed and face down, her words that reversion could lend to positive cards a certain negativity. I suppose the simplicity of the spread Angus laid down should have eased my anxiety, but if anything, seeing those straight-forward cards only made me more nervous.

Even worse, I wasn't sure what I should be hoping for. I understood, at least vaguely, what Angus meant for Veronica to do, but I wasn't familiar with the Tarot and didn't really know how Veronica might counter those cards, or even if I should want her to. That first-drawn card, the sun, with its bright golden face upon the back of a grinning child on a horse, seemed positive; was I really meant to hope Veronica might cancel out its meaning in the deck?

"So we begin," Angus said,

Chapter Twenty, in which we begin

*A*s he gestured toward that first card and named it. "A sign of completion and wholeness. A note of contentment after a long, tiring journey so well accomplished that even the sunflowers follow the rider rather than the sun itself. You have emerged whole from a dark period, and now feel it is time to reap the rewards you have earned."

And that didn't sound bad at all, does it? Wholeness, completion, rewards?

Veronica Geisha-fanned her cards before her, and from it she selected the Moon, which she set down on the desk, in front of Angus' cards. "Because things are not always what they seem, and if those sunflowers follow you, it is because of your own light. You don't need the sun to see by, and indeed, what appears happy in the sunlight might appear otherwise by the light of the moon, which is really just a reflection, anyway. It's up to you to be vigilant and perceptive."

Which didn't sound as happy, as positive, as the earned end of the journey, the emergence from darkness into the light of well-being and happiness, but then again might have been more true. Because, sitting there, in Angus' inner office, just off a lobby whose appearance had so markedly changed since last I'd seen it, how could I believe anything was what it seemed? How could I believe Angus was just an old man helping me make a choice? How could I believe he had my best interests in mind and heart?

Angus indicated the card crossed over the sun, which depicted a man and a woman carrying cups, the man reaching out to the woman. Between them, red: a winged lion's head above a staff of some sort. "The Two of Cups. The challenge of a new relationship lacking real stability, perhaps, but perhaps again the challenge of reconciling two parts of yourself into harmony."

Veronica shook her head, setting down a card with which I was already familiar: the Lovers, but different. When I'd first seen that card, it had depicted a man standing between two women, one a blonde maiden and the other a red-haired vixen; the card Veronica set down pictured a woman and a man standing side by side, hands reaching to join, while between and above them an angel looked down on them. The woman stared at that angel, while the man stared at the woman. "The Lovers. Because the challenge in your card, Angus, is not the man and woman but the staff of Hermes between them. The relationship between my lovers is strong and pure, and the man in the picture has to trust the woman, who is the only one looking at the angel." She looked at me, then: "Your challenge isn't relationship stability. It's that you have to trust me."

Which made me hesitate. Trust isn't something I've ever been good at. It's not that I think everyone's lying to me, not that I think life is one big deception; rather, it's that I'm the only person I trust not to let me down in the end. I'm the one person I know I can rely on. Maybe it's a control thing, not wanting to let someone else have so much power on me or my life. I don't know.

What I do know is that, the moment I heard it, I knew she was right. I realized, of the two, I trusted Veronica, and understood further that meant I had to trust her game. Her results. Even if they didn't seem so happy, so positive, as the story Angus' cards might tell and the interpretations to which he lent them, Veronica was the one who had already been seeing through the glamour and the romance, the magic and the smokescreen. I have always liked to think I have keen perceptions, and maybe that was why Angus had been able to manipulate me so easily.

I swallowed. Nodded. Again, said nothing.

Angus pointed to the card above his Two of Cups: an Ace of Wands. "Your distant past is a sudden and spontaneous burst of furious inspiration and brilliant creativity," he told me. "You prefer to work all in one shot, all at once, hour after hour like a blazing star. It can carry you far."

I thought, then, of those two weeks during which I had completed the novel I had been working on, the furious production that had carried me through to the end. I wasn't sure I could argue with him.

Veronica set down an Ace of Pentacles. "Genius is only one percent inspiration. All the rest is perspiration, the blood and the sweat and the hard work required to set it down. Hour after hour, one word at a time.

Inspiration can't finish a novel, and your past is less furious creativity than long and dedicated craft. Everyone knows overnight success can take years, even decades. Nothing extraordinary was ever accomplished without intensity, but neither was it accomplished without real work."

Maybe nobody wants to really believe that, least of all me, not in our age of insta-lebrity and scandal-inspired publication contracts, authors more likely to have been strippers than students of craft, but maybe that's because we've gotten used to working without discipline and care, favoring the quick route over the more difficult. All I really knew was that Veronica's words felt true in a way part of me wanted to resist, all the more reason to acknowledge them.

Angus eyed her, a hint of a smile on his lips, his eyes slight-squinted with something halfway between cunning and bemusement. He tapped the next card, a man wearing garish clothes and set mid-leap against a blatant yellow background. "The Fool for the recent past, a new beginning, perhaps a new career, certainly a new direction begun light of heart and with great mirth. Perhaps it is time to relish the feeling of a job well done, a journey well accomplished."

Veronica plunked down a Four of Wands. "Careful not to pull a muscle patting yourself on the back, and don't forget every new beginning comes from some other beginning's end. I know you're pleased with yourself, having begun this new job, having finished your book, having found yourself somewhere you are happy to be, but such good things aren't reason to stop. If nothing else, in fact, they're all the more reason to keep things going when they're going so well. Which leads directly into your next card, doesn't it? Because

I'm willing to bet you're going to say your Six of Swords for the best outcome signifies it's time to get away from previous problems, like rejection and adversity and too many agents who don't want to see any more pages, and chart a new course," she continued, even as she set down her own Five of Swords right on top of Angus' Six. "But no, because like I just told you earlier, when Beethoven went deaf, he didn't stop. Now is when you cut the damned legs off and put your piano on the floor and you pound the keys even harder. Greatness doesn't end when you fall; it begins when you get back up."

I wanted to laugh, not because it was funny, but because it was the kind of truth that hit me in the stomach with inspiration. It was the kind of encouragement that doesn't make you feel any better but rather makes you bite down, through the pain and the ache, and keep going, the kind that forces you to reach down and helps you find a little more strength you didn't even know was there when you do.

Angus stared at Veronica's six swords. "I fear I may have underestimated you, Veronica."

"I'm counting on it," she told him. "We can stop now, if you want. Just release our future from your contract."

"The only way to break the binding is to finish," Angus told her, touching his next card, a red-robed woman wearing a crown and holding a sword. "You will in your immediate future meet with Justice, answering for past deeds. As you have sown so shall you reap, and you will confront the consequences of your actions, good and bad. Reward will come without ceremony or congratulation, but punishment will be swift and harsh. How answer you that, Veronica?"

Veronica considered her cards, but I couldn't help thinking I should have been the one answering; I was the one who had made the decision, who had chosen. I was the one who had given up writing to be with Veronica, and I wondered, no matter the outcome of their game, if I deserved to write again. I had turned my back on the page and its words, and I wasn't sure I deserved to sit again at a keyboard; I have always maintained that anyone who can give up should, because there are plenty of others ready to take up the places of any who have walked away.

But Veronica plucked a card from her fan. "I answer the only way I can," she said, setting down a woman holding open a lion's jaws, an infinity symbol above her head. "I offer Strength to stand before such justice, strength to accept any punishment as well as strength to acknowledge your own quiet power and fortitude of character. I offer you the courage to trust in yourself and your deeds."

Angus chuckled as he nodded. "Well played," he said as he swept the already played cards together and aside. "So now we address the influences in the situation, beginning, of course, with the doozy," he pointed to the Devil, that grinning beast standing atop his own card, clutching chains of man and woman, one arm up toward the sky but the other down like he was trying to hide it behind his back. "Not a happy card, to signify a man who has been unhappy. A man who feels he has no control in his life, a man who fears he is losing his own fight, and most of all a man who is ashamed of himself."

I swallowed. I don't know that I was exactly ashamed of having made the decision as I had, but I certainly wasn't proud of it.

Because let's address that decision: the idea of holding one's singular passion for activity, be it writing or music or sports, higher than all others comes with a dual edge. On one hand, the idea of a writer holding his stories above all else comes with some romanticism; when we think of Shakespeare, we don't think of Anne Hathaway and the life the bard ignored in Stratford in favor of the London stage—we think rather of being or not being, of double bubbles and toil and trouble, of damned spots and brief candles and what a piece of work is man. But is that not rather cold? How can people create anything passionate if they themselves have never once known it? How could any artist—and I use the term as loosely as it might be applied—possibly be expected to create great art without loving anything besides art itself?

Because art is useless without faith in it. Art is nothing without something to be communicated. Too many museums are filled with too many canvasses marred by too many brushstrokes slashed by so-called modern artists who never set to canvas anything worth commemorating, favoring instead an attempt at commentary that might perhaps be more effective backed up by citations and references in an academic paper.

But you look at Dali and Warhol, Pollack and Picasso—or I do, anyway, and I feel nothing. Not like I feel for the awesome genius of Leonardo or the faith-fueled dedication of Michelangelo.

We want to believe love is about compromise, quiet dedication over a lifetime, simple work at co-existing with another soul, and it is, certainly, but it's about those things as it is about many things. Love is infidelity every bit as much as it is faithful, avaricious every bit as much as it is committed, belligerent every bit as much as it is patient. Without meaning beyond the colors, feeling beyond the words, art would be merely paintings and books just as a kiss would be nothing more than four lips pressed together.

But that's not what those things are. A kiss exists despite the universe, a moment of singular hope fueled by connection and passion and desire, and that's nevermind a good kiss: a good kiss stops the whole damned world. A good kiss stops every thought in your head like an orgasm blasts them all away in a firework-seizure of delirious pleasure, and aren't those things worth giving up anything for? Tell me what is worth more than fully loving, with your whole heart and body and soul, someone who loves you the same way in return.

I can't think of anything more powerful than that. Call me a romantic, an idealist, and I will simply shrug and tell you I've been called worse. Because I sat there next to Veronica Sawyer and I couldn't deny her beauty, couldn't help feeling my heart reach toward her, couldn't help wanting to just kiss her and be done with it all and live happily ever after. Veronica Sawyer wasn't just the girl with whom I fell in love who did not love me in return, nor even the girl for whom I'd given up the thing I loved most in the world; no, the reason I had given up writing for her, the reason I had fallen in love with her regardless of her feelings for me in return, was that Veronica Sawyer was the hope—however impossible—that she and I could up and leave, that we could walk out of that office and be together and I still might find the desire to write. Veronica Sawyer was the hope that a story like this might find its way to a happy, romantic comedy ending.

That hope. That foolish, romantic, entropy-defying, heart-enriching hope.

I'm sure, however, by now you have gathered this is not one of those happy-ending stories. I'm sure you know by now, as I knew by then, as I have already told you, that whatever relationship Veronica and I had after sitting across from Angus would not be romantic. Really, all that's left, now, is not so much how it ended but whether I am able to tell the story successfully through to completion.

It is not complete yet. This you know.

You know there were more cards. You know Veronica drew a card against Angus' leering Devil if not what she drew, and so I'll tell you:

She set down a Queen of Swords, about the closest to a regular playing card I had so far seen. It pictured a woman in profile, sitting on a throne, looking out on the world. "Really what the Devil means is that if anything is holding you back, it's you, which means you can free yourself any time you'd like. What's troubling you most is not your actions but your lack thereof, and you need to see things more clearly, like recognizing the Devil when he's sitting right in front of you."

Which made me carefully consider Angus. Veronica had already said I had to trust her to see what I couldn't, what I wouldn't, and now I had to recognize the Devil across from me . . .

The thought had already crossed my mind, and Angus had already dismissed it. But maybe . . . if I looked closely enough, I could imagine Angus as he might otherwise appear: with black, slicked-back hair; a long, semi-pointed nose; dark, hungry eyes full of guile and cunning and the sort of confidence that makes you check for your wallet.

Then again, I have a very active imagination.

Angus indicated his next card. "This Three of Pentacles for external influences, because you have so recently found success in your career, success you have sought for so long, and you can build upon it. You may not yet have a position of power, but you certainly have much more room for potential than so many other people, and you might express yourself through your position."

But Veronica was already setting down her card before he finished speaking, and she put her Magician atop his Pentacled-Three. "You have far more power than you have yet given yourself credit for, the power to transform and create the universe at your will. You have felt the sting of inaction, the pain of rejection, but you can go on, and must go on, for a very simple reason: your life is yours to control. Your life is what you want it to be. Your life is what you make it."

Of course she was right, because the same can be said of all of us, of all our lives: our lives are what we have made of them, and if our lives are not what we want them to be, we can change them. We have to make choices, hard decisions, to do so, but ultimately, the only thing in the world we have control over is our lives.

There was also more to her words. My life is whatever I make it and can be whatever I want it to be, and so can this story. From the beginning, this has been my story to tell, and it will end however I say it ends. If I want for this story to have a happy ending, if I'd wanted to reach out and take Veronica's hand and leave that office with her, all I'd have to do is write that I did so and we might just come to a happy ending before we run out of words to find one in.

But that wouldn't be right, or true. I could tell you that's what I did, that I kissed Veronica and told her we were leaving and took my own destiny into my own hands before I set them down on the page, but it wouldn't feel right. Not that it would feel incomplete, just wrong. It's not solely my story to end here anymore: the moment Veronica led me through Angus' door, it became as much about her as it has been about me, and given that I made such an important choice without her input, I can't end it without her permission.

Most of all, it wouldn't be satisfying, and you haven't come this far not to be satisfied. You haven't come this far not to see that game between Veronica and Angus through to its end. You haven't come this far to think that I was going to write myself to successfully telling this story solely by telling you I had, have you?

No, you haven't. You want to see that next card, and it's my job to tell you that Angus next indicated a Four of Pentacles, which he said signified my hopes and fears, and which he said meant that I could have material security, financial stability. "You have a new job and a new direction free from rejection and uncertainty and instability, and why give that up in favor of something in which there is so little security? You can have tradition, but it has to begin somewhere."

At what price happiness?

Veronica pulled a card from her fan and set upon Angus' Four the Hanged Man. "Not a card one normally hopes to see in one's spread, but it means letting go, which is what is necessary here. Letting go of past hopes, outmoded desires, unhealthy obsessions, is important, but real sacrifice requires balance. The decision you made only worked because you loved writing as much as you loved me," Veronica said, "And as much as I love you, you cannot find as much reward through a relationship with me as continuing to write will fulfill you. It's not about publications and adoring fans and book deals; it's about those words you love to set down one after the others, and I love you too much to let you give that up. You need to let go of the idea of safety and security, because they're just happy illusions perpetrated by people too afraid of a little risk. And only where there is great risk can there be great success. Isn't that right, Mister Silver?"

Angus' smile seemed reflective and amused. "Quite."

Veronica nodded. "Which leaves only that last card."

Angus nodded. "The final outcome," he said as he turned the card over, and I wish I could say I gasped when I saw that thrice sword-pierced heart, but I wasn't sure it surprised me. I'd seen it once before, after all. That red-haired woman and her reading had warned me about it, and maybe by then I had already begun to accept that I would never be with Veronica. This story can't end with romance, can it? How could it surprise me?

I wasn't sure, but it seemed to surprise Angus, who just stared at it a moment, then looked up at Veronica as if he were realizing something. "He's broken your heart."

I wish I could say I gasped, but that's not what happens when you're really shocked, is it? What happens is that everything feels more distant for a moment, like the world withdraws from you, goes grey and cold to leave you with a dead stomach paradoxically empty and dense at the same time. What happens is that the desire to cry clenches your abdomen and forces a tiny exhalation like a lifeless autumn breeze trailing dirty grass in its wake.

Of the three of us, Veronica was the only one who didn't seem surprised. When she heard Angus' words, she took in and let out a deep breath as if she were steeling herself, and as she did so she chose one card among her fan to set down. It pictured a cloaked man standing head-down and forlorn by the side of a river and among cups tipped over and spilt.

"The Five of Cups?" Angus said like he wasn't sure what she meant by it. "But that's grief, sadness, disappointment. A broken relationship."

"Not if you look more closely. That man by the river is concentrating so hard on the cups he's dropped and spilled that he is missing the fact that there are still two left, still upright, still full. That man is so focused on beating himself up over what he thinks he has done that he doesn't consider what he can do," Veronica said. She looked at me: "But you've already done it. You've already said you are sorry for what you did, and now I tell you, simply, that I forgive you. That what happened here had to happen, and now your work begins. You can make this right."

I stared at that card she had set down, that hooded man and his spilt cups. That everything happens for a reason, and that maybe I had made a mistake, maybe I had made a bad decision, but I could set it right. As long as I had some space and some words, I could set it right, and staring at that card, I thought I might know how.

"Which I believe concludes our business," Angus told her. "You have successfully countered my influence and broken any contract made——."

"So things will go back to the way they were," Veronica said.

Angus shook his head. "My sphere of influence is for the future, not the past. While you were able to reduce my influence over your collective future, I cannot change what was given up."

"Will he write again?"

"He had the chance. He gave it up. Again, I have no power over what has come before."

"No. That's not good enough," Veronica said.

"I'm sorry?"

"I said that's not good enough. I want a new deal, and a new contract. A new wager. With real stakes. Because if I won our little game and reduced your influence, I created uncertainty. And where there exists uncertainty, as you said, so there must exist risk. And where there is risk, we can gamble. I want a guarantee."

"Of what?"

"Of the future. He said he didn't give up just the writing but the fame and the popularity, too. I want a guarantee he can get it back."

Angus considered that. "I can guarantee only the possibility. The rest would have to remain up to him. I can't fulfill his potential, only offer the possibility of it."

Veronica considered that. "A guarantee, then, of success from hard work."

Angus hesitated, then nodded. I'm not sure it was my imagination that his eyes sparkled, and I can't claim certainty whether they would have done so out of mischief or hunger, anyway. "What, exactly, do you have in mind?"

"Simple," Veronica said as she slipped together the rest of her cards and set down her deck. She moved the top two cards from it, set them just to the side, face down. "These two cards against the next two cards in your deck."

Angus considered her, her two cards, then looked at me. "What do you say? With your permission, I will agree."

And so there it was, and I sat across from Angus and next to Veronica, deciding whether to let my fate hinge on a few Tarot cards, but I only deliberated for a moment, because what had I to lose? I considered the cards Angus and Veronica had played between them, the Devil and the Hanged Man, the queens and the aces, swords and pentacles and cups, and I thought of letting go, of inaction, of choices.

I chose, then, to let go. I chose to trust that Veronica knew what she was doing.

I nodded.

"Very well, then," Angus said, and with a motion quicker and less dramatic than it should have been flipped over two cards: one a dark, foreboding tower spiring out into an inky sky, the other a profiled reaper man on his pale horse, carrying a black flag in place of his famous scythe. "The Tower," Angus said, "And death," and in a voice that I required no more elaboration to know that they weren't happy cards to see.

"But the Tower is the fulfillment of the Hanged Man letting go of his obsession," Veronica said, "And death is just a spiritual transition, a signal not only that there is a next step to take but also that it is time to take it. And if you'll just take that step, you will earn the World," she flipped over what looked to be a happy card, a woman in a wreath surrounded by blue skies and ethereal figures. "You will find great success, both materially and spiritually."

Which made me hopeful, of course. Material and spiritual success? Yes, please. Where might I sign up? Surely there must be a line.

But then she turned over that final card, and while my heart didn't fall, well, that hope caught on me as though I'd snagged a sweater-shoulder on a stray nail: a giant angel holding a trumpet and looking down upon a post-apocalyptic wasteland, a man and a woman cowering as though afraid to meet its gaze, in the distance mountains and river. All caps at the bottom: JUDGMENT.

Before I could worry too much about it, however, Veronica turned to me: "Because Angus is right about the Tower and Death, but only because of the great power of transformation. You will have your world, and you will find your success, because that transformation will be creative rather than destructive. With this card, I cleanse you, wipe clean your slate, and most of all, give you the new beginning you need to earn your world,"

and what, dear Reader, might I do with a new beginning besides take it, because—

*O*nce upon a time I fell in love with a girl who didn't love me in return.

And while that may not be, as openings go, altogether novel (for who among us has not felt the sharp-barbed long-constant prick-pull of unrequited love?), still I've always known it's how I need to begin this story.—

even if I have only just recently realized I would return again to them. I always knew I was going to need the big guns if I intended to make my way through, and now that I'm very nearly there, I am relieved to have established those guns from the start so that I might draw them now.

I always knew it wasn't going to be an easy story to finish. I've always found endings more difficult than beginnings, though many would disagree. Endings must satisfy, and I want the ones I read to transcend, to take everything that led up to them to an entirely new level, and how often does that occur?

Some achieve it more successfully than others—

It is a far, far better thing I do than I have ever done; it is a far, far better rest that I go to than I have ever known.—

or—

Lastly, she pictured to herself how this same little sister of hers would, in the after-time, be herself a grown woman; and how she would keep, through all her riper years, the simple and loving heart of her childhood; and how she would gather about her other little children, and make their eyes bright and eager with many a strange tale, perhaps even with the dream of Wonderland of long ago; and how she would feel with all their simple sorrows, and find a pleasure in all their simple joys, remembering her own child-life, and the happy summer days.—

or—

And then he began chirping his peculiar melancholy song, from which we have taken this history; and which may, very possibly, be all untrue, although it does stand here printed in black and white.—

Because how can you go wrong with any of those?

I only hope I can reach the same here. I believe I started wisely—

Once upon a time—

mainly because beginning with that phrase makes this a sort-of fairy tale, and fairy tales come with rules that might guide us through to a proper, satisfying ending. Those rules may vary from tale to tale, but most are consistent through stories: stray not from the path. Eat no food, and accept no gifts, and if someone asks where you are going, say, simply, in front of you; if they ask where you are from, say, simply, behind you.

Tell no one your name.

Names have power in fairy tales. Revealing one's name gives up one's power to others.

The astute among you, here, will notice I have not. I have tried to be neither clever nor conspicuous about it—writing this account in the first person helped—but I never used my name because I have known, all along, I would use it here. Maybe you noticed I had not used it, and probably you sensed, at least subconsciously, why. Maybe you guessed I wanted to prevent Angus from having that sort of power or control, and maybe you never really trusted him, either. Maybe you have understood, in addition, all along, even just subconsciously, that my reason for keeping my name for myself, for preserving that special sort of power, has been simple all along:

I have meant all along to give it up to you.

But you've known it all along, haven't you? Somehow, depending on how you've read this. It's the website you've visited every week for the past twenty, or it was noted when you downloaded it on your Kindle, or it's there at the tops of the pages of the book you're reading, on its spine, on its cover.

I would say that revealing my name to you, in addition to giving you full power over the story, also fundamentally changes the nature of the story, but if we are to be honest here (and we always have been), that is probably not true. You have likely wondered all along what, in this story, was fact and how much besides was fiction, how much was semi-autobiographical what was actually autobiographical. Maybe you've wondered all along which characters existed and which did not, and maybe you think that Tom and Veronica had to be based on people in my life while Angus and that red-haired woman were simply devices by which to tell a story.

But then, that may be something I would neither confirm nor deny. If I told you I thought Angus was Hermes—you did catch that I called him "Quick" when I first met him, did you not? Or that he wore an Hermés suit?—I dispute that makes him no less real. The god of the crossroads, with dominion over commerce and art, companion to poets and conmen alike. He has always existed, because we have always wanted the choice he offers.

I would wager the character you're wondering most about, however, is Veronica Sawyer. You are wondering whether Veronica Sawyer exists, and who she is, and maybe whether we ever were together or if I ever told her how I felt about her.

Ah, Veronica Sawyer.

I'm sure there is a Veronica Sawyer somewhere in the world. It's a common enough last name (you caught that, too, right? Her brother's name? You might as well call me Huckleberry. One of my old teachers did. Totally true).

And so you say, fine, Veronica Sawyer exists. But you say, did you really fall for her?

To which I respond: well, no. I've never met her.

But the Veronica Sawyer in this story? Her I knew. But then, you knew her, too, or him, didn't you? Because I hate to call her a character or an archetype or whatever term someone with an advanced degree in literature might use, but really, Veronica Sawyer is the person you fell in love with who didn't love you in return, and as was noted in the very second line of this story, who among us doesn't know that tale? Who among us hasn't been there, done that, and written the bad poetry about it?

I did fall in love with a girl who didn't love me in return. I've done it a couple of times, and at least twice with girls I knew growing up, and while the details themselves may be slightly different (and even in this story. I'm fairly certain the descriptions of Veronica's eyes change over the story, and I could probably change it in a revision, but then again, nitpicking her eye color kind of spectacularly misses the point), the story itself remains the same. Because like I said, it's never something so clearcut as chests or asses; it's the calloused fingertips, the slender hands.

That said, this story was inspired by one girl in particular. With whom I did, in fact, grow up, and whose brother was, in fact, my best friend for many years. For many years, I pined away after her, quietly loving her from afar as she dated a succession of guys whose hands I shook even though I never thought they were good enough for her. Instead of meeting Angus, however, I wrote an early draft of this very story, which was substantially shorter and substantially worse, and I gave it to her, and after she read it, I said, it's true, you know. How I feel about you.

And she said I know.

And I said and you don't feel the same way.

And she said no. Sorry.

And I said hey, that's how it goes, right, because it so often is.

That was several years ago, and eventually we grew apart, as people do. I left for USC and Hollywood, and she left for philosophy and Georgia. We have seen each other a few times, and spoken sporadically, and now she's married to a guy she seems very happy with, and maybe some year I'll open the mail around the holidays to find a card depicting a girl I only vaguely recognize standing with her hubby and her children and wishing me greetings for the season.

And maybe, some day, she'll open her mail to find a copy of this book. And she'll trace her fingers along the cover just like she traced her fingers down the title page of that old manuscript (because, yes, that Christmas actually occurred), and she'll think of me, and she'll smile.

One can hope.

It's all that matters, after all.

I don't know if you wonder about other elements of this story, and I'm not sure they matter. Does it matter I went to Saint Peter's College in Jersey City, not Montclair State? Does it matter I never worked as a production assistant at the Weinstein Company but did spend more than a year in the broadcast department of Young & Rubicam NY, one of the largest advertising agencies in the world? I can't imagine it does, and even if it did, well, so many of the details are the same. You can find Cassiopeia, the tattoo place, if you look. Hell, if Candela hadn't closed, you could have followed these pages right to its door (and you would have loved it, let me tell you. I was devastated to find it was gone. It's now called Irving Mill, and its burgers are terrific, just slightly smoky, but there aren't enough gnocchis on its pasta plate, and worse, there's just nothing exactly *special* about it anymore). Grape Street Pub closed a few years ago, not long after I placed Foolish's launch party, back when my best friend Tim's band was called Hero for Nothing; it's now called Sum of You, and if their CD isn't on iTunes, Hero for Nothing's *A Carter Avenue Project* is, and you can download it knowing I danced countless times in countless bars to those songs (Foolish's CD, incidentally, takes its name from one of my favorite book review blogs, *Books I Done Read*, which I find hysterical for its thumbing its nose at grammar; its proprietor, Raych, is spectacular).

We could tick through the rest of the story, point by meticulous point, scene by pain-staking scene, and I could enumerate which details were true and which ones besides had occurred, but I fear that would miss a point as well. I would wager that there is as much truth in these pages as in Dave Eggers' *A Heart-Breaking Work of Staggering Genius* or James Frey's *A Million Little Pieces*, and as many aspects made up as in either, as well. One could probably go so far as to debate whether this was a fictionalized memoir or an autobiographical novel—

or, on the other hand, one could just acknowledge it as a story and leave well enough alone. I'm content enough with that choice, to be candid.

Because I think—I hope—this time I have pulled it off. Have you enjoyed it?

Because you're what counts. You, and the story. So far as the story goes, I have told all I can, and it's about time for me to shut up—

It would concern the reader little, perhaps, to know, how sorrowfully the pen is laid down at the close of a two-years' imaginative task; or how an Author feels as if he were dismissing some portion of himself into the shadowy world, when a crowd of the creatures of his brain are going from him for ever. Yet, I have nothing else to tell; unless, indeed, I were to confess (which might be of less moment still) that no one can ever believe this Narrative, in the reading, more than I have believed it in the writing.—

and trust it. And you.

Because what I said to Angus was the truth: I don't trust critics or academicians, but I trust you. And the best way I know to demonstrate how much I trust you is to tell you my name is William Entrekin, and I hope you have enjoyed my story. I hope it has meant something to you. I hope you have laughed, and I hope you have felt it, in however small or great a way.

And now that I have not so much broken the fourth wall as rendered them all moot, allow me, please, just one more moment. Because if you look back at the beginning of this book, you will notice that there is no dedication. A minor detail, mostly because it's nearly universal—

Who drinks the deepest? Here's to him.—
or—
To. The. Onlie. Begetter. Of.
These. Insving. Sonnets.
Mr. W.H. All. Happinesse.
And. That. Eternitie.
Promised.
By.
Our. Everlasting. Poet.
Wisheth.
The. Well. Wishing.
Adventvrer. In.
Setting.
Forth.—

and just as I saved my name and its power for you here, at the end, so have I saved this moment to dedicate this story to you. Allow me to tell you it's not for Veronica, or any girl who has been there with me through everything, or my parents or my sister; this is for you. I know not how you have found these words, nor who you are, but the whole point has been to reach you, and so, if I have, if you have read this far, to you I am forever grateful, and I leave you with one final gift. I mentioned in beginning that I hoped beginning with

Once upon a time

might lead our way through to three others, and here and now I offer those words to you:

May you live happily ever after.

About the Author

Will Entrekin is a Pittsburgh-based writer. Born and raised in New Jersey near Philadelphia, Entrekin studied fiction and screenwriting in the University of Southern California's Master's in Professional Writing program with best-selling authors Rachel Resnick, John Rechy, and Janet Fitch and filmmakers including Irvin Kershner, Syd Field, and Coleman Hough. He wrote *The Prodigal Hour* with the guidance of Sid Stebel, an author Ray Bradbury called "The greatest writing teacher ever," and received the 2007 Ruth Cohen Fellowship, as well as a 2008 lectureship position teaching composition.

Entrekin has worked as a commercial production assistant at Young & Rubicam NY, an editor for the *Journal of Psychosocial Nursing and Mental Health Services*, and a personal trainer for Bally Total Fitness.

Entrekin studied at Saint Peter's College in Jersey City, where he won the Stephen J. Rosen Memorial Writing award and earned membership into the national Biological, Literary, and Jesuit Honor societies. He graduated *cum laude* as a Gerard Manley Hopkins scholar with degrees in both science and literature, and studied theology with Father Robert Kennedy, S.J., *roshi*, a Jesuit priest and Zen master in the White Plum lineage. Entrekin is also an Eagle scout and a member of the Order of the Arrow in the Boy Scouts of America.